■ □ ■ □ ■

A LAND THE SIZE
OF BINOCULARS

■ □ ■ □ ■

IGOR KLEKH

A LAND THE SIZE
OF BINOCULARS

Translated from the Russian
by Michael M. Naydan and Slava I. Yastremski

With an introduction by Andrei Bitov

NORTHWESTERN UNIVERSITY PRESS

EVANSTON, ILLINOIS

Northwestern University Press
Evanston, Illinois 60208-4170

Printed in the United States of America

10 9 8 7 6 5 4 3

ISBN 0-8101-1942-0 (CLOTH)
ISBN 0-8101-1943-9 (PAPER)

Library of Congress Cataloging-in-Publication Data

Klekh, Igor', 1952–
    [Selections. English. 2003]
    A land the size of binoculars / Igor Klekh ; translated from the Russian by
Michael M. Naydan and Slava I. Yastremski ; with an introduction by Andrei Bitov.
        p. cm. — (Writings from an unbound Europe)
    ISBN 0-8101-1942-0 (cloth : alk. paper) — ISBN 0-8101-1943-9 (pbk. : alk. paper)
    1. Klekh, Igor', 1952– —Translations into English. I. Naydan, Michael M.,
1952– II. Yastremski, Slava. III. Title. IV. Series.
PG3482.6.L42A26 2003
891.7'934—dc21

                                                            2002154470

■ □ ■ □ ■

CONTENTS

■ □ ■ □ ■

TRANSLATORS'
ACKNOWLEDGMENTS

We wish to express our gratitude to several people for making this translation possible: first and foremost to Maria Zubrytska of Lviv for kindly introducing us to Kallimakh and for the expertise she shared with us on the architecture and history of Lviv; to Taras Vozniak of Lviv and to Elena Zheltova of Moscow for their persistence in contacting Mr. Klekh, a not so easy task at the time, to obtain permission to publish his works; to Tammy Lynn Marpoe for her meticulous inputting of many of the translations onto computer disk; and to Valerie Nollan for her helpful suggestions on an earlier version of the translations. Special thanks to Elwira Grossman and Paul Bushkovitch for their kindness in providing information on Polish historical questions and to Charlotte Holmes for her encouragement on this project in its early stages. Thanks to Dallas Skeens for reading the entire manuscript for those errors that even spelling checkers don't catch. We are also grateful to Natalka Babalyk, Myroslava Prykhoda, and Yuri Andrukhovych for assisting us with explanations of various Carpathian dialecticisms. Extra special thanks to the copyeditor, Steven W. Barnett, who did such a marvelous job on the manuscript. We, of course, are responsible for any errors or omissions.

■ □ ■ □ ■

FROM MEDIEVAL TO POSTMODERN:
THE PROSE OF IGOR KLEKH

Michael M. Naydan and Slava I. Yastremski

Although nominated for the Russian version of the Booker Prize in 1995, Igor Klekh isn't yet a household name in the West, partly the result of the stylistic and syntactic complexity of his works. Klekh has published his prose extensively in Ukraine during the Soviet period and in Russia after emigrating there following the fall of the Soviet empire in 1991. He has been a frequent contributor to the best Russian literary journals, including *Novyi mir, Znamya,* and *Druzhba narodov.* In 1998 he published his first book, *An Incident with a Classic,* and in 2002 the Agraf Publishing House issued a collection of his literary essays. Klekh received two prizes in 2001: for best short story of the year and for a book on Ukrainian painter Sergi Sherstiuk, who tragically died a year earlier. Klekh recently published two new books of prose and is editing the Contemporary Reading Library, a series of books—prose, poetry, and literary criticism—by leading contemporary Russian authors such as Evgeny Popov, Ivan Zhdanov, and Lev Rubinstein.

Klekh, who was born in 1952 and grew up in western Ukraine, writes exclusively in Russian. He is as enigmatic a figure as the heroes of his prose. He currently resides on the outskirts of Moscow and on occasion travels to Germany, Sweden, and other parts of Europe as a writer in residence. He completed his undergraduate degree at the University of Lviv in Russian philology and for a time taught the history of Russian literature. He also worked for several years in restoration studios in Lviv, where he intimately became acquainted with the history of the city as well as with Galician Ukrainian culture.

Like Pavych, Eco, and Borges, Klekh represents the lineage of erudite, philologically oriented writers of prose in the modern period. Similar to Bruno Schultz and Joseph Roth, Klekh, too, is a phenomenon of the multicultural environment of Galician Ukraine, and to a certain degree he continues the line of Schultz, whose novellas he was among the first to translate into Russian. Klekh is part of that phenomenon of marginalized colonial writing in which the literary culture of the colonized parts of the empire, with its unique perspectives, seemingly overtakes and influences the center. In English literature, the same thing has happened with figures such as V. S. Naipaul and J. M. Coetzee. And it is only logical that the same phenomenon, in turn, would occur in the case of Russian literature following the disintegration of the Soviet Union.

Klekh emerges from the literary scene of Lviv, a Vienna-like cobblestone city of winding streets, which, as a result of its proximity to Poland and the rest of Europe, has always had freer contacts with the West and Western literature, even during the Soviet period. Most present-day inhabitants of the city speak Ukrainian, Polish, and Russian, with a smattering of other European languages, including German and English. The large pre–World War II Jewish population of the city was nearly completely obliterated by the Nazis. The history of Lviv spans from the thirteenth-century founding of the city through its domination in turn by Poles, Austrians, and Russians, and ultimately to its re-Ukrainianization following the collapse of the Soviet Union. The city, named after Prince Danylo of Halych's son Lev and whose name means "city of lions," has been known as Lemberg in German, Lwow in Polish, and Lvov in Russian.

The stories and novellas in this volume are divided into two sections, "Galician Motifs" and "Carpathian Narratives." The first section includes the novella *Kallimakh's Wake* and the short prose pieces "An Incident with a Classic," "The Foreigner," "The Way Home," "The *Église* by the Station," and "Introduction to the Galician Context." These prose works, whose genre crosses back and forth over the boundary between fiction and nonfiction, are translated from Klekh's first book, *An Incident with a Classic.* The second section includes two novellas, *A Tiny Farmstead in the Universe* and *The Death of the Forester,* which have been published in Russian literary journals and will appear in a forthcoming volume in Russian that will mirror the selections in *A Land the Size of Binoculars.*

We consider the novella *Kallimakh's Wake* to be one of the most refined representations of Klekh's early writing. One might describe its style as a combination of Gabriel García Márquez's erudite, convoluted, magically realistic run-on prose of seemingly endless but fascinating single paragraphs, with a large dose of Umberto Eco's medieval mentality and encyclopedic knowledge of a bygone era. The story itself is a fictional reconstruction of the real life of Filippo Buonaccorsi (1437–96), the humanist, statesman, historian, and poet who helped found the Roman Academy. Later in his life, Buonaccorsi took the name of the Greek poet Callimachus (Kallimakh in Russian) to indicate his desire for the restoration of ancient ways. In 1468, he, along with members of the Academy, were accused of immorality, impiety, and a plot against the life of Pope Paul II. He fled to the east and later to Ukraine and Poland, where he came under the protection of the Polish archbishop Gregorz of Sanok from papal assassins and later became tutor to the children of the Polish king Casimir IV. The real-life events of Buonaccorsi's life closely frame those presented in the novella. Significantly, the word for "wake" (or "funeral repast") in Russian— *pominki* in the title—contains the root meaning "to remember." Thus Klekh's obvious goal in his novella, like the Russian postfuneral *pominki* celebration, is to remember Buonaccorsi, to take him out of dusty, long-forgotten history books, and to furnish a psychological portrait of him beyond pure historical fact, to make him live again through anamnesis, and to show the synchronicity of the past with the present.

The multicultural city of Lviv, under Polish rule at the time of the story, stands at the crossroads of Europe and, for Klekh, serves as a symbol of the profound interconnectedness of cultures and times. The opening of the novella captures a Lviv that has maintained its distinct European character for more than five hundred years. The depiction of the fifteenth-century humanists succinctly captures the spirit of the era that so enthralls Klekh. Klekh clearly sees himself as one in the lineage of those humanists, a discoverer and conveyor of knowledge, yet still a human being with failings and insecurities like Kallimakh, who is confronted with the choice between the life of the spiritual or that of the flesh, or something in between.

The story is, as Klekh himself notes, a covenant between the author and his character, to the spirit of which the author must be faithful. While the facts of history can never present a true and complete picture of an individual from the past, the author can bring that character to life by adding an emotional aspect to an otherwise purely rational depiction. That is why Klekh is far more than a chronicler in his story. While the story fits into the genre of fanciful biography, it is more significant in the manner in which it is told. Klekh tells much more than he shows characters interacting, but the telling is so artfully done that it engages the reader in a profound way. The questions Klekh poses through his hero aren't new, but he does manage to "knock off the focus" of his readers, as he puts it, "to wipe off apathetic eyes," to make this fascinating Renaissance figure of Kallimakh Buonaccorsi come to life with all his human frailties.

"An Incident with a Classic" describes the narrator's (who is almost always an alter ego of the author) attempted pilgrimage to the town of Mirgorod, the location of several stories by Nikolai Gogol. It fails because on his arrival to the town, the narrator drops his keys into the station's latrine. The story becomes a Gogolesque character study of the present inhabitants of the town. "The Foreigner" is set in a hospital where the narrator, an urban intellectual and thus a foreigner to the culture in which he finds himself, observes other patients playing dominoes and begins to contemplate the question of life and death. To some extent, the story is reminiscent of Leo Tolstoy's "The Death of Ivan Ilyich." These two stories can be seen as representative of Klekh's narrative design, which is to a large extent defined by his keen sense of language, as in "The Foreigner," where the name of the game being played gives birth to a prayer about the dead, and in "An Incident with a Classic," which is built on various cultural strata. "The Way Home" explores the relationships between a father and his son. In it we observe the main character wandering through the streets of Lviv, with his physical movement paralleling the mental journey of self-analysis and the realization of the purposelessness of his life. "The *Église* by the Station" conveys the history of a Polish Catholic church at a square near the railroad station in Lviv. The changes the church undergoes over time reflect the transitions in the political and cultural life of the city. "Introduction to the Galician Context," as a sample of Klekh's work in the genre of the creative essay, relates the tragic story of Bruno Schultz, whose high art and tragic death at the hand of the Nazis become for Klekh the emblem of the best and the worst that have occurred in this "border" land.

The two Carpathian novellas represent Klekh's most recent development as a writer. The earlier piece, *A Tiny Farmstead in the Universe,* deals with local Hutsul culture, which has preserved close ties with the ancient beliefs and rituals of the Ukrainian highland dwellers. It describes the narrator's annual visits in the Carpathians to a small farmstead, which belongs to a forester named Nikola. The novella comprises a philosophical discourse on the purpose of human life and its values—and its title echoes Gogol's famous collection of stories *Evenings on a Farm Near Dikanka.*

Klekh's most recent novella, *The Death of the Forester,* is based on autobiographical material from the time Klekh taught at a secondary school in Ukraine. Its plot consists of several stories organized around the narrator's visit with his uncle, who lives in the town where the narrator used to work as a secondary-school teacher several years ago. The reader will discover several narratives interwoven in it: the love story of a mentally challenged schoolgirl Marusya and a carpenter Shchek (whose name recalls the legendary founder of the city of Kyiv); stories of the town's different inhabitants; as well as the history of the region. The result is a complex mosaic in which Marusya becomes a kind of Holy Virgin, Shchek a mock Christ, and the narrator the prodigal son.

The prose of Igor Klekh is not an easy read—either in the original Russian or in English translation. But it is a read that we feel will be a highly rewarding one for those who take that plunge into discovering Klekh's fascinating literary world where the boundaries of narrative and genres and the meaning of words blur and intertwine. It has been a challenge for us to translate. We have attempted, as much as possible, to maintain the idiosyncratic nature of the original, yet at the same time to make him accessible in English.

■ □ ■ □ ■

AN INTRODUCTION TO THE OSCILLATING
PROSE OF IGOR KLEKH

Andrei Bitov

Translated by Michael M. Naydan and Slava I. Yastremski

In 1957 I found myself in a "construction battalion" where all the
debris of our generation used to end up—invalids, people who had
endured the labor camps, plus those whom the authorities didn't
know where to send. I had been kicked out of college and also landed in this category of people. It was the time when Nikita
Khrushchev had pared down the military and simultaneously freed
the inmates of the labor camps. The construction battalions were not
considered part of the military, and, naturally, we were sent to those
very same labor camps. There they had no idea how to use me;
because I had an incomplete higher education, I was given a clerical
assignment. That's how I was spared from logging. The only human
rights observed there were the rights to elect and be elected to the
Supreme Court. I was assigned to rewrite the lists of people in the
labor camp in alphabetical order. In the very first line I had "Adam
without a patronymic . . ." and some last name. He was a gypsy from
western Ukraine. I, of course, rejoiced because Adam had no
patronymic. He spoke six languages without knowing how to write
and signed an *X* instead of his signature. It meant that there was a
place on earth where one had to know six languages. This is the territory of the former Austro-Hungarian Empire. For some reason that
patronymicless Adam comes to my mind every time I read and think
about the writings of Igor Klekh. Geography is of no little impor-
tance in an attempt to explain individuality—although it doesn't

belong to any single person. They used to say that without the Ukrainian *mova* ("language"), Gogol would never have become a part of Russian language to the degree that he did—with such a freshness, at such an acute angle equal to his prominent, sharply pointed nose. They say that the Ukrainians sing better, that they have a warmer climate, and that their vocal cords are softer—that's why there is such a melodiousness in their language. They say that in western Ukraine in particular they have a better talent for design—they paint their houses with more beautiful ornaments, carve lovely wooden toys. Out of all of this (if we exclude our dislike for the militia, the sergeants and corporals), the positive image of the Ukrainian competes simultaneously with a negative one. And if you travel now in a train from the north to the south or from the south to the north, you can feel—more keenly in a train going to the north—that the border of Ukraine is objective. Not because they now have placed pointless tollgates and customs officials at whom people groan on both sides of the border. You enter a different geography, trees curl their branches in a different way, hills slope somehow differently—and you understand that you have crossed from Ukraine to Russia. Ukraine for the Russian imperial consciousness is still not quite south—south is the Crimea, the Caucasus. But Ukraine clearly is not Russia. And here, by the air, by those same vocal cords, by not the bellowing but the purling of spoken speech, having brought all these isolated notions together, I discover Igor Klekh—a man from Lviv who used to be a designer. I have never heard him sing, but by the way he sings out his stories and the details of his prose, all this is connected for me with a geographic mentality. Though you will never catch him being exclusively regional. By the way, he has turned out to be quite a European writer. In addition to his clearly defined Europeanness, he doesn't have any absolute Russianness with all his wonderful use of the Russian language. Instead there is that Eastern European spot where patronymicless Adam lives, which had been erased by the Germans, the Hungarians, the Poles, the Ukrainians, and the Russians, and the air in his throat somehow oscillates differently.

The very first Klekh story I read some time ago delighted me. It was a story about Gogol written with a wonderful understanding of the contemporaneity of the life of the great writer based on the experience of the author's own generation. Everything Klekh writes has its own intonation, its own dialect, its own style, and it is very convincing and manifest. It would be much more difficult to discuss what he writes about. Because as a true master (people are born masters and do not become them), behind his attitude to the material at hand—to that wall of a bungalow, to that rooster to be painted on it, to a sound being sung—he evidently quite diligently and quite skillfully conceals his authorial *I*. That's why it is difficult to surmise what he is writing about, but there is the feeling that he is writing about *something*—a sign of an author who has a detached perspective.

That is why I leave it to you, the readers, to judge what he is writing about.

■ □ ■ □ ■

A LAND THE SIZE
OF BINOCULARS

GALICIAN MOTIFS

■ □ ■ □ ■

KALLIMAKH'S WAKE

HE STEPPED ONTO THE COBBLESTONES OF THE STREET, ALONG WHICH the formerly nonmenacing Polish kings had entered the city. The Galician Gate, the Chapel of the Boims—the cortege stopped at Pidzamche, and later at one of the palazzi of Rynok Square—for two weeks the malmsey wine flowed, the delegations were relieved, the well-groomed patrician ladies slipped out into the night and appeared from out of that night in the illuminated palazzi, shadows glided in the windows.

During the day the market was crowded, near the traps with live fish servants were hired and infidel children were bought and sold, there were baskets with grapes and barrels with fermenting plums; berets, turbans, caps, and yarmulkes, tasting and haggling, disappearing in the illusion of rows of tradesmen beyond the city hall into the forest.

With the law of logic, besides Magdeburg Law, the free city of Lviv, the capital of Galician Rus, was invested by the king's power. And the merchants of all Europe gathered there, all manner of languages intermingled, interest was simmering, deals were struck— the froth of Babylon deprived of grandeur, Brueghel's spittle, the spirit of the onrushing temporal flesh of the Middle Ages.

The city had taken only its name from Leo, it scorned the secrets of Venetian glass, the madness of transmutations, the fiery debates of the Sorbonne, sending its sons to Bologna and Padua and receiving traders thence, lawyers and doctors, dispatching for architects from Italy, a master clockmaker from Peremyshlyany, executioners from

Germany—a secondhand dealer of a city, the temporary nearsighted doorkeeper of Europe. Its power and rule were pellucid, it fell with the fall of Constantinople, Caffa, and Belgorod—the result of an external factor, the sweeping thrusts of the misty crescent moon—in the so thickly stirred cauldron of the city, by name bequeathed, culture had not boiled dry: all the generations of its inhabitants in the future were fed with this pig slop.

One day together with the Wallachian cattle traders, through the Galician Gate, Kallimakh Buonaccorsi, a poet, entered the city.

■   ❑   ■

Kallimakh was cautiously returning to the Christian world after two years of roaming. After the arrest of the freethinkers in the papal scriptorium, when his friends had heaped guilt on the fleeing Kallimakh for his Catalinian oratories, for his being the first to have the idea come into his head about a conspiracy and an attempt on the life of the keeper of the first apostle's keys, His Holiness Paul II—for two years since then the flames released after him licked at his heels, the soles of his feet cracked all over from the heat of the earth that more than once seemed like it would buckle and swallow him, the papal spies and the legates who set off after him like arrows from a papal quiver persecuted him on the farthest islands of the Mediterranean, forcing him to repeat that flight of Odysseus, fraught with dangers, adventures, and literary reminiscences—only in reverse order, to finally reach his eastern Istanbul as though he were a genie from the *Thousand and One Nights,* in the wink of an eye, struck by the city's towers and minarets and a carpet thrown onto the empty, sacred spot of Great Constantinople—so that like the beggar Sinbad he could unrepentantly loiter about the bazaars and squares, avoiding the colony of kinsmen, and when relations between the Ottomans and Rome got better, to lose himself in the wild horizon of the Black Sea.

From Wallachia he exchanged letters with his cousin on his mother's side, Ainolfo Tedaldi, from Lviv, an influential merchant, the head of a trading house, who offered him sanctuary and protection—it was only then by a circuitous path on the periphery of the Catholic world that once again the flying figure of an insolent

Italian reappeared in a dust-covered short cape, in slippers ready to crack apart like a dried-up streambed.

■　❑　■

How many were there then when they didn't even have the common name of "humanists" in fifteenth-century Europe?

Five hundred? More? Hardly.

An informal union of tens, of hundreds of people—bankers of new knowledge and dead languages, torchbearers of language, carriers of a new faith—as though with a mysterious wafer beneath their tongues—and carriers of a fresh ethics beneath the joyful yet still-reverberating burden of them; in stiff Confucian clothes, in the armor of philological scholarliness, they sat long in the rulers' libraries working on manuscripts, with a fragile, composed voice they laid down the law from the cathedrals and stepped out into the gardens of the new Academies beneath new skies. Reverentially they grew numb, chilled, before the profiles of statues unloaded onto piers; before the first observed perfect male body, for the first time in a thousand years, deprived of covers and crates; they were astonished at the dignity of Athenian goddesses and the fortress of their breasts—with their puffy fingers touching cold veins, freeing the marble body from the earth, and feeling, the way an inner light fills up their own forgotten human bodies with warmth.

They loved: subtle wines, imported from far away, healing the spirit with conversation and daydreams of roaming, they loved disputes and glory, they loved women invested with an unfeminine woman's mentality, they loved one another—at a distance—by correspondence.

This brilliant Renaissance assemblage that had torn the Earth from its pillars with Archimedes' lever of Ratio, so that the caravels flew out of the ports and rocked on the waves—the powerful perching Earth, unaware of its own body, being still half flat, not emboldened either to open up or close like a globe, either to enter into an a cappella round dance of luminaries, either to follow after the setting sun, losing its shores. . . . The Titans Putti—the Wunderkinder of Quattrocento—invited the Earth to a dance, without realizing the immensity of their partner, without knowing her temperament, powerful, like an earthquake. And sleeping till now, having turned out to be a sphere, having been torn from the sacral tripod, she rolled swiftly up and down like Leonardo's wheel, with spokes of arms and legs, released downhill, gaining speed, because in this world the ENERGY OF FALLING expands the speed of bodies. Worlds moved from their spot and began to glimmer, unwinding with centrifugal youthful hurling power, so that in five centuries it can fuse in a single solid white glimmering shroud . . .

■ ❑ ■

A completely different text occupied his consciousness, seeking an exit, swirling in him and depriving him of his last peace, he lost his strength, it didn't stop making him feel sick to his stomach; a white sheet of paper swayed before his eyes. Trying hard to grab onto its nonexistent edges, to hold on to his lightheadedness, he again swallows the nausea moving up to his throat—a chunk of chewed papier-mâché in which there was only bile, spittle, and bad blood mixed in with dreams and letters of the alphabet. He stirred his whitened lips, tightening—till his bones hurt—his unneeded fists and with difficulty disengaged his teeth.

Sensing that only direct speech can help him.

DIRECT SPEECH

(descending into the cellar of a bread store opposite the Latin church)

"Girls clutch their knees, and little boys flex their muscles."

And they clench their fists.

Here is an illness from which we all suffer. The covering of the mind (we write *mind, fear* is in the mind) has made us gloomy. Has thickly covered our faces, has wrapped us so that we cannot breathe or live; those who were nearby have already suffocated with their face in a pillow (he recalled a friend of his who from childhood was fearful of just such a death)—he's on the contrary—". . . I'm just fearful of the guillotine. In a wondrous way I'm tied to the eccentricity of my head—a bony growth, a thinking fist with the whimsical hairy growth and the mass of the soft loathsome appendices of a human face, only the absence of imagination and conceit of a man force him to find beauty in the construction of his own head, and all the same I impetuously fear losing this appendix, this throwaway of the body, overgrown with the organs of feelings, with timid tiny bridges to the external world, which nurtured that brain in the bone of the head, I'm still afraid . . . This is Avidia, the antonym of Nirvana, another name for Klyosha, my schoolboy nickname, the name of brain centrism, an illness, a thin, tiny chain, like a notation in a passport: Registered in Avidia."

"What are you clenching in your fist, fool? Let go—you'll see—it's not EMPTY!"

. . . In observing small mammals—dogs, hamsters, the neuroses of feline love, the parsimonious life of people, it's difficult to rid yourself of the thought that life is a quivering, the slight quivering of the rhythms of survival, torn away by birth from great energies and rhythms (how do wasps know what kind of winter it will be?)—splashes of life, which become obsolete in their own way, in crampedness and in the commotion of everyday life, in a droplet of a preparation beneath God's microscope.

A man wouldn't survive a summer—not even a week—in his limitations without the freshening emptiness and grounding, without the intervals of sleep, the gift of dissolution, depriving us of freedom to force our body, leaving our soul only a memory and a sum, and then kindly depriving us even of this last burden. What can you—a point—know about a line, like something as simple as eternity and infinity, what can you—flatness—know about a sphere, when it passes right through you: a point, an expanding circle, a contracting circle, a point, flatness . . .

. . . Autumn. Flies are freezing, are clinging to a man's head just to warm up. White circles swim up in a bowl above peeled potatoes. Spiders close the affair and hang themselves on their own work, as though completely bankrupt, tired of eternally dying and resurrecting.

"How an extinguished cigarette suddenly becomes lighter! . . ."

A woman-child, in white curls and wrinkles of antediluvian skin, smiling, took away his coffee cup, wiped off the table, leaving the wet traces of a snail. He followed her back, moving farther away with his gaze—at times the disappearing silhouette with a basin of filthy dishes . . . a transparent blouse . . . the double trail of her bodice on her shoulder blades. . . . Then he moved toward the exit, scrounging in his pockets for a cigarette lighter, then stopping, lit up a cigarette.

And already at the tight turn of the stairwell he suddenly remembered the dreams of last night: about the caves of death—about underground terraces that move away downward in wide steps into the blackness of passages—and about a talking dog—a shadow lay from it in the form of a short ladder. His head again began to spin.

■   ❑   ■

Toward a green hillock on a plain the distant wasteland tracks rushed, the nearby paths from the farmsteads and farms were crawling like grass eels and intertwined around it, streams and rivers flowed away from here along the plain; in its depth among the diverging earthen ramparts, it was as if in a harbor above a mountain there stood at anchor a cumbersome flagship—a fortified city, in the masts of towers, in Gothic rigging, in scaffolding and pennants, encircled with a double belt of walls, earthen ramparts, and moats, closed by the declaiming rhythm of bastions and defending towers, each one erected and defended by one of the trade guilds of the city; this is a list of them, it is like a deafening load of hay, frozen forever in the Middle Ages, but the scent of which penetrates centuries and makes the head swirl to our prose:

1. above the Krakow Gate: the furriers;
2. sack makers, tinsmiths, and soap makers;
3. sword makers;
4. weavers;
5. hat makers and saddle makers;
6. brewers and mead makers;
7. harness makers;
8. masons;
9. rope makers and turners;
10. boot makers;
11. potters and cauldron makers;
12. above the Galician Gate: tailors;
13. coopers, carpenters, and wagon makers;
14. carvers;
15. blacksmiths, lock makers, and toolmakers;
16. shopkeepers;

17. bakers;
18. goldsmiths.

The entire flotilla of settlements, of fortified monasteries, churches, and water mills swayed around the flagship from both near and far.

On the oars of the counterforces an ark of poor people—the hospital floated up to the walls of the city—a Polish church and the monastery of St. Stanislav.

The helmets of the church of St. George the Dragonslayer were ablaze at dawn, who, with the narrow spear of an idea, was smiting a coiling serpent on a mountain.

Above the orphaned, princely Old Rus city of Pidzamche left outside the walls—above the city of Leo—Leopolis, Lemberg—and above the entire landscape to the horizon towered, occupying the peak of the cliff, a guardpost fort—Vysokyi Zamok, put together from rough stone blocks. A secret underground passageway linked it with Pidzamche. In the middle of the courtyard a deep well had been dug. In the year 410 in its dungeons the knights captured at Grünwald waited out their ransom. The garrison of the castle consisted of fifty soldiers. Leaving them for the defense of the city, the king didn't forget to set aside for them the right to free bathing in the city's bathhouse once a week. Attached to the wall of Pidzamche, the bathhouse was a crowded place.

The Klekhs used to bring their schoolchildren here to bathe, accompanied by the singing of "De profundis," merchants arranged for meetings here and concluded transactions—people came here to rest, to clean the pores of their skin, to trade news, to spend time, to copulate.

The city oozed with sewage, with the stink of bulls' intestines—the stink coming from the plank troughs of the sewage system—it reverberated with rat passageways made beneath it and in it, as though a parallel city-bone eater were built into it and rapidly expanded, an insertion, dissolving its bone and brain, threatening to change the main city into an empty set decoration, stone into papier-mâché, into a shell ready to collapse into itself.

The city was cleaned up twice a year, at Easter and at Christmas, and for greater zeal among the population in this matter, the city executioner was installed to manage the cleaning. In another time on his squeaking heavy wagon, he used to cart off out of town and burn all kinds of junk and carrion, in expectation of his starry hour on the main crimson platform amid the spreading dead rippling of heads.

The heart of Leopolis was the stomach that occupied its center: the market, the square. The merchant bazaar element simmered and spattered around the eight-sided tower of the city council hall—casing for clock and power, with totems of stone lions at the entrance to the morose mechanism, with a tidal wave it pressed the clock, haggled on the steps of the scaffold, swelled with tents and the covered carts of rows of merchants, with entire streets of warehouses, shops, and workshops, as though in a seashell colony, it overgrew the stones of the pavement, the rear facade of the city council building. From the basements of the city council building wine was sold, from them the bars of the prison holds looked out. The lapping of subterranean lakes carried from the prison holds of the medieval republic. The ground was like a deck partly dried up above an abyss, and not even the archbishop could be assured in it.

As though into a Cossack's thin gruel they threw everything they had in their pockets or bags—lard, dried millet, tobacco—this way into the city—into a circle—they were tossed and divided among themselves by the Germans and Armenians, the Poles, the tramp Ruthenians, the Jews and the Italians, the Wallachians and the Greeks—into a city alien for them all, a haven for nations and hearts torn loose—in order to overcome this beggarly world disconnectedness, his own and its. The Armenians erected stone houses, paved the courtyards, rebuilt the church, the Jews locked their street at nights with a chain, the barefoot Ruthenians crowded beneath the eastern wall like parasites, trading in salt, in the city council building German speech reverberated, the Poles quickly finished building a cathedral—beneath its walls, still in scaffolding, the patricians of the city were already being buried. Into the words of the prayers at times there interwove shouts carrying from the closest tower of the masons—from the torture tower of the executioner. Carpenters' hammers knocked along the roof. At the slaughterhouse, cattle roared. An organ hollowly droned—the high voice of a Polish Catholic priest covered up the hum of the organ pipes—a liturgy was going on. From a tiny chunk of land so many sounds emanated, rose to the heavens, superimposing and interweaving, intermixing on the way, fusing—already in the ear of God—into a single indistinguishable lowing: the agony of the earth.

Fate, having broken loose Kallimakh from his chain, tossed him out onto this clod of earth.

■   ❑   ■

The clock on the town hall was beating the hour of ten. The square was unremarkable and empty. The stores were just opening up, in various places the streetlights were beginning to work. At gate 26, the nauseous odor of eau de cologne from a neighboring door. The hair salon opened at seven in the morning: it was difficult to imagine its clients at that hour.

In the semidarkness of the entrance, infused ammoniac intermixed with the eau de cologne. In the depth of the cement floor before the shackled tin plate door, in the darkness for some reason, an empty bottle was standing. The door was locked, no one was there. In any case he tugged at the door, drawing out of its body warped with locks the sounds of frozen iron emptiness. At that hour they could be drinking coffee in Virmenska Street. He again stepped out onto the square. The morning happened to be chilly and overcast, several times it had already begun to drizzle. The dank Lviv autumn had arrived. He started to cut across the square, having decided to go down to the toilet beneath the city hall—to urinate for later. He had a lot of things to do ahead of him.

"What's stopping you from being a puppeteer of good prose?" he thought. "Where have all the plots gone? What kind of fertile soil for a plot can your life of avoiding give you, *socium*, and its meager offerings? What can be more dead and more fantastic than the working day of a working man, and, if not for us, then for the mentality of the Russian language, the essence of work is well known and accessible—the hidden antonym of labor. How many macabre stories occur somewhere on the boring periphery of life, wherever literature goes seeking the typical? Can you build a plot on the fact that without any kind of Wolands, a young female student during work in the fields in the fall had her head cut off by a potato combine? And neither

Gogol nor Zoshchenko would risk jotting down the plot of how a bride-to-be on her wedding day was given a silver-plated watch — everything that was left of her fiancé, who, after a bachelor's bash the night before, had fallen into a tub of acid. Phew, Lord! Who, besides life, would be bold enough to present us with such a joke? Or here, a sign, already forgotten, of the beginning of the "Andropov Era"— at that time no one doubted this—a thunderstorm in January: Icy sleet, a downpour, thunder and lightning; after six o'clock in the evening from the colossal figure of the Statue of Liberty sitting on the roof of the former Galician bank, illuminated by the thunderstorm, the hand with the torch fell off, fell down and killed a young woman on the pavement, for some reason also a female student—a lot of people study in this country. . . . And Andropov managed only to come to frighten everybody, to give everyone hope and to die— and already from beyond the grave, suddenly extending his hand like a vampire to drag off with him to the grave the name of an ancient Russian city on the Volga—Rybinsk. Who wouldn't feel themselves to be a complete idiot here? . . .

"A horde of questions crowded behind thin partitioning, beyond the torn door of your study, in the corridors and rooms of the workers' dormitory. And the first one of them: What are you doing here?

"But they keep silent and lead their eyes away. Galicia is here, they're tolerant of foreigners here.

"The swinish heaviness of lead and the sharp edges of glass hid your life from them, having taken you as a hostage, having designated the allowance and soldered up your freedom and your time, having forced you to look through several dim pieces of glass not fired quite long enough in the oven at the luster of Soviet sidewalks, to capture at four-thirty in the morning the sun reflecting in the windows of the buildings on the opposite side, to listen to the annoying drone of tractor-trailers, their unceremonious horn blasts at the checkpoint, to guess by the sound of water that it's raining, to guess it's the murky streams of time, turning the pavement for half an hour into a noisy mountain river that runs down from the Austrian Citadel—which is the color of baked brick—the warehouses of a television factory.

"Your life is shifted toward evening, and you step out to see how the wind rinses the wash on the towers of Magdalene—on the balconies, carried off into the sky—the world and evening enter a quieted-down city, as though someone in an empty room had set down a glass of water onto the windowsill. You've already forgotten how quiet it can be in the world when all the building sites fall silent, when all the truck transports and deliveries cease, and the universe rests until morning. The tram cars roll along the streets like children on roller skates, just barely jingling on the turns with the coins for a tram ticket.

"High above the city like the scattering of tiny black seeds, flocks of ravens and rooks circle, gathering from the outlying areas in the city parks to spend the night, in the sky capturing the final warmth.

"And the city has already begun to get dark, like water in a pond, when the air is still lightly saturated and warm, and you make your final insatiable inhalations with the day that came up to you just like a cigarette butt.

"Why are you tugging at the hems of Kallimakh, then heaping up introductions, what in general do you have to do with him and his time, with whom did you intend to argue, and what kind of refined lie are you preparing in your heart? What kind of desires are inflaming your guts and your imagination? Do you really know how to undress a woman of the fifteenth century?"

(But the more he asked himself questions and failed to find arguments, the more he continued his writing with despairing decisiveness.)

■   ❏   ■

The fate that had saddled Kallimakh didn't even give him the chance to catch his breath this time. Barely having hidden himself in the walls of the city, he was struck by love.

Was he wounded by the rusty arrow of the redheaded Faniola, the tavernkeeper, did the poison begin to wander along his swollen veins, in a net of deep blue snakes twined, salted through and dried by the deprivations of the body of a thirty-two-year-old Italian man—in a tangle of arteries and veins that clenched his throat, that dried out his larynx—what was this sweetest of all septicemias, this threatening transfiguration? Who knows? Who remembers?

It's as though everything is the same, only you're five centimeters above the earth—and it's impossible to get used to this.

Once in the spring Kallimakh sprightly ran to the wine cellar on Rynok Square to refresh himself with a goblet of wine, and he was inebriated by another much stronger wine, from which he will be unable to tear away for two whole years. The sweet wine fermented, and went bad, it poured and spilled in the cellar of the merchant woman Faniola—a magnificent redhead, a flying enchantress, a beauty—where the wine trade moved along swiftly, in smacks and pinches, in fleeting kisses and slaps to the head, Fanusya was not greedy with her bounties—business would be good and her mother satisfied—but at the last instant she slipped out—your arms caught emptiness—and she was flying, to the envy of all, to meet her fate, toward the table of a strange, shaggy Vlokh who was losing his liveliness with every passing day, scribbling Latin verses that were sonorous but unintelligible to her, sitting at the tables with wine spilled all over them—she gathered them almost into a pile, he was turning pale and wringing his fingers out of jealousy for her, ridiculous in his undivided passion and attractive in his gloomy faithfulness.

What's wrong with you, Vlokh, is it you, Kallimakh? You're a complete adolescent in your thirty-two years—smile, savage—Is this really the way you conquer maidens' hearts, can't you see that she can't understand anything in your Latin?

Enraged, Kallimakh runs out of the cellar and—through the Krakow Gate—from the borders of the city, having forgotten that he doesn't have any money with him to return, and, after circling around the hills, the orchards, and the vineyards, he'll hang out after sunset at the city gates, waiting until the city patrician Ainolfo Tedaldi, himself in clothing with fur trim, surrounded by servants with torches, approaches the gates from the other side, to convince the guard to allow the frozen Kallimakh into the city and to pay the police constables a generous recompense. Tedaldi, saddened by the conduct of his relative, all the same understood that it was difficult to make a merchant out of a poet, especially when he's over thirty years old, and, although he looked at his service in his office with closed eyes, he wanted him, at least, to be concerned more about his future. So he insisted that Kallimakh try very hard, although it was unknown how long he would have to live in this region, to set himself up with influential patronage. He named several candidates to choose from, and Kallimakh, who always treated his gift as though it were an instrument, obediently got his cherished trunk with his writing accessories, where his texts also were kept, and, having chosen two of his Roman dedications with particularly immoderate hyperboles in fanciful syntax, he meticulously rewrote them, inserting other titles and new-sounding names. Having right then and there put them aside for the night, jotting down a verse consummated yesterday beneath the walls of the city and nurtured on the hills, he turned to a hallucination, to the "unfaithful" redhead Faniola, to profess his beloved to death on paper, because of the impossibility of doing this in bed, so that tomorrow, pale from sufferings, he could once again hand her his poetic credentials in the sound of pure Latin, and, reading it aloud, will he be awarded a kiss or a bite?—on his earlobe, which, like thunder, as though he were placed beneath a bell, blinded him.

Kallimakh spent the entire day getting besotted with wine, trying hard to cool off his burning ear with various vintages, not hearing anything, and only seeing—from the distance—how Faniola, laughing, was winding through the other tables, avoiding his corner, and how the heated-up honored merchants were joking and embracing her waist, how she spun away from the hands of the drunkards, and how, beaks opening, the heads of the hatchling crow apprentices endlessly followed her rear end.

Italian curses again rose in Kallimakh's throat, forcing him to choke on the wine. He had already had enough today. Reeling, he clambered along the spattered steps while up behind his back the thunder and laughter failed to quiet down, and through the fumes of her broad flesh on bone, through the steam of the wine, Faniola's eyes shimmered gaily. Urinating right on the door, in unsure steps Kallimakh crosses the emptying square. The night watch is warming himself by a fire. Shutters are being shut, light is making its way through their cracks.

He met all the Tedaldis together by the fireplace in the dining room. Ainolf invited him to the library. He is leaving tomorrow for Krakow on the business of his mercantile firm and is taking with him Kallimakh's panegyrics, to pass them along personally and at the same time to determine the possibility of setting him up with a position at court.

"Phillipe, I'm surprised at you," Tedaldi finally says, "at the carefree way you're spending such a gift to turn the heart of some female barkeep! Wake up! A brilliant future is waiting for you in this barbarian country. Mark my words."

He embraced Kallimakh to say farewell and began to pack up papers.

In the dining room Tedaldi's little boys throw themselves at Kallimakh, asking that he tell them a tale about the Janissaries, about pirates, or about the scaly nereids that live in the depths in the shadow of the cliffs right at the very shore. Moving his tongue with difficulty, Kallimakh asks that they warm some water for him to bathe. The servants, gathering in a crowd at the door, disappointedly disperse, and young Mrs. Tedaldi takes the children away to sleep. Unlike her husband, with great understanding she relates to the sufferings of the new relative and, mocking him, tries hard to teach him a little bit of Polish, surmising fairly that several *c*-sounding and hushing locutions—which were much more pleophonic than the voiced Italian and the so distant and so beautiful Latin—will turn the fiery Faniola's little ear to the curls of her countryman wounded with love.

Kallimakh stretched out his legs to the embers, and quickly, in the fireplace's warmth, the room began to rush about beneath him, like a deck. He spitefully guessed whether Tedaldi's wife will bring him his towels herself or send a female servant instead . . .

■   ❑   ■

Quite unexpectedly on one of the final days of spring Kallimakh Buonaccorsi was suddenly made one of the happiest of mortals. Closing up shop and chasing out the last of the customers, Faniola, cleaning scraps from the table of the Vlokh, who had grown weary and thin, suddenly grabbed him from behind by the neck so that his hair fell on his face—his shoulder blades instantly felt the divided taut points of her breasts—and placed her finger to his lips.

The Vlokh, having turned deaf, blind, and nearly breathless, stepped after her, and it wasn't until the third floor, right before her door, that he managed to exhale some air. Blood thrust him to the assault, spreading his hands, coupling them onto the bulges of her breast and the inward curve of her waist—pressing her and bending her in two—she was barely able to drag him past the door, whispering something and shutting his mouth with the iron key in her hand.

Being inexperienced in these subtleties which Roman courtesans commanded perfectly, Faniola, it seemed, had been created for the business of love. Already half-crazed from restraint, the Italian gathered speed and pulled the love harness close, forcing the inaccessible and shameless body beneath him, before him, above him, to move from moans and complete exhaustion to swallowed shouts to tears and moans again—it seemed to him that bits of pepper had been scattered between them, which he should have collected and crushed with Faniola together in that mortar of love, and, just flushed, burning, stiffening—he hadn't noticed how he had ended up pushed onto the stairway just before the arrival of her mother from vespers.

Muffling himself in a short cape, carrying like a clasp the traces of a bite on his shoulder and the mystery of her tiny tongue—the afterbite of a parting kiss in the doorway—he slid in the early twilight along the high sidewalks of Rynok Square toward the Tedaldi hearth, where he could calm his throbbing shudder with a goblet of wine, and, having thawed out and suddenly become limp by the fire, in the insatiability of desire—after two years of wandering—he could unexpectedly feel himself to be the happiest of mortals.

Tedaldi's wife was winding a silk thread by the light of the fireplace. Ainolf was readying to depart. Drinking one more goblet of warmed-up wine, Kallimakh moved over to the library, lit a candle, and set out a piece of paper.

Still one more poem, addressed to Faniola, will emerge today from his quill. These centurions obedient to him and their cohorts of lines and strophes will greet the Lviv redhead in triumph, as a goddess.

■   ❏   ■

Tedaldi returned with a stack of news, tired, frightened by the accounts of the frequent attacks of the Tartars on the borders of the

Polish-Lithuanian Principality—as if they had been seen in the out-skirts of Peremyshlyany, near Lviv—the entire neighborhood now sat on bundles, having packed up their household belongings, and at the appearance of any two riders on the horizon were ready to rush to the city gates to trample a few dozen people, to hide in the walls of the city from the savage calamity—the slant-eyed, biblical locust.

Now back to things. Kallimakh's dedications were accepted gra-ciously, in the court, they say, the Hapsburgian lady, Queen Elisabeth, concerned with the education of her growing sons, might become interested in him, if the business were promoted correctly. . . . And everything would have been fine if, while Ainolf was in Krakow, the papal legate from Rome had not arrived at Wawel Hill and had not demanded the return of the political criminal and the most evil enemy of the Christian world, the heretic who had made an attempt on the pope's life—you yourself know who it was.

Kallimakh's heart began to despair on thinking of Faniola. It was difficult to drive it into a corner—fate had given him light legs and had taught him to be prepared for everything—he thought despon-dently how his former friends would blacken his name at the inquests—erudite and sharp-witted revelers—the friend and teacher of Plotinus and the great Pomponius Leto himself, having turned up in the dungeons of the papal fortress of the Holy Angel—what kind of demonic criminal they would make of him, so that this puppet within a puppet, this nothing with the broken egg of a tiara on his head in a fury could scrape his claws in every corner of Europe just to get to the most unnoticeable of mortals, some scribbler on demand, a poet in a circle of friends, a certain Philippe Buonaccorsi (a Florentine? or a Venetian?), who acquired for himself by vainglo-rious custom of the newly appeared academies the name of a certain Kallimakh (an Alexandrian? a Gnostic? a librarian?)—just to get to him and, pressing him in a callused paw, to squeeze out his young life drop by drop, to crush him rather than part with his . . . Ainolf rushed to reassure Kallimakh.

"Do you see, Philippe, the Polish kings have never walked under the rein of Rome, the Polish kings since long ago have cut short the interference of popes in secular matters, as well as their pretensions to spiritual matters, in their own domains. All of this is a long story and grand politics. Now the Polish-Lithuanian Principality had very serious reasons for alarm in the eastern and southern regions. In the very near future, it would have been impossible for us to escape a clash with the Ottomans and Tartars."

(With surprise Kallimakh noticed this "us" in the speech of Tedaldi, his cousin, the Italian.)

"Their strength is like the locusts—you saw yourself—and the Polish-Lithuanian Principality in light of this threatening danger cannot remain in isolation, we must now in every way strengthen our alliances and ties with our neighbors and with the entire Christian world. Here they still haven't forgotten the resounding defeat at Varna. It is natural therefore that the king doesn't want to ruin relations with Rome."

Seeing how Kallimakh's face was stretching, Ainolf, evidently not expecting such an effect from his foray into grand politics, hurriedly continued: "Philippe, my friend, you've understood me incorrectly, the king evaded a direct answer, offered to look over your matter at the next Seym in Petrokov. You haven't heard, surely, that the Polish gentry is extremely daring and willful? I think, I'm nearly convinced, that they will be unable to make an agreement about anything. All the same from our perspective we need to be concerned about guarantees of your safety. You need ties and protectors, and the more the better. You should manage to dispose everyone to your use. You should also think about a sanctuary in case of the worst. Who would have thought, Philippe, that your misfortunes would follow you even here to our godforsaken Sarmatia! . . ."

"They tattled to him quickly," Kallimakh responded gloomily. "Now I can at least run to Moscovy, there's nowhere farther to go, just to the Tartars right away . . .

"Why to the Tartars? And Moscow's not the end of the world! I can always, in the worst case, disappear for half a year or a year with a merchant caravan, and after a year a lot can change. And then afterward, everything isn't as bad while it's taking shape, nothing new or awful has happened, and there are no reasons at all to look gloomily at the future! . . ."

Chatting for another half hour and reassuring each other as best they could, the cousins parted preoccupied, Ainolf to his study to return to his business, Kallimakh to Faniola's cellar, to share the news with his beloved, to think up something together with a flagon of good wine to wash down the bad news, to wait till the cellar closed.

■   ❑   ■

Kallimakh continued to write Fanya poems filled with rapture and reproaches and finally found a path to her heart, and—although not thanks to them—she was prepared to listen to them and even to try to understand what he was talking about, for they clearly did not have enough words in common between them.

On the other hand their dictionary of love expanded with each day. In good order the tables and benches in the cellar served them; after it closed down, they knowingly used the departures of Fanya's mother, who every other day stood through vespers, and although she suspected her daughter in whatever she could, she wasn't emboldened to proceed against her, finding herself dependent on her—and the business didn't go any further than admonitions and threats addressed to the dissolute Italian. Fortunately, not being in contact with the Italian colony, for the time being she didn't know a tenth of the transgressions of the godless Deviltalian Kallimakh, and she was largely unaware of what brought him to Lviv, much less able to guess that her daughter had become a victim of such a refined corruption and such monstrous caprices—undoubtedly, she would have considered him the embodiment of the devil. Her daughter had already completely lost her mind over her Italian and barely took care of her business affairs.

On Sundays after matins, and even during the light of day, Kallimakh came for her and took her away for a stroll beyond the walls of the city. It was a hot summer, and walking far away through the hills along Hlynyansky Trakt Road, leaving behind them Vysokyi Zamok and passing the outskirts of town, they found a glade and a small stream in a secluded thicket and began their lessons of love. Kallimakh unlaced her sleeves, unbuttoning them, freed her of her skirts, took off her undershirt and finally the transparent cups holding up her breasts, and then he allowed her to do the same with him, beginning with his cape and ending with his tight sashes. They're naked, like the heroes of myths, like a satyr and a dryad, like Hermaphroditos and Salmacis, they intertwined, playing out the eternal mystery of love, in the end not restraining their cries or moans, caressing each other half to death and coming back to life again and again. Then, coming across a mushroom growing in moss, Fanya carefully and cautiously, the way one tests cold water with the tip of the toe, licked it first, and then Kallimakh. Thus they ended up cast into an abyss of salty mermaid caresses, a submersion into which the horizon shudders and capsizes with a ripple widening into a complete ring, taking off the bitter juice of life from between each other's legs, from their gates opened wide.

They returned to the city at sunset with armfuls of field flowers and grasses with which floors are covered in houses, and Faniola's always lowered hair, decorated with a fresh wreath, burned like a fire in tangent rays of the sun, and although her knees and the small of the back hurt and her skin itched where pricked by the grass and bitten by insects, like a tsarina, lightly and freely, she passed through the guard who yielded way, glistening in his chest armor in the melted gold of the arc of the Krakow Gate.

Kallimakh was mad over his Fanya. His inflamed skin melted from not finding for itself a release for his tenderness for her.

■ ❏ ■

The spacious room of the public toilet was filled with the roar of cast iron Niagara-brand troughs that had been conceived by the disease control station's standards as an attack of mustard gas. The chlorine ate his eyes. Trying not to breathe deeply and looking away from the attuned pursuers of same-sex love who were hanging around the stalls pretending to urinate, he rushed to Virmenska Street. "They probably got sloshed yesterday . . ."

Not finding them in the coffeehouse, he nearly accepted the unavoidable defeat of his movements today, of his planned meetings, the purchase of cigarettes, glass, a light bulb, and of all kinds of rubbish as well, jotted down since evening on a piece of paper. It's true, he managed to drink some coffee since morning, but this was such great luck, and something—was it experience?—was telling him that the day would not favor his undertakings. The probability of finding someone in the office at that hour or running around half the city to stock up on cigarettes that had disappeared again seemed to be minuscule. Deciding to take a look into the office just for the sake of a clear conscience, he turned the corner and set off again in the direction of the city center along the street of vegetables dangling in the wet baskets of balconies.

"Forget this plot! You took it . . . now put it in its place. You yourself don't believe in it. Because your time has so unlearned how to relate stories, it has stopped believing in them. What worries you in this story of yours? Only its vanity, strictly speaking. It's not in Time that a meeting with Kallimakh is enticing you—a meeting with this Lviv phantom of Italian blood—indeed! . . . The startup and clang of the narrative machine of Time—won't it be the end of both of us? Why disturb the shadows without having the means to distinguish and tie together the past and present? Trying hard to tie together the laces of two shoes, you won't even be able to move a single step. Something keeps you from forcing the plot to live in the violent world you brought forth, to force you to repeat it, ruthlessly, as though in an investigative experiment, words that have stopped reverberating long ago, words that were already completed actions, once again to live through vanished passions—to walk through Lviv, through a disappearing Leopolitana, along the ruins of Dunaev with a tape measure and transit, and to appropriate someone else's life that is incapable of defending itself. The wavering of the air could disturb—and even does disturb every day—that suddenly appearing link, that thinnest immaterial sticky spider web, a filament strained between you and it. You would not wish to meet them in Time, but in another place— there where the wineskins of space are folded and Time calms down, where you can drink some tea—and already you don't have to talk about anything . . .

"Skeletons, dancing skeletons, appear, wrapped up, hidden in the whiteness of the pages of your prose, and right here they disappear in the caustic darkness of today, overexposed by a countless stream of escheated days."

O sour city of sauerkraut and sausage, how you've tormented me! The city is on a river hidden beneath the earth, with walls and Gothic foundations that had long ago submerged beneath the pavements and sidewalks.

In the cellars of Lviv where they keep potatoes for winter, where the ceilings have lancelike Gothic articulations—with the ribs of Leviathan, Leopolis—ceilings whose gray, cracked skin is adorned on top with discolored rusted patches of slogans and banners.

How tired I am of trampling your cemeteries . . . !

■　❑　■

Fate did not let Kallimakh go, intentionally it led him along the circles of trials, each time wondrously saving him, making him understand that another lot is intended for him, so that he even doubted the absence of predetermination—or was it Providence?—and doubted the ponderability of his personal merits in the salvation of his life. This time he raised his godless eyes to the heavens—in perplexity and thanks—when in Petrokov in the Seym after a speech of the legate, who also accused Kallimakh of being a spy of the Turkish sultan, the fatal decision about handing him over to Rome was made, and when all the gold and connections of the house of Tedaldi were no longer in a position to save him, the Lviv Archbishop Grigory of Sanok decided to hide Kallimakh from the wrath of the Roman pope in the archbishop's castle in his little town of Dunaev, a day's trip from Lviv.

At that time Kallimakh understood an important thing that he did not know in his previous hungry, happy, greedy life, something that his wanderings and deprivations had never taught him and about which later, after the lapse of one and a half years in Dunaev, in his new, highly uplifted life in the capital, he would not disclose to his cruel and nefarious time.

He will repay Grigory with what he can, writing for him seven years later the first saint's life in Poland in a new time, where for the ages the image will be kept—the example of the first Polish humanist, in which there will be everything: the frenetic events of Grigory of Sanok's life at the Sian River will be described, his temper, his customs, his views, his appearance, his means of spending time—there will be the main things that Grigory, who was twice his age, made his young friend understand, and things that will forever remain between the two of them in their year and a half of life together in Dunaev, and for that Kallimakh, even with all his wishes, would be unable to repay him, because something—so valuable and rare—in this life created by the Lord God will not be subject to its laws and can only exist as a gift.

■　□　■

On a gray autumn morning a carriage rode out of the Galician Gate, harnessed to a pair of horses, and, making its way onto the Hlynyansky Trakt Road, in the accompaniment of servants on horseback, it rolled along the stony ruts, in the cold rays multiplying its reflection, in the direction of Dunaev, toward a thinning, clearing sky to the east.

When the walls of the city disappeared from sight, having gone into the ground behind the next rise and fall of the road, and the road began to bend around a mountain and then go off through the forest, the carriage stopped at the mass of the basalt cliffs rising like the castle on the slope of the mountain—completely in the billow of gray fur, in clumps of morning fog and rain. From behind the trees several riders stepped out and carefully began to descend along the road. When they approached the carriage, they cursorily greeted the black-bearded portly man sitting in it. Two of them dismounted and, leaving the reins for the third one, crossed over to the carriage: a young man in a short cape with winding wet hair falling onto his shoulders and a young woman with strands of red hair sticking out from beneath her hood. A servant also dismounted and placed two fairly small suitcases at their feet, and, holding their horses in rein, for a long time gazed after the carriage going off in the distance, even after it, along with the people accompanying it, had disappeared beyond the turn of the road that went off down the mountain, bending around a forest lake.

A slight gust of wind shook him out of his stasis, blowing along the treetops and echoing below with the hail of droplets and the soundless slowed snowfall of leaves. After he urinated in a puddle, so that bubbles and a dirty yellowish foam began to run across its surface, he suddenly began to hurry—tying the reins to the saddle of his horse, he jumped up on it, urging it on at times with blows of his heels into its sides, rushing beneath a low-hanging sky on the way back—in the direction of Lviv.

After the descent from the mountain the road moved along a monotonous plain—once again the crosses and the towers of the city rose up and sank down in the distance—and soon the road and with it the carriage became lost in the folds of the wet sackcloth of the boundless expanses. It was just near Peremyshlyany that they began to come across tiny villages on the plain, but beyond the Peremyshlyany that flashed by, beyond the tiny bridge through Hnyla Lypa, the desolation and the backwoods continued.

The carriage rode into a dense forest that was just beginning to decay along the edges of leaves and curling into a funnel, the black wet tree trunks like coals holding up, for the time being, a growing latent heat—into a forest that didn't end until you reached Dunaev itself. Wet foxes cast a sidelong glance at them; snorting and growing furious, it must have been a wild boar running headlong through the bushes; a noble, antler-topped deer stepped out onto the road and darted into a thicket.

The day first was bright, then it began to drizzle, and it was only toward evening that the sun for a little while glanced out into a gap from behind the clouds, as though deliberately, so that on the border of the forests beyond the last thinning trees it suddenly illuminated for the weary travelers shaken by the road and splattered by dirt their goal and haven—Dunaev, with a moist imprint appearing on the friable closing page of the day.

Kallimakh and Faniola, closely pressing to one another with uneasiness in their hearts, looked out into the tiny city on a hill that was within a half mile of them, separated from them by the overflow of water—by the cooling meltwaters fusing on three sides. The western part of the hill, an island that turned out to be a peninsula, was enclosed with an unexpectedly powerful wall, above which rose a Polish church that was gazing through embrasures and several defensive towers. Beneath one of them, on the landlocked wall turned toward the town, there were gates, in which the road beaten by tiredness disappeared, having encircled the hill and opened to hundreds of little white houses.

■   ❑   ■

Life in Dunaev quickly began to flow at a measured pace and not without small pleasures. Grigory, despite his old age, was filled with that clear and peaceful energy, that male energy that can draw strength from experience, illuminated by understanding of the equilibrium and mature proportionality of an active beginning, which, perhaps, can only be achieved at such an age. Having led a stormy life, at the age of twelve he ran away from home, where his father with birch rods tried to turn him away from books, wandering along German cities and universities like a savage ferret, a schoolboy, a choirboy, returning to Poland and exiting from the walls of the Krakow Academy with a baccalaureate of free arts, and after spending two years in Italy at the court of Pope Eugenius IV Condulmero, he became the teacher and confessor of kings and lived through the awful defeat of the Christian army at Varna, was saved at the crossing over the Danube by the Hungarian commander Hunyadi, then finally received through the protection of the old queen Sonka Holschanska, who had a weakness for Lithuanians and Ruthenians, the Lviv eparchy, and, despite the opposition of the cardinal and primate of Poland, Zbigniew Olesnicki, at the age of forty, he donned the violet soutane of archbishop.

Having received from his predecessor, Jan Odrowaz, an impoverished and pillaged eparchy, he began by publicly shaving in the cathedral Polish church the tonsures of the drunkard, shaggy, despairing chaplains. His rhetorical talents, his ability to handle business and achieve stability, his concern over his flock and, not in the least, especially, his concern for the female half—the imposing appearance of a black-bearded prince of the church with a gray streak won him such authority and recognition that soon money and gifts from parishioners poured into the eparchy just like longed-for rain. The influx of means allowed him to renew works and complete the building of the cathedral in Lviv, to expand and then settle the abandoned farms, to fill up the fish ponds, to build bridges and roads, and to buy several villages near Rohatyn.

In Dunaev Grigory erected a stone church and a castle, and he planned below the walls of the castle a little town and settled it, acquiring for the inhabitants the king's privilege for two yearly fairs. Along the outside, the little town was encircled by a rampart and a ditch. Damming up the Zolota Lypa, Grigory turned his Dunaev into an impregnable fortified peninsula—a European chestnut too tough for the Tartar's steppe teeth.

Two years after Kallimakh's visits, when in a sudden attack the Crimean Tartars were devastating Rus and Podolia, bristling up with cannons, catapults, and crossbows, encircled from three sides by water, bristling like a wild boar chased into a swamp, Dunaev remained the only fortress in the Rus that held out under the pressure of the Tartar epidemic. The archbishop, still stately and black-bearded, and even refreshed—as though the horn of youth had summoned him—himself took charge of its defense from the walls. . . . Surviving a prolonged war with the mighty Odrowaz family and emerging from it as a weary victor, Grigory toward the age of sixty managed to restrain his ardor for building. For the most part he now lived in Dunaev, leading a peaceful life of concentration. He visited Lviv only on great holidays, when his liturgies and fiery sermons as before helped gather crowds of many thousands, leading them to a paroxysm of despair, a mass lament, a sense of fraternity before the face of the coming Judge. This scene was repeated time and again, and Grigory was never unfaithful to the flagellant passions and expectations of the crowd.

On Rynok Square, on the eastern side, a three-story home, his city residence, was rebuilt in Italian style. Here Grigory took care of business that had piled up, had audiences for members of the chapter of canons and the magistrate, petitioners, emissaries, and passing travelers. Tedaldi, who was only briefly acquainted with him, once brought his good-for-nothing brother here, knowing that the archbishop loved poetry and conversations about poetry as much as he loved Italy and Italians. With the intention of giving satisfaction to the host, he might secure for Kallimakh high protection. This is how their acquaintance took place, immediately, from the first glance that drew together the archbishop and poet. Tedaldi himself did not suspect this time the extent to which his tactic would drag far-ranging consequences along with it.

■   ❑   ■

In Dunaev Grigory used to get up early and in the morning usually wrote letters. He very rarely resorted to the aid of his secretary, finding a timidity and a certain woodenness of hand in his calligraphy and entrusting him only with managing the accounting books.

Having given his household instructions, Grigory got dressed for matins in the accompaniment of his lay brothers in white lace shawls. He set off through the courtyard toward the entrance into the sacristy of the church. In a puddle that never dried up, ducks bristling with feathers romped.

The first words of prayer resounded in a hum in the stone of the church that had chilled overnight, forcing his empty body to awaken, with the friction, clash, and swinging of bronze Latin spheres and a storehouse of breath forcing the church to gradually warm up, covering its walls and round stained-glass windows with condensation and echoing human words, supporting it suspended, bringing forth and not allowing it to touch the floor, out of words—THE WORD—a sphere: by pressure a swallow of the mountain air compacted, a silver bubble of oxygen beneath the water that, having achieved a critical size, suddenly breaks away from the bottom and quickly is carried up to disappear on the blinding border of two worlds—on the cutting edge, which is sharper than the sweep of a saber.

Stepping out of the cloud of the liturgy and again treading on the sinful earth, having crossed the courtyard, Grigory had breakfast in the dining room of the castle—usually alone. If Kallimakh should already have awakened by that time, then together, and sometimes the three of them—with Fanya—they made their way on a stroll along the groves and fields, moving away along the shore of the river far away. Grigory always took his walking stick with him, but almost never used it, just after a rain—on the clay rise or downhill.

Kallimakh brought with him Lucretius's *On the Nature of Things,* and he and Grigory now had long conversations about the possibility of a god that consisted of atoms and strolled like the wind in fissures of the universe's space, about the "Ultimate Goal" of the Epicureans, about the ability of poetry to inform a philosophical thought with sharpness, energy, and strength, about the clear-as-ice prose of the Roman historians: Titus Livius, Tacitus—as well as Kadlubek—Cicero—and the wild gluttony of our Sarmatian conversations, "the golden mean" of the Romans in everything, even in extremes, and the impulsive, unmeasured barbarianness of a Europe abandoned by Jupiter. Here they concurred in their evaluations, in Italy alone, in the hammered-into-it hundreds-of-years-ago healing memory source of thought, in its cleansed for breathing, chilly, infectious air finding the only hope and guarantee for European life, its future freed from tyranny and ignorance of the present day. Two large swamp birds: a gray violet crane and a red legged stork on fragile knees.

Two bird peripatetics—wandering about the outskirts of Dunaev, suddenly becoming frozen on a hill and gazing above the bend in the river, above the forests stretching to the horizon and growing dark, as though remembering suddenly their migratory nature and estimating—by the only visible signs—the distance to that autumn day when standing on a hill this way they would have to awkwardly draw in their legs beneath them and, shooting upward with several powerful sweeping movements, gaining in height several circles, straighten up their bodies like a compass arrow to the sun and set off on their path in the direction of eternally greening Rome.

But this winter, and the next after it, they both spent in Dunaev.

■　　❑　　■

In the bureau, in fact, he didn't catch anyone in.

They had taken apart the stairway in the House of Scholars for restoration, and the doorwoman sent him across the courtyard toward the back door.

The courtyard was empty: a dismantled motor scooter stood on bricks, water was pouring from somewhere. Only swifts etched the sky above his head, striving at least a bit to push apart the walls of the stone well, flying like bullets pell-mell into several black slits gaping in the solid wall where bricks had fallen out.

At last finding the entrance and penetrating into the building through some kind of "courses on self-financing," he immediately lost his way in the multitude of floors—the eternal mystery of back stairs, in the tangle of corridors, making his way through breaks in the walls, along floors torn apart, avoiding the hanging ends of electric wires, stumbling finally on a landmark—a scaffold with a chandelier wrapped to keep it free of dust in something like tablecloths or shapeless garments, suspended from a single main beam—and finally coming across in the much deeper bowels of the building the bureau that had moved. But in it he found only a secretary bored as a carrot kept in a cellar and a supplier calling for a car that had not come out of the garage today.

Tearing her sleepless face from the typewriter, the secretary told him that it seemed like the chief engineer had gone to the warehouse "at the church," where they brought something, or, on the contrary, had to take some kind of boards. This sat well with him—with some luck he could find the chief engineer and the stockkeeper together. He rushed back to the street.

The trolley bus stop was just opposite the entrance into the House of Scholars—a former casino. Two hollow zinc Atlases, holding up a cardboard balcony and gazing across one shoulder, stuck out their naked heels in its direction. Beneath the roof of the stop with its corner torn off, about ten people were gagging about. Rush hour had just ended not too long ago, and the trolley buses could stop for a break. Gazing at the corner of the house, behind from which, braking and rocking, the snout of a trolley bus, flattened like the nose of an old carp, would appear, he lit up a cigarette.

"Finally you've gotten to the very heart of your history—that point where parallelograms of power converge, from where grow, rocking back and forth, the shoulders of your story, the point where life freezes for a moment, as though in the thin swirling nerve of a whirlpool.

"The archbishop, the poet, and the slut gathered at the same table—they gathered together in some distant century. With a jug of wine, conversing by the fire, they whiled away the bad weather, the evening, the year, the wilds, life—has the archbishop decided to hide the lovers? Or his young helpless friend, entangled in his passions, whom he found suddenly in the wasteland of old age? Behind, was past life cooling down, largely measured by decades and years, and ahead—was its valuable remnant, living in harmony with the seasons, secretly breathing the weeks, the days, the mornings, and evenings—insomnia, the expectation of the dawn—next to him—the poet, for the time being—Kallimakh; opposite him—the blushing beloved Faniola.

"Blasphemous like life itself, and, like life itself, an illegitimate ecumenical synod, three carved figures stood behind the archbishop's oak desk, star-studded with meteoric dust, grown into eternity, three lives interwoven and soon to be swept by someone's hand, three fearful, delicate bodies, struck by shortness of breath, by the vague but distinct premonition of changes."

■   ❑   ■

Like two streams finally fusing their waters in a single bed, like a river emerging into the open from its confines and uncontrollably over-flowing—this is how life at first flowed for Fanya and Kallimakh in Dunaev.

The weeks passed in the heat of love. Kallimakh's beloved turned her dazzling behind and her slender back toward him, and with the twinkling of her flesh eclipsed all the miracles of the universe, the heavenly bodies and luminaries, all the kings, all the walks of life and glory itself, and like sweet death the ardent Vlokh grew weary in it, languishing and gathering strength, overriding his consciousness, so that all this was only a respite in the middle of life, so that no longer would he drink this way when he wanted to, gradually overcoming mortal love with her in a draft, affirming and accumulating precious bitterness—the knowledge of approaching ends and limits—of the spicy seasoning of maturity. For the first time in his life the Vlokh wasn't hurrying, in the damp walls of the Dunaev castle, in the bed-room and on the stairway, in the wine cellar and in the library, he again and again pressed to the white stomach of the sweetest and most insatiable of mortal women, of sponges and mollusks, of medusas and cuttlefish, which followed one time after their pilot, Venus, to the shore and subjugated dry land to their salty domain . . . the faces of the wild lovers, distorted with lover's wrath, hair entan-gled like snakes, the convulsions of an exorcism, the cramps of gout and agony, the streams of tears, which flowed a second ago from the bowels of her body, scalding his loins and filling Kallimakh's palms, a warm wave which rocked the body of Faniola for the last time, car-rying her out onto the warm shore next to the body of the exhaust-ed Kallimakh, and with a soft splash slipping through the sand . . .

■   ❑   ■

Every evening the master of the house and his guests came together at dinner in the dining hall of the castle. Grigory didn't have any particular attachments, nor either any prejudices, as regards food. He rarely fasted, considering old age in and of itself adequate penance. He ate when he happened to or when he had to, occupied more with his internal life, living in a world of other meals—the unleavened bread of unending studies, seasoned with acerbity of thought, the perplexity of his sleepless nights, washing it down with a drink of the intoxicating wine of his favorite books. His bedroom was filled with books, they lay everywhere—on the bed, on a bench, at the head of the bed, on the floor, mixed up with weapons, with pewter housewares, with dried bread—the maidservant was forbidden to touch anything here. Preparing the bed and moving all this disorder onto a bench, Grigory was jokingly saying that he can't allow himself in his whims to be the servant of his servants, that order is apropos in the shop of a tradesman and not on a bench in his bedroom, that everyone ultimately lives for themselves.

The feasting was another matter. Here Grigory was becoming extremely fastidious. The physical disorder most likely was called for to allow the master to hide his mental fastidiousness. The gathering of people at the table, as was customary in his homeland, of those who simply decided to have supper together, seemed to him an idle waste of time and a profanation. For him it wasn't in gluttony or in the connoisseurship of food, but in the small secular congregation that he could see the sense of feasting. Therefore, he avoided like fire meeting at the table with his nonsensical compatriots—that's why he was a xenophile, finding especially among the Italians lively, intelligent, often subtle conversationalists, and for them the archbishop's table bloomed with luxuriant blossom—for them were served dishes of baked, jellied, and stuffed fish, a suckling pig with garlic sauce oozing with juice, quail, smoked eels, olives, cheeses of various sorts and consistencies, baked eggplants, and various other select and refined dishes, all for the sake of conversation. Grigory himself oversaw the brewing of the mead for the table, he ordered Tokaj wines to be dragged up from the cellars—to which he had taken a liking in his youth at the Renaissance courts of Hungary—and also his own wine from the vineyards planted on the Dunaev slopes, which was, as a matter of fact, quite bitter. The appearance of Kallimakh in Dunaev gave Grigory the unexpected opportunity to display his hospitality in full fashion.

Warming his blood with the wine and feeling uplifted by the recitation of Kallimakh's poetry, Grigory himself picked up the lute, and with the deep, agitated, voice of a professional cantor who had maintained the timbre of his voice to old age, he sang, turning often to Faniola—"the glory and honor"—of his Dunaev. Competing with Kallimakh—lighting up his literary passion with the impulse of another—he even penned her some poetry dedications as a gift—in reality to sacrifice them to the poetry of his friend, easily succumbing under the pressure of the rights of its indisputable primacy. As for philosophical disputes and scholarly conversations, Faniola patiently whiled away the time through them, finding in herself the art of being able to overshadow the emptiness of her gaze with the luster of moist eyes and a mysterious sidelong yawn just in time with a polyvalent, slightly shy smile, managing at the same time to place her small bare foot into Kallimakh's groin under the table and exciting his beast, hoping for a quick end to an extraordinarily prolonged supper . . .

One question occupied Kallimakh more often than others—how and why Grigory, a man so close to him in views and in spirit, chose at one point the spiritual walk of life, for it made no sense to dispute it with him—the higher truths of reason and faith differ variously and greatly.

"It is not I who chose," Grigory answered, several times avoiding an answer, "but I was chosen. I think you don't become a priest any other way, you shouldn't, in any case. But this is a much too delicate and personal matter," he said, emphasizing with his voice the word "matter," "to be able to discuss it. Much greater a power must be given to a man for him to talk about God and revelation without falling into idle chatter. We prefer not to cast the touchstones of reason into the spring of religion, forgetting that we won't have anywhere from which to drink other than from it . . ."

"The higher truths of reason and religion don't differ for us much," Grigory continued, throwing himself rearward toward the back of the chair, "as their rights. A few people, like blessed Augustine or Hieronymus, knew how to not violate either the former or the latter—the power of their triumphant conviction is in this. The power of their delusions was equal to the power of achieved divine revelation, which had caught up with them, moving from opposite directions; thus, in any case, is the way that I, an old man, think. My modest powers do not allow me to swim that far in the ocean of faith, I find myself on its human shore, and I'm already satisfied, if I succeed, fulfilling my duty before God and people, to take care of the flock. After all, one shouldn't argue either that everything in the world moves by power and profit, except for religion—and, perhaps, poetry—religion after all softens and preserves morals, being an example of another power, reminding men about something greater than the trough of their needs."

"But, my friend Grigory, is not reason cognizable and cognized by God, and is it not in religion that darkness and sluggishness are found, the slothful ignorance of priests and the fallibility of bishops, do they not justify themselves by it, and are not the filthy intrigues of the Curia and the pope-scoundrel washed in it? In limiting the rights of reason are you not protecting by the same the preserve of evil? Aren't you yourself the rarest of exceptions in their circle?"

"My young friend, you are too young and hotheaded. I agree with you in many things, with the exception of your hotheadedness and unconditionality. Reason is certainly capable of illuminating dark corners of the world and cleansing them, but its meaning is instrumental, and rights are finite, by its very nature it can give only finite answers to finite questions. In contrast, the divine word is infinite, and the Bible, forsaken in dust, will remain the Bible—the undusted word of God, and our task is to raise it and be a witness, for what is man without God . . ."

"Is that so! . . . And is not the Holy Writ itself rife with contradictions, with impenetrable and intentionally obscure utterances, does it not suffer from naive anthropomorphism, is it not translated repeatedly by people from one tongue to another? Is human indolence not evident in it—the smell of the sweat of its authors—is there not too much revelation in it?"

"Everything has its limitations in the world of appearance, Phillipe, as well as in human letters. The naïveté, even the rudimentariness, of the ancient gods, the contradictions and obscure passages of Homer, do not disturb you. What meaning and truth do you find in that made-up world of the Greeks?"

"Be that as it may, but in my short life I haven't seen, with the exception of 'church miracles,' any presence or participation of God in our lives, and haven't felt even, by the way, special need for that, and, inasmuch as I can judge, Christ's deputy on the earth, man, who should be connected to heaven directly, is still further removed from Him than I am—much more so!"

"You're too embedded in the world and enticed by human affairs, Kallimakh, you gaze into it with a much too undiluted attachment. But the way poetry tears you from the earth, opening up for you and for us for one moment another seemingly nonexistent world in the distance, so, I think, with time, a different distance will appear to you—a form of farsightedness, pardon the pun, which will allow you to more accurately judge the world, people, and the existence of God."

"But doesn't farsightedness appear as a defect of vision, does it not distance us from the essence of the world and ourselves? The Lord God is foreign to me, and Nature is close. Here she is given to me—was He not expressed in her, if He is her creator? Isn't He himself Nature—by principles of reason constructed Nature, living and developing, which, having nurtured and raised man—her Gardener—and now transformed by him? How wondrously all is arranged in her, so proportionate and thought out. A tree grows by itself, grasses sow themselves, in an egg an embryo is formed, has not *Divina Natura* herself at one time developed from a certain embryo, which we now call God? And has not man, frightened of his own freedom and responsibility, thought up this name, separated the world from responsibility for it and with this introduced into it evil and disorder—having strayed from his role in the fulfillment of the law of nature? And the entire matter is in this, and not in the fall from grace of some kind of Adam and Eve who are unknown to me!"

"Phillipe, haven't you noticed that in such an interpretation there is no room for the freedom about which you speak? Elevating man—you turn him into a slave of faceless law, into a prisoner of Nature who falsely thinks himself as her master. This is rejection of the face of God, according to whose image and likeness he is created. What sense then is there in a brief slice of his life, is it any loftier—besides conceit—than the life of an ant? Everything is quite different, God is not confined in Nature and does not live according to the laws of Nature. Her laws are not His laws, she is a creation of His, and she herself lives according to the law of His will. Man is born according to the law of His will, but not as a slave—for what joys would God derive from slavelike devotion, for this He has stones and snails, but man is endowed with a soul and is free. Losing bearing in his heart, resting on his will, man immediately turns upside down, head to toe, and then he walks away, as it seems to him, because of the flow of blood to his head as he goes along his paths, but in reality he is floundering in the air with his legs, remaining in the same place."

"I give up, Grigory, you speak with great power, and I imagine how your sermons in the cathedral can bring the mob to such giddiness if the subjects about which you speak surpass my understanding to such a degree. It's possible that if, during an argument, should I stand on my head, several of your suppositions might reach me even better!"

"You're at that age, Kallimakh, when I myself experienced similar doubts, and in struggles with myself my soul was dying; you just have to listen to it—it itself with time, God willing, will find an answer. Your life, perhaps, is positioned now at the sharpest curve."

Thus Grigory and Kallimakh argued, in essence agreeing more on the humanities, worldly, and applied questions of faith: on the purifying action of reason on it, of the new philology, in part; on the necessity for the building of theology according to the laws of grammar and rhetoric; on the demand for unification of worldly and spiritual power in the person of the king—in spite of the pope—and on other things, passing on finally to the affairs of pure philology and poetry, and finally reconciled, having softened from unanimity and from friendly agreement, they raised the last toast—to Fanya.

After which the poet—in the play of the shadows—accompanied the archbishop, carefully supporting him by the elbow, to the door of his bedroom, and, after waiting there for a bit until Grigory lit a candle at the head of the bed, and then wishing him a good night, himself rushed to the field of nocturnal battle—to the flesh of Faniola, who had hungered for him all day, glistening in darkness on the sheets.

■   ❏   ■

In the trolley bus while it was rising along the steep street up alongside an old park, remnants of slippery dreams bothered him. . . . About the splashing of the waters of the canal beneath rotten floorboards, and about a sewer boar living in them . . . about Gogol, who cleaned out his nose at the supper table with a white towel, passing it through the nostrils of his huge plaster-cast nose and dragging on both ends the way they massage shoulders . . . and the most terrifying of the dreams—that he was living in a fascist country . . .

He pulled himself together. Just opposite him like a scofflaw with two large hands holding a briefcase on his knees sat a man about forty years old. A validated ticket shone through the chest pocket of his short-sleeved shirt like the poor but honest soul of an engineer. While sitting, he also searched through his pockets and, not having found any tickets, fastidiously shook his fingers, having glanced in a flash right into his face. The eyes of the passenger looked through him, along his cheek. With the close-shaved, inflamed skin of his left cheek, with the soft edge of his ear, he sensed the nearly uncowering, sluggish nature of that gaze. Having overcome the ascent, the trolley bus in a smooth wide arc rolled toward St. George's cathedral. The doors began to hiss . . .

". . . in which abyss is your consciousness found, at any given moment and in any given place slipping off the world for the leading of your mysterious parallel life . . . already several months have passed since you stopped to seem to be a simple fever blister on your lip, which you could brush aside, brush away the bush that is grown into you, sucking your life and time, feeding on your juices, breathing with your lungs, so many times tormented by it, you struggled to squeeze it, to make it smaller, to reduce it, and like a miraculous spring each time it unwound in you, allowing you to feel its temper, not wishing to disappear into nonexistence, imperiously widening its limits, branching out and already beginning to cast a shadow, in which your own tiny shadow lying there—swallowed by it—all the more often is lost . . .

"How long did you have to wait for Grigory to begin to stir on your soul for you to awaken from a five-hundred-year-old dream? And while you were learning to converse with the dead in the language of the living, how many temptations and enticements, how many ready-made paragraphs had you to reject in order not to aggravate with fiction and false witness your guilt before the mysterious homeland of all the living? Here is one, for example, which has submerged in the rubbish of rough drafts, about the fact that . . ."

In Grigory there met and came together—for the time in an individual's life—the charm of life and grace. In his daily life he easily and freely left God aside, the way he used to leave women, still not understanding that he himself has been left this time, that the woman abandoned by him—is he himself, that they turned away from him; and only at night did doubts torment him while he was fingering rosary beads, he read St. Augustine, St. Hieronymus, walked about, prayed, and once again began to read, he prayed as he was going to bed, but the bud of the restless sleep of a nightmare ready to burst into bloom, began to ache in him somewhere in his solar plexus, it never has risen up, never has freed itself from the secret depths of his soul, and never has taken the shape of a dream, a vision of how generations will proceed and will give way to one another at the humanistic table, so that after five hundred years in full measure to sense suddenly the drama of the abandonment by God, so that the namesakes of Grigory in his city would be born with blood poisoned with the syphilis of ancestors, with a head made heavy by someone else's hangover, so that they would measure the new asphalt-covered land beneath a glimmering new neon sky with some of the letters falling out . . .

"But what Jupiter can do, the bull can't, and the fearless arbitrariness called art does not have the power to violate the prerogative of Time, to get involved in that game in which it plays, so carelessly and horrifyingly, with the fates and designs of the city. Two bas-reliefs have survived on the stone fence of the former infirmary of the monastery of the Holy Spirit—today a driving school—on both sides of the monastery wicket gate: Abraham with half a lamb and a little dog, a raised chalice, and an isolated standing foot—and the Lord, holding in His arms the resurrected Lazarus. Time had eaten through the shape of the frame, it had rubbed off the faces, eaten off the beards, torn off Lazarus's hand, and the Lord Himself had been changed into Cronos, holding on his lap the scraps of his own son . . .

"But while there is enough time, my nonexistent reader, there is plenty of time, let's return for the time being to the damp walls of the castle, sitting in the forests and swamps, to the constrictions of the narrative locked within them, to that far-off century, which like a darkened inhospitable home in the wasteland—into which it is impossible to enter, which is even all the more difficult to abandon. The labor of reading is no greater than the labor of writing. Be lenient, reader—toward the end I've prepared for you a quite nice surprise that will be something like a wedding, well, or there, a baptism . . ."

■ ❑ ■

As before during the nights the quieted-down castle was disturbed by the repressed shouts and moans first of either kegeling and of the fighting blows of ghosts, or lovers wallowing in wet sin, to the delight of the servants.

But Faniola's love gradually withered, unreinforced by the signs of attention from Kallimakh, who was poor as a bird. And even more so than from the absence of gifts, Fanya began to be disturbed by the indefiniteness of her future, and she was already beginning to reproach herself in her heart for her thoughtlessness, for not giving all of herself in the sacrifice of love for Kallimakh, and she had hardly received and would no doubt never receive anything in return. With each passing day this became all the more clear. Kallimakh preferred to spend more and more time in conversation with Grigory, and all the more often they went out on walks together, early in the morning, even before she got up, simply forgetting to invite her. Fanya roamed without anything to do throughout the castle, for hours she gazed from the window into the courtyard: she'd see the cook come out onto the threshold to sharpen his knife, and in an uproar and in feathers, he'd catch and slit off the head of a chicken; a dog would bark inopportunely; a maidservant would gather a basket of coal in the barn; a courier would hop in with the mail from Lviv once a week and, leaving his horse at the tethering post and hanging on its muzzle a bag of oats, sit beneath Fanya's windowsill to pull the wool over the eyes of the gullible servants with news and rumors—in expectation of the archbishop. Several times Fanya walked to the town, but the market was usually held in the early morning, and the peasants had long ago departed for their homesteads and settlements, and at the market only the wind sauntered. Dunaev quickly grew wearisome for her.

The winter passed unnoticeably. Snow fell only in the middle of January, and already began to recede in February. The fields blackened. The wind began to blow, mixing in its breath the warm spirit of fascination and decay with streams of chilling coolness. One day a covered carriage drove up to the gates of Dunaev along the slushy road. From beneath its curtain wandering comedians in tattered costumes poured out, with roughly painted faces, with drawn-in stomachs and ribs sticking out, and right there in the snow they began to turn somersaults, to fling knives and hoops, to swallow fire, and they raised such a ruckus that the inhabitants of the little town gathered together, and some of them even armed themselves: some with oak clubs, some with spears, some simply in a work apron with a hammer and pincers—together with the gate guard they took to asking them to leave the city immediately, knowing the harshness of Grigory on this account, trying to convince them to leave in good time, since the archbishop's residence was here and he did not tolerate any kind of vagrants and rogues.

Spitting and cursing, putting out the hissing torches in the snow, cursing everything in the world—even their starving bellies, thanks to the sanctimonious person there entrenched, like demons into a barrel they crammed themselves into their carriage, and, accompanied by whooping and angry town dogs less emaciated than they were, they took off kneading the dirt and snow, along the road to Peremyshlyany, dreaming of getting there while it was still light— they drove away, tossing aside the curtain, having lashed a dog sharply with an iron rod across its back, so that, splattered with dirt, the wet dog fur stuck together and bloomed in a crimson spot, and the dog spun around like a top in the snow, lightly whimpering and—as though by and by remembering its puppyhood—trying hard to catch its tail. Having swayed at the gate, enraged and hesitating whether to set out for the chase, and having waited for a while until the carriage had disappeared in the forest, the crowd little by little dispersed.

Fanya, having seen everything from the wall, went back to the castle to tell Kallimakh about the incident, but both he and Grigory already knew about everything from the maidservant and calmly continued their argument over some point in the manuscript spread out before them. Loitering from corner to corner, once again Fanya returned to the city wall. Every day now she stood out on the wall for a long time, avidly admiring the approach of spring, filling her lungs with the invigorating, putrid air, letting the wind play in her hair, turning her neck to it, capturing it and feeling it with the ringing comb of her thighs, and her heart, suddenly skipping a beat from the vague promises of some kind of otherworldly freshness, of youth returning.

After the beginning of spring, quickly packing, Fanya went for a week to Lviv to see her mother and remained there for three weeks. Kallimakh was consumed for those weeks by the jealousy which unexpectedly grew in him, by the surging sense of emptiness—an obliging fantasy presented him with monstrous pictures of Fanya's unfaithfulness, and toward the end he, similar to Fanya, found himself loitering about the castle, not finding for himself anything to do, nor peace, and tormented by bitterness.

After Fanya's departure, Grigory, it's true, succeeded in occupying Kallimakh for a time, rousing him to pen a memorial to the noble Sandomierz Commander Derzhislaw of Rytwiany. The fatal decision of the Seym remained in effect—no matter that it was just in words—but if its execution turned out to be in anyone's interests, in the turbid waters of the Polish gentry's democracy, at any time, unnoticeably and quickly, an intrigue could be acted out, once again leading Kallimakh to the brink of death.

Fencing with words, moving right away to the attack, Kallimakh flew onto the fields of Polish political journalism. "People who have never seen the pope," he wrote to the commander, "hear from everywhere as though the Keeper of the Keys and the Guardian of the Heavenly Gates is sitting on the papal throne, having power over souls, the intermediary between God and people, and that he is a heavenly being. And, meanwhile, he is subject to all human passions, possessed by hate and the thirst for revenge, and is rather a cruel and merciless tyrant . . . Poland is a strong and free country, and one should be concerned that precisely in such a condition it should be passed on to its descendants, a condition achieved by the efforts of ancestors who did not lower themselves to vassalhood and who defended the country more than once from being subjugated by foreign powers." To the apologetic part there was attached a sheet of calligraphically executed poesy, a description of the ordeals of the author and an appeal to the proposed protector: "Give me a short life, I beg of you, and Yours will become eternal, for, believe me, I will raise You to the stars. You will shine similar to the eighth guardian of the midnight Ursa Major, which today consists of only seven stars." Such was the approximate meaning of Kallimakh's impeccable, as always, Latin. Discussing in the evenings as it was written Kallimakh's voluminous work—the first text, after a long break, written by him in Dunaev, both Grigory and Kallimakh remained satisfied with it in all respects. Derzhislaw was close to the king and linked by birth to the upper echelons of the Polish church hierarchies. Together with Tedaldi he maintained the largest part of Russian salt mines, which allowed him to hope for favorable, to a certain degree, relations with the latter's side, and mainly, as an educated man, who quite often had been attached to embassies in various countries, he himself was not alien to the literary profession and even at one time had translated from the German into Latin an account of the English knight Sir John Mandeville about his pilgrimage to the Holy Land.

But the concentration and strength Kallimakh found during work were soon dispersed by the worries of his passions. Periodically tormented by the thought of a life that has not worked out, by anxieties of all kinds, by uncertainty about everything, Kallimakh unexpectedly wrote two new poems in his cycle "Fannientum," which, for a while, had been laid aside, once again endeavoring in love to find the fulcrum of his life that was falling apart. The new unusual sound of them struck Grigory. The timbre of the verse changed, which was immediately captured by his sensitive ear, a split and a hoarseness appeared in the Latin, either the gasp of the middle of life or the distant hum of inner self-destruction, something new and unexpected and yet indistinctly grasped by Kallimakh himself.

Grigory experienced toward Kallimakh that caring, understanding, tender feeling, never found between father and son, but, as happens, sometimes is demonstrated toward a godson. Not having a means to help him in his confusion, and commiserating with the movement beginning inside him, Grigory, led in his relations with Kallimakh by a special scrupulousness, decided to rely in this case on letting things slide, on the passage of time, on the fact that his friend himself would soon begin to see clearly the artificiality of the supports with which he so painstakingly and blindly strengthened his life, for his thirty-three years not even once having tried to penetrate the evangelical maxim about a lost and saved soul.

But there was too much in Kallimakh's nature that had occupied the place of too little, too much had been set aside and hardened, that could not allow him to strive, headlong, where no one freely goes. Once having stepped on it, he immediately stepped off of that frightening, unfaithful soil. He considered his poems unsuccessful and, as a result, did not include "To Fanya" in his cycle.

■　❑　■

Easter passed without Fanya.

She returned at the end of April as spring was in bloom, she herself was blooming, fresh and somewhat guarded, with a golden chain on her neck. The worst fears of Kallimakh were confirmed. He was beside himself, Fanya denied everything—and there were no means to obtain the truth from her or to force her to lie—in scandal, in tears, in humiliation everything ended with an erotic avalanche, from which Fanya emerged slightly shaken, even somewhat not herself, as though having begun to be afraid of herself. For several days she started at any sound, she slightly limped while walking and complained about a ringing in her ears and a weakness in her knees. But Kallimakh's revenge was expended on this—he personally didn't have any other means. Several days passed, and everything began to flow as before.

A joyful bit of news reached Dunaev toward summer, introducing a certain ferment into the life of the inhabitants of the castle, soon changing the content of life completely, if not its course. Kallimakh's persecutor—Pope Paul II—had died, so now all three of them could breathe more freely and peacefully wait for what would happen next, hoping for changes for the better. It seemed that the threat of death, accumulating in the air during the last years, had finally cleared and melted away forever. At the same time, with the disappearance of this external pressure, which at some time about a year earlier had pushed and pressed all three together—somehow unnoticeably, but tangibly, the internal bond among them had now weakened. Uncertainty remained, nothing was said, but each one now thought more about their own affairs.

As before, at night Grigory read nonsecular texts and during the day secular authors of antiquity, but now he went to the fields alone more often to gather healing grasses, without parting from his thick book *On the Use of Herbs*—his favorite reading in the summer.

The Krakow correspondents of Grigory wrote that Commander Derzhislaw, the court, and the king himself very favorably viewed the means of defense chosen by Kallimakh, and everyone in Wawel Hill now spoke only about his memorial.

Cheered by success, Kallimakh sharpened his quills and his rapacious publicist's beak, ready at the first sign to fly at any extended governmental hand. But for the time being there wasn't any sign.

Fanya warily, with a constantly aching heart, gazed at the changes in Kallimakh.

■   ❑   ■

Just before the Moscow Olympics, in a single day, the Church of Elizabeth was surrounded with a plank fence, then during unpaid work on Saturdays, they painted it with oil paint. For the Intourist people, this freshly painted fence should have indicated the most serious intentions of the authorities to begin the church's restoration. Several years before this, those same city authorities considered the project, suggesting that the church be broken up into pieces and hauled out of the city; in this country people have been crazy about clearing immense blocks to make way for their frame-house veneer ideology, infected with manic giantism and dropsy—but, since all the same, the city had no money, and the tank drivers, with the sole thought of armor-piercing Austrian brick, got headaches, and the project remained just on paper, as something like a poem or an oratory about the lofty spiritual swells of our epoch remaining in musical notation.

The inhabitants of the nearby houses dumped garbage behind the fence, where it glimmered through the slits as though in a television tube, and the people in a rush to relieve themselves also ran behind it; all manner of drunks—the sensitive bottom of Privokzalny Square— lightly sighed, finding at last peace and quiet in a little restaurant beneath the open sky to their taste.

At the side doors of the church stood an empty truck with a hatch folded down, but there was no one in it or next to it. Having tugged the doors and looked into the keyhole, the windows in the church were broken, and from the keyhole a resilient draft put pressure on the eye, chilling the eyeball and forcing it to tear—and being convinced that there also was no one inside and that no voices could be heard, he decided to walk around the church.

Locks hung on all the doors; having turned the corner twice, he frightened a woman with a flabby swollen face in the niche amid the trash, who had begun to querulously lift up her underpants. She staggered and nearly fell. Her eyes were tearing. You could figure her to be thirty or fifty years old.

Having wet the wall himself in the next niche, he lifted up his head and walked around the pseudo-Gothic church. The wings of flocks of pigeons and crows rustled the air above his head, fusing with the fluttering and stirring of leaves. White and black angels, having flown up to the window, disappeared suddenly on its unseen edge and reappeared just as quickly, as though touching a translucent barrier at the passageway between two worlds, sometimes losing a feather at the crossing of it. They made themselves at home in the emptied resonant nave of the church with a modeling of white guano, continuing the business of its builders, strengthening with petrified encrustations the buttresses of its arches, the broken reliefs and sculptures, the broken window frames.

Buttressed by the fluttering of the birds, by low atmospheric pressure, by the morning, by giddiness, with a gaze touching the tip of the faceted spires in moldy copper hoods, with the flourish of crosses above them, his soul began the flapping of a domesticated bird in a cramped cage, as had always happened to him since youth, or even since his youngest childhood: he needed to escape the daily grind.

On the crag of the facade above the plicated Gothic caves and the rose carved of stone, there was a hanging, carved, crucified God the Son turned to stone. There was no ascension this time. His eyes were closed. Beneath His feet, which had now stopped hurting, the Street of Peace swarmed, ending in this spot and butting up against Horodetsky Street—the former Novy Svet, the former Hitlerstrasse, the former Stalin Street—but from His place of execution, He had long ago stopped being aware of the commotion on the sidewalks below, the fleeting, apprehensive rushing with some bundles and bags—like dolls—from back doors to stores to hawker stands beneath the canopy of trees, to kiosks and to the long bodies of tram cars.

A Polish woman dried up by time stood on her knees in a tattered raincoat on the steps of the main entrance; a shopping bag with two two-liter bottles of milk stood at her feet. Having crossed on her chest the relics of her arms, she prayed at the two folding doors beneath the binding of which a mass of dried colorless flowers protruded, with a single fresh cheap little bouquet distinguishing itself from the rest. The doors also were, judging by everything, closed—they kept cement here and rarely opened them. The Polish woman was about to energetically move her lips, when he, speeding up, passed her quickly, and turned the last corner.

No one was at the truck as before. You couldn't see the Zhiguli car of the chief engineer. He had decided to wait in the square by the church. During this entire time his brain didn't stop working even for a second. The trap of memory snapped shut on the shadows in the mansion of shades, sorting, storing all the nuances of his experiences, grasping his tricks with the tendrils of the mind, with the feeble impulses of ferocious tentacles.

He strengthened his resistance and continued the competition with himself. His head was ringing somewhere on the edge of a brief short circuit. Beyond the gates an especially profound thought came calling:

. . . There isn't a thing more uncomfortable for a hunchback than a knapsack.

"That truly is a profound thought! . . .

"—Build your invisible city, set out the curved frames of your ark—the barge of the dead—here its cleansed skeleton stands on beams in the depths of a continent, in the very core of it, looming in a terrifying desert like a mirage, an obsession, a delirium . . . Come to your senses, and you will finally see what you've lost and what you're seeking here!

"Aren't you seeking support like ivy and vines? Not a hideaway like all other rodents? Do you need a guarantee, do you need God understood as a staff? Or a line of poetry understood as a ladder? Or a life understood as rungs? Or Man, carrying off his essence somewhere far away like a Goal?

"Isn't it the tree of death that you've grown in the desert of your heart, generously nourishing it with the juices of all your infirmities? . . . Live on, stupid body!—It can't. How does it still breathe under the oppression of your arrogance? . . . Uncover for the reader your sadistic secret, admit that you haven't read a single line of Kallimakh!

"And still, you intend to continue to wander in the regions of a werewolf city escheated by you—after knowing what a joke your characters have played on you?"

■   ❑   ■

Dunaev now was burdening Kallimakh. By the idle turning of his mind, by the emptiness of his heart, by the desire for movement, for activity, by the changes overcoming him once again—he understood that he had stayed too long. There was a woman in whom there was no longer any mystery for him, with neither anything unexpected nor any unpredictability; he had an elderly friend who was still in some other dimension of life, as though he were in another corner of the universe, from which the steady, unwarming light of friendship dissipates, unable to warm the cold white body of the Italian who was yearning for the burning rays of glory.

Like a wolf wound up in this life, seeing a shaft of light beginning to glimmer in it, with his previous unreasoning unconsciousness he rushed to it, aiming at quickly widening and staking it. Once again his talent was given for gain, and there was left only to count up the percentages, to hope and wait. After several months he wrote and sent off the dedications to Dlugosh—the king's chronicler—on the occasion of his brother's death, the young Wladislaw Jagellonchik—on the accession to the Czech throne, the praise of Bishop Jan Targovicki—God knows why—and amid all this production two dedications, possibly for the sake of his own soul.

Grigory approved this activity of Kallimakh, just as clearly understanding the problems of thirty-three-year-olds, as well as the fact that the time to part was approaching. His indispositions, which he usually overcame in the fall, allowed him to distance himself, unintentionally and unnoticeably, so that quietly returning to his usual solitude, it would be easier for him to endure the looming loss of his friend and guest.

Fanya had already thought up something—you could see that she had a plan—she calmed down and now cold-bloodedly, outwardly, in any case, was waiting for a denouement.

■ ❑ ■

On a clear winter's morning, awakening alone on the cold sheets, Fanya finally put into action the mechanism of her plan.

Having wiped herself with a wet sponge, she then dug into her trunk, and after some hesitation, she put on her dark green dress, considered to be Kallimakh's favorite, she carefully combed her hair and let it fall along her shoulders, and after a brief search, she discovered Kallimakh writing something in the library—here she told him that she had received a proposal from a certain young Lviv merchant, he had left with a caravan for Caffa and promised to return by Christmas, by Christmas she should give him an answer; how should she act?

Kallimakh reluctantly tore himself away from his work, and then led her away, holding her by her cold fingers, back into the bedroom, did with her there what he always did, himself not understanding why, was it to make sure that from the hot coals on the brazier of the bed there remained just decaying gray ashes? . . .— And, lifting up his pants, he left in silence.

From the corner of his eye while dressing, he saw Fanya, who had remained lying there, biting her lip—in tears, in her sprawling hair. He coldly thought that she was just as attractive as before, perhaps even more than she had been before. To the scent of outlived love, which saturated her and was deposited by the shadow beneath her eyes, imprinted in the depths of her gaze—not a trace, but a sign of ripeness and undoubtable depravity, other men would fly there now, the same way as moths always have flown for ages.

The vixen is a thunderbolt!

His heart and throat clenched simultaneously: his throat from deathly longing.

■ ❑ ■

Fanya left before him, on the next day in the morning.

Having collected herself in spirit and in strength, she very cheerfully and sweetly made her farewells, holding her palms on his chest—for the last time she called him "beloved," she swept away a tear that had inadvertently run down her face, then she kissed the hand of Grigory, who had stepped out, he kissed her on the forehead—she couldn't figure out his lengthy joke, he blessed her with the sign of the cross. Kallimakh sat her into the carriage, the coachman snapped the whip . . .

Fanya jumped out of the carriage that was already in motion, twenty steps away, she ran up, and for the last time embracing Kallimakh, hung herself on him, she just couldn't tear herself away, then she returned to the carriage, smiling: "Poor Kallimakh! . . ." In rolling tears, she finally let go of his fingers. Kallimakh waved his hand—the carriage darted and rolled away from the courtyard, through the gates, carrying away Faniola from Kallimakh's life forever.

. . . Having hesitated, Kallimakh ascended the wall and remained standing there until the carriage had disappeared beyond the river in the thinned-out, bare forest, delivering him finally from the soundless howl, from the look of a lover directed back toward some past life.

The chilling wind cut to the bones, and he couldn't prod a single swallow of air into his lungs, it was as though his pleurae had died and were no longer utilized for breathing, they shuddered several times—something with a dry paper crackle tore in them—but they were no longer even utilized for crying.

He passed his hand along the chilly, rough stone, as though he didn't recognize it.

■　　❑　　■

Sixtus IV long ago had proclaimed an amnesty of the College of Abbreviatores.

Returning to their pulpits were Platina, who had nearly been impaled on a diamond stake, and the pupil of Lorenzo Walla, the academician Pomponious Lito, to his villa in Quirivelle. The library of the curia and the university once again were put to their disposal. The much-intrigued Krakow impatiently awaited the appearance on its parquets of the brazen Italian, the stiletto-man and stylist, who had managed to tweak the nose of the very pope of Rome.

Kallimakh, however, unable to make up his mind in choosing Rome over Krakow, delayed the moment of departure from Dunaev . . . from his friend . . . as long as possible . . . with an entire period of his life coming to an end, closing, as though catching Kallimakh in its magic circle, in a new way making intelligible for him the sounds of silence and desolation, the taste of water with ice, the rim of a wooden mug, the sweet smoke of pinecones in the hearth, the lightness of ashes and the wet and soapy heaviness of ashes, the cold of clean pieces of paper, overflowing into his fingers, the translucent, formless warmth of candle ends, of the vision of the love he had experienced, did it happen? Or didn't it?

A neat ream of calligraphic Latin—with red initials, with grandiosely large margins—lay before Kallimakh, sixty-one verses of his completed and entirely rewritten final draft of the cycle "Fannientum."

The overcast wintry morning crawled into the crack of the narrow window. Having thrown his shoe, chewed up by someone, to mice bustling beneath the bed, Kallimakh collapsed into the cold, unmade bed, he pulled onto himself the edge of the feather blanket. The fray beneath the bed quieted down for a short time and then more intensely became renewed, he could hear knocks, squealing, a dragging across the floor and the crunch of a rusk, apparently it wouldn't squeeze through the hole; it'd have to chew it on the spot . . .

The air of the room grew dull, turning green, the heavy wave of the feather blanket—first carrying him onto the crest, then covering with his head and pressing into the abyss—it carried off Kallimakh into the open ocean of dreams . . .

From day to day he put off his departure; he slowed down, slept, dozed, for some reason dragging things on. He felt uncomfortable and too lazy to move from the warmth of his sleepy, lumpy bed, from the delirium of feelings and mysteries of half sleep to the shameless communality of the day, to become driven into its brilliant, revolving, rumbling epopee, onto a wisp of hay into his creaking carriage, making its way amid the crowds to the place of trade and executions . . .

Kallimakh's Dream

Suddenly he returned to his parents' home in Tuscany, he pushed the door and without a knock entered beneath its canopy in the hour just before dinner—Lord! From where in a dream do such details become known to us?

In the silence and twilight of the summer day, walking through the empty rooms, he didn't immediately notice his tiny mother standing under a table in the dining room, she was so tired and weakened by life that it became all the more difficult for her to maintain her natural size, and, when no one was looking, she, shrinking to the size of a flask or a flagon of perfume, rested under a chair. Slightly confused, putting herself in order and returning to her customary size, she, embracing her son, led him to his long-dead father, quite tidy and rosy-cheeked, lying in a spacious bedroom, and she told him that everything with them was fine, father when he's better gets up and even walks around, only he doesn't speak, as though making efforts to confirm her words, father smiled, it was evident that he was agitated; but today he didn't have enough strength to get up or at least to pull his son to his chest, just his eyes began to glimmer more intensely, and his ruddy complexion acquired a feverish shade; mother washed him every week, taking him apart at the joints, every bone separately, into the washbasin, with soap and pumice stone, then again carefully put him together and dressed him, on those days he happened to be especially lively, and, while he was lying after bathing, so washed, so clean and fresh, he made efforts to say something to her, and in his eyes tears of thankfulness and a love demanding nothing . . . with these words his mother again went down, embarrassed by her weakness, and she stood beneath the leg of the chair, next to the copper washbasin, turning away her face and lowering it to the ground—a slovenly little hunchback.

Kallimakh began to feel faint and, losing his stability on the floor, once again he was suddenly swallowed by the dark wave of the featherbed, which swelled up from nowhere, choked by the salty foam of tears, of down, of phlegm—and splashed out onto someone else's bed, in a bedroom empty to the point of torpor, in tens of thousands of days from the roofs, the hills and the turrets of Gimenano, where his childhood had passed and had forever remained, where white dust mixed with rain had kept sending chills for more than a thousand years and caressed the soles of little boys, in little mud fountains squeezing between their toes, in scratches and red spots, running to catch up, to tease . . . to do battle.

■   ❑   ■

"The time for Kallimakh to grow has come, and for Grigory to become smaller." This was how the archbishop unhappily joked, coming out during one of the last wintry mornings into the empty tract, to see his friend off on his way to the capital.

Behind Kallimakh, they carried an enormous decorated trunk with his things, his clothing and household goods, given to him by Grigory over the past two years. Grigory crossed and blessed Kallimakh for his journey—the friends embraced for the last time. Kallimakh jumped into the carriage, settled himself, clutching his inlaid chest—with Grigory's letters of recommendations inside and sixty strange seeds never seen beneath the Sarmatian sky, which were destined to give sprout to the Polish Renaissance, and for the time being to guarantee the literary glory and the near future of their erstwhile creator, Kallimakh Buonaccorsi, the poet.

The carriage moved off, carrying away another, already new Phillipe Kallimakh Buonaccorsi—Kallimakh "The Tested"—"The Much Experienced"—in the cocoon of poetry imprisoned for a time by "His Eminence's Voice," the "Gray Grandeur" of the Polish-Lithuanian Principality, summoned to soon become the tutor of its kings and their secret advisor—strategist, adventurer, who would make terrible breaches in the stereotypes of its medieval conscious-ness, a man, who for two decades would direct the entire foreign policy of Poland, the object of equal hate, worship, and indifference of its future historians.

Five years later in a certain other kind of geometry, which would seem arbitrary for an untrained eye, one more time the paths of Kallimakh and Grigory of Sanok would intersect.

January 1477 would find Kallimakh in Venice, where before the senate of the republic he would deliver a brilliant speech, constructed in the spirit of the New Philology—and containing a grandiose threat: that if the Venetian Republic and the Hapsburgs did not unify with the Polish king in a battle against Corwin, then the Polish-Lithuanian Principality will have *no other choice* but to sign a union with the Turks, and then ALL the above-mentioned will be in terrible shape. (In regard to the Turks, Kallimakh bore in his soul the cunning to settle accounts with them at the hands of the Crimeans.) Poetry was cast aside, and Mnemosyne was exiled as a maidservant to the palaces of Demogogy—to carry firewood and water to her for washing. New times for some reason always happened to be crazy over the passion of eunuchs—the will to power. If only not one . . .

That winter Kallimakh worked on his *Curriculum Vitae and Mores of Grigory of Sanok,* counting on presenting it as a gift to Cardinal Zbigniew Olesnicki the Younger as a prophetic exhortation on the spirit of the New Time, and as an example for imitation for all those wishing to follow it . . . but this text was for Kallimakh also a tribute to friendship—breathing, as each gift of God, where it wants, unlawfully, and its sample made out of clay, partaking of the mysteries of its communion, enlivened with every line and page, filled up with self-proclaimed power, came into motion—and became just as careless in usage and imperceptible—just as every living life.

. . . In the middle of January, having suddenly sensed the losses of his life, driven by an unintelligible longing, Grigory would abandon Dunaev and go to Rohatyn. Having inspected for show the holdings of the eparchy—the church, the monastery, and the nearby villages—he would remain here for several days.

On one of the last days of January, in the morning, he would be found in his bedroom, lying on his back on the floor, spreading his arms like a crucified man, torn from the rosary beads of time. Death's pleasure would be to take him without lengthy preparations, without a confession and without repentance.

His life would be described as frozen for a second, lingering too long forever, on the very edge of an abyss swallowing bones. For a thousand miles from Rus, from Rohatyn, Kallimakh in his manuscript on that morning will place a period.

The Agony of Characters

(The abrogation of the convention between the Text and the Author, following the last visit to the scholarly library.)

"Here is this thunderous fiasco—an utter debacle!—and not any contrivances of even the newest prose will save your text, which hardly have descended into the water from the shipbuilding stocks.

"In your head alone, daredevil and delirious, certain Eskimo revolutions are still possible—the miracle of a cork-tumbler—designers, officers, captains, engineers, even secretaries of the local government committees shoot in such instances!

"Show the measure of your doubt and shamelessness in a futile attempt now to see victory in a smashing defeat!—and to convince at least one person of this—to begin—you yourself."

Testing the Soil

In Dunaev Kallimakh was not alone in visiting and hiding. There was still one other fugitive from Rome, Glavk, Marino Condulmero, a friend of Kallimakh even before his pre-Roman times, who had shared with him the misfortunes of roaming. But being completely superfluous in a given text—the shadow of Kallimakh—he painlessly disappeared from its pages. One can consider that the depiction of Kallimakh at times doubled, was it necessary for us to learn about Fanya's marriage from Glavik's letter addressed to Kallimakh?

Further, the suspicions of the legate Alexander Forli about the collaboration of Kallimakh with Turkish intelligence was not without basis. Whatever was there, thanks to his "uncircumspect" letter, the skin was torn off two of his close acquaintances—Mark Antonio Perugino and Galeacco Gistiniani—participants of a Turkish plan to take the island of Chios. However, at that time people looked very flippantly at unions with the enemy.

And it is completely trustworthy knowledge that in 1483, Kallimakh, being in the service of the Polish crown, became a spy for the Venetian Republic and until his death regularly sent coded messages to the Council of Doges. (As a matter of fact, being concerned about progress, he also introduced—perhaps even the same—cipher into Polish diplomatic correspondence for which historians of diplomacy give him credit. Polish historians, to the contrary, to this very day cannot forgive him for the campaign which he inspired of the young king Jan Olbracht, in which near Chernivtsi, an entire generation of the Polish gentry was butchered by the Wallachian nobles. This occurred soon after his death.)

Much more colorfully, however, is drawn the figure of the Lviv archbishop in the less-accessible literature. Grigory indeed was an impotent, and "debilitas naturalis," as Kallimakh writes, largely was conducive to his turn to the spiritual walk of life. From the age of twenty-five on his appendage called the foot, a fistula opened up, through which, as his friend and biographer surmises, all the juices departed that were harmful to the organism and to the reputation of a spiritual man. The meaning of the signs on your body is not always revealed and not all at once, and not everyone is given to discern and understand them. Grigory constantly was concerned about his fistula, never attempting to rid himself of it, being satisfied with Goulard water lotions and the daily washing of it with alums until his death. This was a very clean, exemplarily functioning fistula. Stronger than any argument the presence of it refutes the opinion of the disingenuous critics of Grigory and shared by his heir to the archbishop's eparchy, Polish chronicler Jan Dlugosh, that Grigory excessively loved to be in contact with women, as though the latter had poisoned him.

The famous historian, raising such a wrongful accusation against the archbishop, didn't manage to get to the pulpit himself—for nearly two years he tried to get it, he prepared for it and was about to get it, but then he died unexpectedly on a trip, orphaning a quite luxurious cortege.

Resigning at a certain age from the world, which was beginning to seethe—the impotent with a fistula on his foot—getting off his hands the entirety of worldly and economic power into the hands of the stewards and members of the order, and no longer being interested in their affairs, so as not to fall into frustration, Grigory found for himself many useful and worthy activities in Dunaev. Besides reading and self-education, he loved counting—so in the storerooms of the castle he counted all the heads of cheese, all the hanging sausages and hams, all the eggs—one by one—all the reserves of butter and mead and wine—on the flasks and bottles he left notes—intricate snares, sound-making gadgets and traps, set out by him everywhere on the animal trails of the maidservants, they changed the storerooms into an enchanted forest, and the battle with the servant, of establishing her guilt and punishment in the most fascinating activity.

With the simpleminded wiliness of a sex maniac he followed his goal, bringing himself to an explosion of unbridled anger, followed by a thrashing of the maidservants again, lifting up the skirts of the female cooks himself and moistening the birch rods—their strong, ruddy, peasant backsides—in order to do so, then leaving for his bedroom, feeling a sweet languor and ache in the small of his back and all the joints of his body, and falling face down onto the bed, experiencing a lengthy and sharp condition approaching happiness. He called such a prophylactic flogging—for himself—"a school of thrift," but it is doubtful that it was miserliness here—a human attempt at arguing with death—Grigory was neither miserly, nor wicked—his servants lived with him in warmth and were well fed, and they, like children, reconciled themselves with the games and eccentricities of the child—the old man. So, not long before his death, for three days the archbishop feigned to be mad, he excreted in bed, and, taking pleasure in his own inventiveness and slyness, and learning the intentions and designs of his milieu, he organized a single general flogging—a holiday, bigger than Easter, for himself.

The archbishop also had a brother, thrown out at one time by his parents from home, who started his independent life in the bathhouses and barbershops, gradually reaching the very bottom—the snakelike laying of vices, there was not among them any one which he would not taste. To those who were surprised at such polar opposites of blood-related brothers, the future archbishop modestly noted that very often both roses and thorns grow on a single bush. Three times Grigory gave him clothing, a horse, and as is the custom for a Polish nobleman—money for opening up a store or some other kind of enterprise, but all the assistance got lost somewhere, as though into an abyss, and once again he appeared on the threshold of his home, always drunk, ragged, a loud and impudent extortionist, and the fourth time when Grigory ordered him thrown out on his neck, he consummated the efforts of his brother with the wise maxim about the salty sea whose water always remains salty however much rain, however many streams and freshwater rivers carry their waters to it from every direction. Actually, his brother ended his days in a shelter for beggars.

In general, Grigory, distinguishing himself with great steadfastness, was conscientious as very few people were. At the request of friends, since, having ordained an uncouth and dull-witted village lad, he kept him with himself, occupying himself with the hopeless business of his education, in this way atoning for the guilt for the moments of weakness of the spirit—before God and the people.

The calf-idiot for long years took the place of his family, having taken onto himself either the load of his birth-giving longing or the pain of repentance for the death of his brother.

When an ambassador arrived incognito in Dunaev from Prague in order to find out a little more about Grigory, to offer him the miter of the Prague archbishop, in the town, despite its love for rumors and scandals, there was found not a single person of a debasing nature who would speak badly of their archbishop—including the servants. Grigory was touched, but he refused the Prague throne. He valued his found peace, and being also tied to Dunaev and its inhabitants, he bequeathed his last years to it.

Kallimakh also writes that he was a proponent of free divorces, and enjoyed stopping on the streets, talking with women, and he loved modest puns and the forging of handwriting, not misusing his talent too much, even in his youth; being of his will, for some reason he suggested banishing all lawyers to uninhabitable islands.

Among his maxims was the following: ". . ."

However, that's enough.

Here are two versions—two descriptions, obtained at different times from different sources, and both are real and false, not more than the very desire to write.

And who will say whether they are in contradiction, is there between them the tiniest gap into which a judging human thought could enter? Two truncations—two colored sectors, emerging from two points of view—there could've been three or four, or even better—seven, but two is enough in order to, having spun them on the disk of a plot, to transfer the length of their wave into absolute pain, into emptiness—into the viviparous emptiness of "now" and "here."

This is not the present that has swallowed the past, that past every second devours our present through us.

Life and death are one.

The end and means are one.

And I only want to knock off the focus—to wipe off apathetic eyes.

There is time—and here it is—and it's gone.

. . . He was walking beneath the low-growing linden trees, along the trampled wet path, past the iron barrel with leaves, past the field altars of autumn that were smoking here and there, he was walking in the unsure and unsteady gait of someone fearful of spilling something which filled him to the brim: with the sense of life force suddenly passing through him, occurring to him, dissolving and transfiguring everything around, full of meaning, light, and pain.

Silently the window blinds of tram cars approached, carrying off group photographs of the tram stops, filling up again with extras, again disappearing in approaching tram cars.

Not having the strength to further endure the pain from his eye socket flowing through him, a power greater than he himself, than the ability to cry and the faith in openness and the fullness of meaning of everything living and dead, he raised his hand to his eyes.

Beneath his finger on his forehead a vein throbbed.

Here we leave him, on a bench at Privokzalny Square, at the best moment of his life, ready for everything.

■ □ ■ □ ■

AN INCIDENT WITH A CLASSIC

THIS WHITE PAGE BLINDS ME LIKE AN UNSPOILED MOVIE SCREEN THAT casts its image into the auditorium onto the raster of heads and shoulders, remaining snowy white itself. In the moving reflected light, the auditorium becomes similar to a swarm of white worms seen by a young boy in the hole of a train station's latrine about thirteen years ago. You step out onto the platform—the scent of railroad ties, steam whistles, rails in both directions bending toward the horizon, the heart pounds in the little body, shaking it like an empty kerosene can. O my native Ukraine!

■   □   ■

A certain man, writing poetry, crushed by the riddle of Gogol, decided to take a one-day trip to Mirgorod to suck into himself from the viscous, fluffed-up-featherbed-like air of all those strong-as-death dreams, which had penetrated some two hundred years ago into the blood of the genius and gradually *changed* its composition.

He wanted to walk along the shores of the not-made-by-human-hands puddle, which eclipsed the glory of that of the Marquise with the small boat of Peter, of the Moinaks, of the lakes Elton and Baskunchak, and even of Baykal and the Caspian—with his hand he wanted to touch the yellow walls of the city hall. He didn't want anything bad. But, as soon as he arrived there, he lost a bunch of keys, his own and others', in the train station latrine—the Kyivan keys to everything. In the heat of the moment this seemed to him even to be worse than losing his passport. This was an awful blow to the solar plexus in the struggle for existence. Remaining a citizen, for several months at a minimum by virtue of the confluence of various, among that number odd, circumstances, he stopped being an independent person, merging with the class of street people and hobos. The life of the capital is cruel. Don't expect any mercy in it.

The keys lay above a thick stratum, teeming with life, with half of them being caught on some kind of scrap of newspaper—the lucky half, which barely outweighed the other half, which had already sunk in the dregs. He didn't have a minute to lose. Any movement of the thin surface stratum, the smallest tectonic fault, could lead to the irreparable. It was impossible to reach the level of excrement by hand, the difference in height was about two meters—so that a strange and unaccustomed view opened up, as though out of a porthole of a spaceship, where an envoy of the noosphere hovers with his head pointed down above the flat surface of an unknown planet, and where the signs of long-awaited life can be read so distinctly.

The versifier became lost in thought. He needed some simple device, yet one of genius, born of folk wit, which had always come to the aid of our ancestors. The feverish sorting out of variants gave way after a minute to the expression of decisiveness on his face. He needed to find a thread and a magnet in an unfamiliar city. The business became complicated by the fact that it was Sunday—the stores were closed—and the siesta hour—the city slept soundly after the lunch break.

Without losing time, he ran off along the streets. The perplexed, the awakened, the angered inhabitants could in no way make sense of what a new city madman was trying to get from them. Never, if they had even had it, never would they give you what you asked for right away. The hero hastened on. Being an intelligent person and at the edge of his consciousness understanding himself the absurdity of his request and the growing absurdity of the situation, but no longer of sound mind, he continued to rush around the city, rousing from sleep entire streets and alleys, rushing a couple of times past the central square without noticing it, thus beginning to repeat himself, running through the already once-awakened streets, from where from behind the fences, from both sides, there gazed into his face the judging faces of the inhabitants of the peaceful city who had long ago forgotten about any kind of haste.

Finally in one place he got lucky. At one of the town residences where he rushed in, they were enjoying the last day of a wedding. The groom's ushers, equally disposed to good and evil, under the influence of drunken-up liquor, but finding themselves in a temporary dissipation of will, unscrewed a magnet out of the radiola, and on his word of honor gave it to him together with a spool of thread, forcing him to drink a glass of the warm and murky homebrew to the health of the newlyweds. They liked themselves at that moment. Nothing, after all, uplifts a person like generosity.

Our hero rushed off to the train station and, oh, happiness, the keys were in place, the latrine wasn't occupied, and, having made fishing tackle with his trembling hands, on the third attempt he finally caught the keys. Then for more than half an hour he washed his hands, the magnet, and the keys in the flowing stream—he fell into a stupor, like a raccoon, the splasher, again and again rubbing them in turn and still not daring to lift them to his NOSE.

He returned the magnet but refused to drink, clearly recognizing that the response reaction of his organism wouldn't even allow him to touch the glass with his teeth—as the entire wedding party would be barfed out, including the ushers, the parents of the bride and the groom, the guests, the neighbors, *half the neighborhood*, the greater part of the streets stirred up by him, and perhaps, even the entire glorious town of Mirgorod. Generosity grows savage when it clashes with ungratefulness. And only the quick wit and cleverness of our hero, which slightly forestalled the course of events, in combination with a slightly backward-stumbling thinking ability of the tiring wedding party, which was lagging behind the course of the events, permitted him in good time, unharmed and quickly, to leave the place of the arising aggression, where at one time two heroes of the similarly named writer squabbled so heatedly. It cannot be ruled out that the writer himself, when he was a child, threw a stick of yeast into the outhouse of one of them to see what would come of it. And it turned out boring.

The entire way to Kyiv our hero lay keeping vigil on the upper bunk, trembling with the thought of a cigarette, so he wouldn't take leave of his senses accidentally, so that this impossible, turned-inside-out, inhuman vileness that today so mocked his completely unselfish love for great Russian literature wouldn't come up to his eyes and throat.

Just a several-hour-long bath with pine extract after he had returned to the capital and a week of work routine, which lulled his imagination, at the service to a generally useful life, allowed him to forget this incident in time.

■ □ ■ □ ■

THE FOREIGNER

HEPATITIS HAD CARRIED HIM TO THE SIXTH FLOOR OF INFECTION
Hospital 2 in a place named Falcon Mountain. A snowstorm had been
swirling, blinding his eyes, plugging his ears with snow. Guttural
crows announced the arrival of the first clear hospital morning.

The windowpane has become covered with crystals of frost
overnight. Scattering light poured through the wide white screen—
a projection of a geographic map: Was it the Land of Antarctica?
Greenland? Or Scandinavia cut out with fjords?

He was the Foreigner. Just in case he had decided not to ask any
questions. By the way, not to ask questions of others became his life
credo over the past few years in this country. They analyzed his
urine, blood, punctured holes in his veins for IVs. He humbly toler-
ated all this—he finally stopped feeling queasy, and he just dove
deeper into his hospital sheets, into the bunk, to observe the life of
this strange people from there.

. . . Alyosha Parshchikov in his poetry office, for the time being getting by without a Dictaphone, composed an imaginary ancient
pneumo-hydrometer-cannon for a new long poem, "Poltava" . . .

. . . in a moss-covered hole beneath a mountain, where in a petrified state a gray-green Central European city lay like a river mus-
sel, a Central European city . . . by the way, it already long ago (it's
already been forty years) has stopped being Central European,
because the geography in this country is the first and foremost thing
that is being annulled . . .

. . . frigid women with middle and higher education greedily
searched for personal happiness among the cities and villages, the
resorts, and new building projects of the country . . .

. . . Nikola—on a homestead covered with snowdrifts in the mountains—cooked some potato moonshine and waited for guests from a far-off nearly nonexistent city, he waited for binoculars for Christmas, for Epiphany. . . . The guests always appeared unexpectedly, they would appear suddenly below on the last rise from the fir wood: two or three figures with skis, with backpacks, which resembled foldaway beds; they would have a smoke only when they had caught sight of the farmstead and would slowly, ponderously tumble into the hut, filling it with steam, with a muddle of odors, with things so scattered all over that you didn't know where to look first; would pull bottles of vodka out of their backpacks, stoke the wood burner, and the holiday would begin.

There were no guests. The batteries had lost power long ago. Nikola drank one, then a second shot glass of moonshine, longingly gazing at the snow through the ice hole of the window, at the forested slope, at the damp gray photograph of the gloomy day, chewing off a bit of salted corned beef, already bitten off on the corner by someone, washing it down with a mugful of water with ice. Then he took off his boots, and, remaining in two pairs of equally torn socks, he clambered onto the stove bench with his legs, got the shepherd's flute—a brass tube, cut at a slant—stopping it up with one finger on the end, he extracted sounds out of it, he drew out a not-very-yielding melody: plaintive, primeval, festive, like the life that once used to be in these mountains, when children returned once a year with their father from a fair that spread out along the bank of the rushing mountain river, and the father, who stopped by a bootleg tavern—a cleanly shaven Hutsul, whipped the horse in the straps of a fragrant new harness, the rims of the wheels jumped up and down along the stones and pebbles, and at home Mama scraped and washed the floors with a yellowish extract of beech ashes, and then the children's linen pants were once again taken away from them and hidden in a trunk, and the children were left to run around just in their shirts, until they grew up . . .

And Nikola saw the Binoculars—black, covered with little bumps, unnaturally large, even obscene, with a sixteen-times magnifying power, if this kind exists in the world, and his fingerless hands clench, and yearn, and in his strong as a shovel, as an ax, nimble palms they press a narrow little reed, a piece of ice, a stupid little piece of iron, being warmed by his breath, by a vodka spirit, by warmth, which moves from the raspy sounds to a much more piercing, but nonetheless possessively hoarse, like an escaping recollection of something that you can never bring to your memory and were never allowed to recall, that only teases, teases you, you reach for it with your hands—there's nothing in them, only the brass horn, which is getting in the way . . .

Twilight pours into the window, it crawls from the corners, it's getting darker, the optical deception sways—a crayfish—a mossy binocular half the size of a house—and all this drudgery is only the vain languishing of the spirit . . .

Because one and a half thousand kilometers away Nikola's acquaintance, his friend—the Foreigner—has the revolting tint of urine, and for the time being this is the only thing he finds in common with the people, who were overfilling the ward and who remained incomprehensible to him.

In the meantime the Foreigner slept for entire days at a time, and even when on one particular day, it began to appear to him in a dream for the umpteenth time, . . . he began to grope carefully for a map of dreams: in the oblivion of the endless sequence of a dream, having been locked in the optics of a dream when, even while waking, you don't leave its boundaries—in his mind and imagination, dreamy landscapes, streets and houses became linked together; the visions congregated; little groups of people who were for some reason familiar, but not giving the appearance of that, ineradicable, but persistent, and of whom we dreamed for decades; a land was being constructed, the size of a small district, but a strange one, built of a deceptive, semitransparent substance; a Shelterhaven for Broken Hearts; a homeland of children, sleepwalkers, and adolescents—Ghel-Giu, brutal, like all port cities;

. . . the journey of a beetle along a Möbius strip.

You can also say it this way: A land the size of binoculars.

His broken, burning body at last found peace, being thrown by the raging elements of a Midlife Crisis onto the tiny little island of a cot in a hospital for infectious diseases on the outskirts of a Eurasian capital. He lay there motionless, with his face in the depth of his pillow, with a dangling hand and lungs hurting from the water, with his aural cavities filled with sand, with algae in his tangled hair and his youthful beard. The small of his back was sweetly aching where he was beaten and where the jaundice was appearing.

O former fifteen-year-old captain! O eternal Foreigner!
O bilious vegetarian!
Well, what don't you like about this—precisely this—land?
Which journey have you planned?
Catch your breath. For the time being sleep, sleep.
There's no Africa or Patagonia—there's only your Homeland.
She alone—is a magnet—while we're with her, we don't need any kind of compasses.
She—is a single Great Kursk Anomaly, deflecting and attracting our hearts, magnetized by her nightingales, blast furnaces, Baykonur, the Bolshoi Ballet, by the printed Russian word.
Sleep, my boy, I don't love you, sleep.

And he slept and slept, for so long as he had unlearned to do, as he no longer could, without drilling the mattress with his penis, without tormenting the pillows and not being tormented by them, relaxing all his aching muscles, his urethra, his sphincter, stepping out in roomy pajama pants and a shirt with the hospital stamp printed on it (but without buttons) just to the bathroom—to catch a smoke, to urinate—across the wall of the booth an inscription stretched: ALL HAIL HEPATITIS! and besides feces forgotten by someone there were no traces of the work of intellect.

The Foreigner in amazement turned his head from side to side, to the point of giddiness, suddenly noticing that neither this form of lapidary nor the leakage stains from beneath the door embarrassed him any longer; so what if the bucket with cigarette butts was slightly bespittled; so what if the washbasin had standing water in it; so what if the window was cracked and covered with nicotine as though with gelatin film; what a trifle all these things were in comparison to the first spasmodic inhalations, to the warmth of a radiator, to the whiteness of Dutch tile walls, to the abstract feeling of gratitude to everything and everyone. They didn't talk to him, they just felt—he was a Foreigner. He was thankful even for this.

He propped his forehead against the glass. Evening was approaching. The streetlight below swam in a pool of light, illuminating the floating landing platform, the stairway, the brick warehouses. The hospital was huge, there were a minimum of eleven buildings in it, the eleventh being the morgue. The visions didn't leave his tired brain in peace. He became tipsy from the cigarette, it was beginning to burn his fingers, when below, it seemed to him, a small figure appeared for a moment dressed in a chessboard tricot and a short Renaissance cape—it crossed the yard, it rushed about in the light of the street-light, pressed against the landing platform, fused with the shadow—a carnival figure from the Comedia dell'Arte at a snowy Moscow freight station, at the Moscow Switchyard . . .

He again fell into a dream, managing only to make his way to the bunk and touch the pillow with his head. The light of reason and memory was not capable this time of penetrating the thickness of sleep; the snouts of deepwater fish swam right up to his face several times, but a minute would pass, one and a half, and—it was as though an ink tablet had dissolved—pitch darkness completely overflowed, into which they disappeared forever.

When he awakened, he felt that at last he had slept his fill for all the previous months and, perhaps, even years. And he felt good. And it was the third day, the eighth from the beginning of his illness . . .

■   ❑   ■

These people around—in essence, they were not incomprehensible, they were inconceivable to him.

In the ward the aesthetically trained Foreigner immediately caught sight of Breugel's *The Expert*—a proletarian from Red Presnia: the slit of a smiling lipless mouth as though it had been carved with two sure cuts on wood; with domino pieces in cupped palms, with a joyfully surprised look he gazed at the unheard-of composition—a black cross growing on a table, like a polyp.

The entire thinking ability of the lathe turner from Presnia was spent in the unassuming power of gazing, that difficult power, from which the perforation of the ancient game—of carbon domino pieces—begins to glow phosphorescently in the darkness.

The spectacle of freakish turns and crisscrosses—the movement of hexagrams of fate little by little began to stir the imagination of our Foreigner as well. Days passed in the game. The meaning of this game, its rules, were completely unknown to him, despite the fact that he had spent a number of years in this country, and even had been receiving money for it, although in rubles. From the very beginning, nearly from awakening, he began to suspect that its meaning was not so simple, just as those people playing it were not that simple. And maybe, they're not playing—maybe, the game is only appearance, form?

Through different eyes—but how?—he had to look at the Expert's partners:

—At the aggressive, jerky *Padalka* (Fallen Apple), whose eyes were crossed from the tension of following the game and his partners. This *Padalka* suffered from a rare variety of asthma: If not for three or four "lubricating" words, he would have suffocated long ago, unable to utter a single phrase—he would have difficulty breathing, his throat would go into a spasm—and he'd collapse dead. Thank God there were those words! To each neutral word the *Padalka* gave two or three companions out of their number, precautionarily supporting the word from all sides. He cherished these words for their faithful service, and in his own way, certainly, loved them, caressing them with suffixes, rewarding them with prefixes, creating verbalized nouns and innovated verbs of rare boldness. Thanks to his unbending strength of spirit, to relentless and exhausting verbal exercises, each day he came out victorious in the battle with his suffocating illness.

—At the "Cossack Detachment" guy who every morning spat into his own little policeman's eyes and, rubbing them beneath his forelock, polished them with his sleeve so they would shine; he massaged his plump shoulders—puffing like a weightlifter—with eau de cologne, understandably for what purpose; who with inspiration and in a ringing voice recounted for the ward about the pose of a "swallow" in handcuffs and a "figure eight" straightjacket assisted by a rawhide belt, his girlfriend had passed her examination, and he—

his analysis, soon they'll release him, and he'll be a "Don"; for days at a time he sang two lines—just two!—

"The gravity of the Earth . . .

"The gravity . . . of the fields!"—which was a symptom of echolalia, resulting from his service—and shrilly spurred himself in every undertaking:

"A no-o-ormal pace!"

Try to understand them! The Foreigner thought to himself: "I see yet don't see them . . ."

The Medium—the fourth—sat always with his back turned (so therefore a description of him is omitted), and with two sweeping, counterflowing, circular movements, like a virtuoso pianist, he mixed the game pieces. This was a serviceman, a lustful intestinal worm, a poor wretch cheated by his active position in life.

Becoming latently very involved in the game, the Foreigner all the more sensed how under the banging of the pieces, the contours of his own cherished "I" creaked and blurred. Over the course of the game what the players individually represented of themselves became less and less important. In the fullness with which they gave themselves to it, in the totality of the game itself, behind its frightening accessibility, he caught the presence of something spilled, uncatchable and mysterious like the Slavic Soul, like the Truth, which could find a room for itself on the tip of the nose—just shift your gaze and you can touch it!

Everything that wasn't a game was preparation for it, a warm-up and the raising of the team's spirit. The ward could be easily taken for a locker room before an important international tournament. A brief after-lunch nap—the renewal of physical strength—a loving retardation before a new immersion into the game. Then all the sluggishness disappeared, the emptiness of gaze dispersed, a light trepidation ran through the ward, the weary air freshened up—the body of the world impetuously grew younger.

There was, if you will, yet one more thing, besides strength, besides common passion—they all were Russian people, in their eyes you could read their readiness to fulfill any order of the Homeland. The Foreigner was embarrassed that he didn't love them. But another, more complicated feeling was already awakening in him, it opened a path for itself, it pressed his diaphragm . . .

The meaning of the game began gradually to become clear to him—as it always happens, the stubborn and long-enduring were rewarded; the many days of observation of the game from his cot, secret note taking, comparisons, sullen sitting in ambush, diet, exhausting intuitive efforts were not wasted—suddenly—something flashed, scattering sparks inside his head, something turned over, moved out, illuminated—and EVERYTHING suddenly got in its place.

Woe—Foreigner, why are you a foreigner?

Well, why couldn't you understand it earlier! You were unlucky to be born here among us, where everyone from early childhood knows and anyone can explain that the meaning of this Game, the highest achievement in it—is the "Fish!" And what is the Fish?—This is IHTIOS!—This is the signature of Jesus Christ, IHS.

Did you see the faces of these people incomprehensible to you when to one of them, the one who succeeded in praying and fasting, in participating in black masses of "blasphemous" conspiracies, the "Fish" was suddenly revealed?

Here is the true crown of the Game—a moment of open contemplation of the truth! In what an ecstatic state are the "players," jealously envying their brother-in-arms, who left them behind on the path of a spiritual feat!

The prompting is included already in the names of the Game; on the most profane, demonological level it is called—"the slaughter of the GOAT"—which was the name of the Unclean One from the times of antiquity.

But was it for you, shackled in karmic chains, following blindly the footprints of the Game, bewitched by its symmetry and asymmetry, by the magic of the "six-six," the mystic perfection of the "blank-blank" game piece; was it for you with your consciousness, disemboweled in phenomena, with your immigrant's arrogance; was it for you to comprehend that this ancient and eternally living, all-conquering GAME—that it has a profound God-searching,

God-constructing meaning, that it is nothing other than our secret, treasured national religion—a synthetic belief, which absorbed and reworked Catholicism, Orthodoxy, astrology, spiritism, *I Ching*, several sectarian beliefs, the cult of Avesta, combination theory and crystallography, fortune-telling by cards, Hesse's guesses, the traffic rules, and still tens and hundreds of components—and on a new level resolving all their apparent contradictions.

It turned out that the game was brought out of sealed-off Arab courtyards, from packed London pubs and exclusive clubs in Holland, from the quad of Trinity College in Oxford to the expanse of Moscow boulevards to where the center of the world's religious life had moved long ago.

The very etymology of the word ДО-МИ-НО, do you understand it? DO-MI-NO, "anno domini"—do you understand Latin? You should! You've seen it—you were given to see it!—Benedictines, a black cape with the white lining—Monte Cassino? Marco Polo? "Dixit dominus domino meo!" . . .

With bitterness the Foreigner jotted down that evening: "We are lazy and not curious."

A week later he made his last diary entry, writing somewhere in the margins to the side in the universal human book of suicides: in the predawn twilight, he took an electric water heating element, which he himself had constructed the night before for the needs of the ward out of a wire, two shaving blades, a couple of matches, and black thread, into his mouth, firmly clenching his teeth on the parallel plates of "Schick."

It was one minute to six. The radio began to clear its throat, getting ready to strike up the national anthem at the end of that minute.

■ □ ■ □ ■

THE WAY HOME

THE LIT TRAM CARS SWAYED LIKE CHINESE LANTERNS ON A WIRE AND vanished in the darkness of deserted streets. Sparks showered down when the trams made a turn. He was astonished by the trolley bus. First, it was working. Second, the genie of optics reigned over it. When people disappeared, it became evident that it was conceived as a system of semitransparent mirrors and bent looking glasses reflecting each other, mounted even into the black plastic details of the straphanger's railing. It moved forward and backward simultaneously, anyone who got inside was folded in half by it and unfolded fourfold, the trolley poked everyone in the back of their heads, whacking them, punching them with a ticket punching machine. Suddenly gaining speed, it began to pass through the walls of the nocturnal city, panting and hissing, slamming the mirror shutters of doors at stops, tossing several passengers dangling on the plastic straphanger hooks like dresses on hangers, a dresser enraged from six hundred volts, being dispersed to thirty-two electric chairs, covered with trash like a movie theater after the last showing—a nuthouse—the driver in a black corner was spinning a torn-off fifth wheel . . . ahead it was dark.

His shoulder was tapped by someone. She ushered him along. "Arrived . . . last stop."

His legs carried him to the doors. Still standing on the steps, he gulped some fresh night air. He walked two steps and stopped. Something hissed, a clap, and turning back, he managed to catch sight only of a sparking path, the trail of the trolley bus disappearing, extinguishing in the darkness beneath the trees. He drew in a chestful of chilly night air, thick as standing water. "Shit, how is this the last stop?" He looked around. He didn't recognize the place at all. The road ended, bumping into some kind of wall beneath the trees. Parallel to the wall another street stretched on, wide and paved with cobblestones. He walked a bit ahead and looked to both sides: In both directions the road disappeared in the darkness, in both directions the cobblestones glistened equally and the wall stretched on. There were no landmarks. He turned around. To the right and left a hundred paces away poorly lit nine-story buildings stood sideways, turned to him. "So, stay calm, this has happened to you lots of times, you didn't know, just like here—or somewhere else, how you got here. Too lazy to walk to the buildings, to look for a sign . . ." He glanced at the sky. The stars were barely visible through a certain aureole of glimmering semidarkness. Nothing visible either below or above. Quiet. Crap.

He stood in the middle of the road at the point of tangency of the perpendicular with the straight, as though nailed with this perpendicular into some kind of giant's blueprint, he stood motionless, allowing the unnamed, for the time being unclear thought to ripen in him and to be formulated. He didn't really get frightened, but he suddenly woke up completely and nearly sobered up. It was as though a mixture of anxiety and long-forgotten semibliss clutched his stomach with its cold hand just below the ribs. The seat he was sitting on wasn't hard. With a certain inner feeling, not with his eyes, with his animal intuition, he clearly felt there wasn't anything alongside him and above, and neither below. Beneath him there was nothing supporting him.

How he ended up here became unimportant. The situation was much worse. He didn't remember *who* he was. Not his name, not the place he lived, and so on—this was obvious, but what was even worse—what kind of creature was he? What gender? That is, what in general do they do, and what's accepted for creatures like him, and for the time being he didn't see a single one like that around him. There, well, what to do now, for example? He could continue to stand there for a while, of course, but somehow he understood that this wasn't right, that he wouldn't do it right. Much worse than those over there, who show up darkly, from time to time seemingly sighing along the edges of the road, they were a lot taller than he and more patient. He was completely alone and wasn't being artful.

Continuing to grope the limits of his own consciousness, with surprise he was discovering that he generally knew a lot of these . . .
words and—most striking—knew how to use them, but he turned
up in some dark room from which he didn't know how to exit. He
firmly knew a minute later that such creatures as he, in principle,
existed somewhere—this very day he still lived among them—he just
had to find them. He remembered and laughed—he hemmed that
he even once saw ones just like him—who had forgotten everything
. . . in a movie theater . . . and at that time didn't believe it. That is
those who, of course, hadn't forgotten everything—those recalling
on the way—a fork, a fly on their trousers, those who maybe forgot
something that was most important, and this made them helpless
and ridiculous, off-balance, and kept them from understanding and
knowing anything in fact themselves.

As before, he had no address or profession, maybe, look here in
this thing that's hanging to the left? For the time being he didn't
even have a question that he should ask . . . if there were anyone to
ask. "Where am I? Very good. Who am I? Even better . . . gotta go."

He went to the spot where he had been just recently—maybe even
very recently—from which everything began. He ends up on the
sidewalk with his second attempt, because in the lamplight, shadows
from branches moved beneath his feet, crisscrossing and *moving,* and
it threw him forward, then shook him away, but he had already
guessed that these were shadows, and overcoming giddiness, trying
not to look at their play, with his gaze he grabbed at the brown slabs
of the pavement showing through behind them—and gained a firm
foothold finally in the end. Now to wait. To breathe a bit.

After some time, from under the trees a figure stepped toward
him, somehow quite similar to him—same arms and legs, a wrinkled suit, an unhealthy-looking, wrinkled face in the lamplight,
unsteady legs. The guy asked:

"Excuse me, do you have a smoke?"

Smoke? Sure, right. Sure! His hands first—even earlier than his
words—groped through his pockets. There it is, maybe, in a paper
pack, that's it. The cigarettes.

"Thanks! Got matches?"

He sensed himself that the action that had been carried out wasn't
complete. These sticks getting in the way in the mouth of him and

of the other guy, something had yet to be done with them. Puzzled, he slapped one, then the other pocket. There was nothing like that there. He scrounged in his bag, on the side of which there was a kind of lock that only his hands knew how to pull. A thumping cardboard box turned up there. By the stranger's satisfied face, he knew he had found it. He struck the match, and it lit easily for him right away. The other guy cupped his hands holding the match and said something or other. But he didn't hear or listen. Something dawned on him.

If he ended up here somehow, it means he could make his way out of here. He just had to wait for the thing that brought him here and ride on it, just in the opposite direction. Maybe on catching sight of something he'd remember something? Of course: He'll be riding along, intently thinking, and little by little he'll remember! . . . His body wanted something, but it couldn't distinctly explain to him what it was. Maybe it was just tired? But in order to help it, he had to work at it a bit more and find out something. He sensed that he was acting properly and that someone or something would help him. Wait a bit more—he couldn't help but get lucky.

He recognized it, the one exactly like the one that brought him here. Maybe the same one, but that could hardly be. Rushing along completely dark and empty, it turned and was about to gather speed, in order to disappear, but at the wave of his hand—braked. The doors hissed. "To the park," the driver said. "To the park . . . unpark," he didn't remember what it was. It had to go, so he followed. After several minutes he began vaguely to recall something. One past was now being lined up behind him, another—being carried along to meet him. It's warm, it's warm—the air was becoming hotter and hotter. He sensed that he was getting close . . . to home. "Home!" He remembered the word.

He was recognizing the places where he used to be, literally just a few days ago, almost yesterday, somebody lives here, at some point in the past he had been here, you could take a shortcut here! The places that had passed identification were lining up inside him and rhyming to the reluctantly rejoicing refrain—"Home! Home!"—he still didn't know where to place the period in this spatially tempo-rary opus, or how the speed of his turning was tied to the length of the plot, but confidence grew in him, his breaths became shorter, until there flew out at him suddenly the last straightaway, severing the park on his right hand—wrong one! a different "park"—regulated and murderously accurate, like the fourteenth line of a sonnet, leaving no doubts, and he heaved a sigh at the yellow light of the intersection: "There!"

From here to home, where his cot awaits him in the dark, it was about two hundred paces. He could cross them with his eyes closed, without remembering his address today, or his name, or his gender—distinguishing himself little in fact essentially from anybody, captured by the beam of the traffic light, on the line between death and birth.

■   ❑   ■

. . . The first thin, swift, multicolored she-serpent appears in the door of the train compartment. You jump up, trying to fly up, flapping your arms, but they fail to keep you in the air, you're sluggish.

A second one crawls in, wide and flat, like a boa constrictor.

The thin one rushes at the other, a quick encounter at the door. Can't jump out, you're locked up. So you're forced to observe from the upper bunk, where you had climbed up nevertheless, to watch the outcome.

The big one tears off the tail of the smaller one, and with it the latter's entire lower half, and with one hand choking its throat, with another scooping and carrying into its mouth the hot, still-smoking entrails. Judging by everything, the first she-serpent was going berserk—she was moaning, as though in orgasm, and deprived of the possibility of doing anything herself, hurries with her free hand to bring from her torn-off stomach to her mouth, stuffed already with bits of intestines, pieces of her own liver, or spleen, choking on it.

The big one, victorious, settles in on the lower bunk, spreading out her bed linen. She settles down for a spell. Your bare feet hang a meter from her face. You drive her back with your barbell-like feet, with the weak-willed pants swaying onto the corner of the bunk. But she doesn't get angry, for the time being she's sated and knows when the time is right, continuing to make her bed, she says over her shoulder: "It's your own fault. Your blood hemoglobin is falling because you drink so much."

An eternal simian fatal dark horror congeals in your veins, on the third bunk of a fruit tree, inside the clay hut compartment, in a distant railway siding.

It's getting dark. You can hear only—maybe it's imagined—the stirring of serpents, crawling over the railroad tracks, crawling off into your garden.

Nearly half paralyzed, in a certain peaceful terror, as though in cold silt at the bottom of a well, he awakens at three in the morning.

"Are you a witch? Or are those the boots of the she-guest rising above her knees?

"Or are you keeping a nameless son somewhere far away? Or have you crawled into a telephone wire as though into an open mouth while you were asleep?

"What are you, soul, like a witch, why are you tormenting this poor seminarian's body? . . ."

Back from your hangover—and ready to have fun again?

From the kitchen, shouts, crying, and more shouts were heard. A plaster mask on his face. The London Powder had run out, a ca-pi-tal-istic acquisition, indulgence for a country where intoxication is mightier than the frost. He had to take a shower, first to wash away the alcohol from the roots of his hair where it had accumulated.

He got up and, plowing through the utter chaos of things and rooms, locked himself in the bathroom. There was water—great luck. Under the shower he remembered how he had been drinking yesterday one after another by chasing them, by sniffing at the sleeves of his shirt, tearing them with a single jerk, sniffing his pocket, sniffing his collar. They clinked glasses. . . . Disgraceful.

The eyes were vulnerable, but alive. But his mug, God, his mug! After shaving, it tightened as though by a beauty mask. Gotta get out of the house as soon as possible.

He didn't even begin to grind any coffee and, grabbing Rodya, who had already been dressed, by the hand, snatched up his grocery sack on the run, and like firewood rolled down the stairway into the courtyard. Here he took a deep breath. His lungs gratefully drew in the fresh air, still unspent from the night. It wasn't clear yet what kind of day it would be, though the sun had already risen quite high. The spring weather was windy. All of this would explode into bloom in no sooner than a week. For the time being there were leaves; a separate thank-you for them. Rodya picked up something from the ground—

a beer cap, "a little wheel"—and firmly grasped it in his hand. His gait was businesslike and slightly comic, as that of a man who knew exactly where he was going and why. He looked like a tiny businessman from the Country of the Rising Sun. For the moment he refused to give his hand. "I'm a book, I'm being read," he said a few days ago. Only recently he stopped jumbling syllables—"timmohopamus" instead of "hippopotamus," "qoubet" instead of "bouquet."

There was more meat and feathers on the bushes than leaves. The sparrows bawled as though they wanted to peck out his brain, as though that morning he was preparing to boil them for bird bouillon. Rodya had already solicitously inspected someone's Zhiguli car, stooping down and being reflected in the hubcaps of the wheels, approvingly touching the bumper, leaving the traces of his little fingers on its dust-covered, dirty surface. So. Without shouts. He stopped and lit up his first cigarette. Holding Rodya by the hand he crossed the street. He decided not to drop into the store an extra time—there'll be another one along the way.

Rodya warily stepped along the asphalt road that stretched along the park.

It was only now that he looked closer—the pavement was completely cluttered with the shells of the bodies of thousands of rain worms—why did the earth vomit them out in a single night? There were almost no living ones, among them particularly those that were going to continue to live. A portion of them was crushed by the feet of passersby, in holes filled with rainwater some kind of colorless strings floated, out of which life had already left. Here and there a fragment of a body still stirred, a few ringlets, here half a centimeter, there a centimeter. Rodya became agitated by the vision of such unprecedented carnage, he mumbled something to himself, stooped down at times above something, touched it with a twig, without letting go of his father's hand, then he rose up and stepped over the worms, continued on his way. It was really hard not to step on them, the worms were lying there so nicely, you couldn't fit the foot of an adult between them. This stretched on for hundreds of meters, maybe a kilometer, there were millions of them, crushed, they came across their squished bodies—as though someone had tested a fountain pen—even on the route leading to the airport, where they soon turned.

Here Rodya let go of his father's hand. His good mood had returned.

He turned around and showed his father: "See, we've come from far away." He kept quiet for a bit and added: "We're no longer there."

The first strong gust of wind reached them, which brought the younger one to ecstasy. Spreading his legs and in a set position, he extended his arm and, putting it on some kind of indiscernible dial, turned it sharply.

"I'm turning on the wind!"

A tremor seized his father, the cold wind penetrated the sweater that had been stretched hastily over his bare body.

"What are you doing? Turn it off right away!"

But Rodya was implacable: "The turn-off switch is broken."

The dial quite freely turned in this then that direction, without having any visible effect.

Grabbing each other's hands and huddling over, they crossed onto the other side. Somewhere not far away with a doleful roar, planes were warming up their engines. Occasional cars passed.

Walking a bit further, chased by the wind, they took cover in a store, jostled into the recesses of nine-story buildings.

After several minutes Rodya once again appeared on the doorstep, chewing off the end of a loaf of bread, holding it with both hands, and his father, clanking bottles of milk, put away at the bottom of the bag.

"Well, what, the airport?" his father asked.

"Erport," even categorically, his son confirmed confidently.

For a time they walked in silence, avoiding the undrying muddy puddles, halting at several unfinished building sites, stepping over pipes, gazing into ditches.

A cheerful Stalinist spire with a blue and yellow flag was getting closer to them. Torn little clouds swirled above it, the sun was warming, a light rain began to drizzle, drying right there on the skin, on the sidewalk under the sunlight, in the wind. A voice, carrying from a loudspeaker, disturbed Rodya. It was impossible to make sense of its instructions.

Several taxis waited beneath branchy willows, their drivers smoking not too far away. An open little window, from which they were selling beer, could be seen to the left of the airport, next to the passenger disembarkation area. They rose along the steps of the main entrance and in a glass kiosk bought the schedule for the week. At the end of a corridor you could see the corner of one of the waiting rooms, all the chairs were occupied, the heads of those waiting craning—some kind of film was on.

They stepped out of the building and walked up to the cherished little window, which his father had noticed right from the start, and while his father leisurely was drinking his beer, the son, craning his neck, incessantly gazed at the honey-colored foamy glass, pierced by sunlight, capable of quenching anyone's thirst, and thought about the cruelty of fathers.

. . . Here this Adam's apple, raised to the sky, is hard as a pistol cock. This greediness . . .

His father was strict, but just. Pushing aside the beer glass and a half-liter bottle, he took his son to watch the planes. At the service exit through a wire net you could see an enormous Tupolev plane, beneath the wing of which an army fueling truck was moving back and forth. A little man in coveralls walked about the wing, dragging a really fat hose, flipped off some caps on chains, and stuck the hose inside.

Rodya forgot everything and forgave immediately. He sucked in this vision, this dream come true, with a recoil not less than a jet blast for a plane, or a beer for his father. Here everything was important and surprising, and he wouldn't miss a single detail. He was distracted only for about ten seconds by a plane landing on its roost and a yellow toy jeep that soon after passed along the landing strip—a moving accent, binding for a moment the whitened azure of the sky with the poisonous green of the grass and refracting all this in the giant gray mirror of the strip. A fly, crawling on the glass. It was riding, not flying, just because it wanted to. He could get his son away from here now only with a trick, only with promises. This morning—as sometimes happens after a hangover—turned out to be constructed according to the laws of art and did not require anything of those wrapped in it besides attention and responsiveness. Maybe you can only live when you don't need anything? someone living in his father thought.

. . . They came upon a dirt road. It looped, winding around the garages, the trailers of the builders standing all over the place. Then there was soil turned upside down by bulldozers, overgrown in spots with weeds. Standing on end a cistern with doors cut all the way through and a grated window floated off somewhere along the hillocks here and there. It long ago and joyfully had rusted. In the bay of the door you could see the azure of the sky.

A fossilized tar buggy was moving in place on iron wheels, with a long pipe, like a not-quite-incarnated nostalgic daydream about the first steam locomotive—it was covered all in tar snot, in black oil, in creosote.

Passing piles of trash, debris of parts from decommissioned planes—some kind of nests hanging on wires, panels torn off with chunks, they finally came upon a path leading to the fields. A ditch stretched to the left, half-filled with calcified milk, covered with reeds and dry weeds. It stank slightly. Avoiding occasional gardens, they stepped up to a little bridge—a sheet of welded iron, thrown across the stinky river that came here to its own natural end, finding peace in the dead and rotten swamp beneath the concrete fence of the airfield.

The technotronic vision receded bit by bit and the fields began. They bubbled like the washing machine foam of dandelions, as though blown through straws of stalks by colossal lungs of the earth raised here.

Rodya dragged behind him a bent bicycle wheel that he had picked up somewhere, refusing to part with it, and cursed, grumbling in irritation under his breath: "Some kind of mommykins, poppykins, Rodyakins, storykins, wheelykins, beetlekins (*stumbling*), lands, worms, some kind of volcanoes . . ."

They really had come to the hub of this part of the world—a muddy little volcano, discovered by them and, probably, having erupted just a month or so ago. From fifty paces away you could hear its gurgling and burbling. The hollow, continuously swelling hum was heard from beneath the earth, and as you approached it, turned into a hum, into a quaking of the soil under their feet. Between the stems of grass watery dandelions were puffed and popped just like during the rain. But there was no rain, the sun beat down from behind the clouds. In the low spot under the hillside, a large puddle had formed, in which fountains of water spurted out, as though the puddle were boiling, small stones rubbed against one another, bounding and grinding in this cold brew.

Judging by everything, an underground river passed in this spot, coming close to the surface of the earth, swelling up from spring runoff. It had found a weak spot, grabbing the roots of a small decayed tree, the species of which was now impossible to determine, and shot it upward. In the earth a fistula had formed—a hole about a meter wide, in which there now floated, like a wooden spoon, the tiny body of that tree, beating and trembling, spattered with wet dirt, bounding up from the incessantly popping giant bubbles made of thinly ground silt. The thick slush splattered from the crater, creating around it an undrying half-meter-wide earthen wall. There was something ominous and obscene in all of this. Beneath the dancing and convulsing dirt you could infer the swift flow. Several tens of meters of soil could collapse at any moment through the earth and end up drawn into and carried away by the waters of the subterranean river—together with father and son. So it seemed. Stepping carefully, they left the spot. Now it began to drizzle from the sky again.

Along the edge of the meadow cows were grazing, and in the copse a cowherd was strolling. Glancing at the quickly darkening sky above, he suddenly pulled out from somewhere a polyethylene poncho. His body, dressed up in a crumpled suit, was transparent now through the gauze of the polyethylene, like the skeleton of a fish.

Father and son entered the not-very-dense forest.

Rodya disturbed the quiet all around, finally throwing his bicycle wheel into some wolf's pit, filled to the brim with water, and with last year's leaves floating in it. This thick layer of those decayed leaves covered the entire ground, not allowing the grass to burst through, and felt soft beneath his feet. Dried underbrush crackled beneath the weight of his body. Rodya picked up an old newspaper on the path and bid that it be burned. Stooping down, he accidentally farted and, slightly embarrassed, grumbled, "A truck passed."

His father shook out cigarettes into the pocket of his satchel and tossed the empty cigarette pack into the fire, they warmed themselves at the leaping fire a bit, sitting on their hind legs. Several raindrops soaked through on the paper and disappeared immediately, not even managing to begin to hiss.

When father and son left the forest, it was no longer raining. Was there any altogether? Once again birds opened their beaks, jays, thrushes—but their shouts hardly meant anything—if they were anything, then, they were air punctuation marks rather than sounds or letters. Rodya was already trampling on the minefield of mole mounds. Above one of them he sat on his hind legs and got agitated: "Poppa, a mole pushed out some kaka!"

It was, of course, dog shit—from some kind of half fox terrier, a nervous mongrel of dog that hunts out lairs. He didn't like dogs that deposited sperm sloppily, as though it were urine, and urine carefully, as though it were sperm. Neither those obedient ones in overcoats, nor those purebred dimwits, nor those generally accessible plebeian bastards—you walk, and right at you a wise guy six meters high, your death in its jaws, or a giant bitch in heat—what other way can they be? That reddish young collie, twenty-two in dog years, that always lay at your feet at the table, that captured every glance, measured every word on itself. And it never will speak. Useless. Its mound is here somewhere. They're like children that never grow up. Lord! . . .

Rodya walked in front along the path in the park, cutting dandelions down with his twig; a bit behind him his father followed, thinking about his own things.

Like a dog with its nervous constitution and even with the very choice of breed revealing its owner, dragging out into God's world his secret, don't children to a greater degree do something similar? Doesn't a son give scale to a father and grandfather, doesn't he finish drawing, joining with them, something invisible, doesn't the masculine line outline the break of one rival character with itself? Of his projections, postponed depending on their place in a row, in different directions? How, say, does a magician bang with his fist along a black cylinder, that cylinder then becomes white, then he wrenches it with a blow, and it's black again? To manage to see just this . . . like a contour map, in order to capture the meaning of mutability, the structure of supplementariness, more abruptly: to plot the line of a front.

Unexpectedly he remembered how for the first time about ten years ago he fell onto one knee like a lay brother in a church, in order to lift from the carpet a speck of dust invisible to the world, but bothering him, without getting up yet, with a mixed feeling of terror, delight, and repulsion—almost from the side—he noticed that he had repeated his father's habit exactly.

With suspicion he looked at Rodya.

Rodya was already barging through the grass, to the side away from the path, like a quick-moving land rover, like a gallant little soldier, like a man who absolutely knows exactly what he's seeking.

His father kept up next to him, stepping solidly and weightily, slightly sideways on his way. The gait of a forty-year-old man somehow recalls the run of a rhinoceros. Only a bullet can stop either of them.

■   ❏   ■

One satisfaction remained for him, that squeezed out and occupied the place of all other satisfactions that had left during the past year—this was the daily dream of a day off when you fall through the body's weariness into silence and lay down, like a drowned man in shallow waters on a sunny day.

He shut the door of his room and, pulling the blind, accidentally noticed with the corner of his eyes a man preparing to do exactly the same thing.

Moved by a sudden impulse, nearly a caprice, he left the blind and approached the mirror. This face, familiar to drowsiness, long ago for him wasn't anything other than a subject of shaving—a polygon for a shaving lathe, being only half awake. Toward morning a bright short bristle will pop out like on pigskin.

He was struck by the attention with which that man from the mirror gazed at him. Their undisguised interest was mutual. He suddenly felt like examining this face and trying to understand something through it, something slippery and inaccessible, as, say, the constantly present odor of one's own skin—its secret in a direct sense. From the proboscis appendices of the human face a just as searching and exacting glance was directed at him.

To what purpose, why was this uncut shackle of hair, like a hanging lock, halfway down his face? This sensual schnozz, at which it was hinting, what was it looking for? And these shells—were they taken out or screwed in from outside, gnawed into the bone of a temple? This for the time being elastic skin, taken on rental, which of course, when the time comes, will slip off, decay, fall off? And this pale, as though it's someone else's, hair-smoldered hand? He didn't know a single thing finally—all overgrown, all a mask, put onto someone's hidden, mocking finger . . .

And just this slight shining of his eyes, washed with alcohol, two poppy seeds, drowning in salty sea water, two black holes, into which every second the world turns upside down, and, pushed away from the eye's bottom, dives into the scriptorium of the brain in order to be deposited there for eternity, as though in the library of Alexandria, doomed beforehand.

As though hypnotized, he gazes into the eyes of the other one, that's the way two worthy enemies look at one another, two powers colliding to death, knowing the strength and weakness of each.

He knew the most embarrassing and the most secret about this man, all the profoundest, all his most hidden movements, his wishes and intentions, all his faults and foibles, all his wounded places, he knew what was simply forbidden about him, what was impossible to know about another person without parting from him from earliest childhood, he remembered every step of his, penetrated his dreams, his tongue knew every hole in his teeth!

He looked into his eyes—perspiration welled on his nose—and with despair, with great terror, with surprise, he saw that he, in fact, did not know this man drowning in the mirror behind the glass.

■ □ ■ □ ■

THE *ÉGLISE* BY THE STATION:
A GALICIAN MOTIF

IT WAS BORN AT THE BEGINNING OF THE CENTURY TO THE PIERCING whistles of locomotives, to the screech of the first generation of tram cars—dandyish cars, looping around its childhood spot—a square at the intersection of Horodetsky Street and Novy Svet Street. The elevated location was selected by experienced midwives in soutanes, conforming to the recommendations of the leading lights of genealogical science—as sometimes happens with the conclusion of dynastic, and equally scandalous morganatic marriages—with compulsory trips to Rome and Venice for consultations. The neo-Gothic dandy was supposed to have lifted up its spires eleven meters higher than the cupolas of St. George's Cathedral that milked the sky, which for several centuries plagued the humiliated but still haughty Polish eye, in order to prick God, who had forsaken Poland among the neighboring nations.

In steamed, starched napkins, among the clots of placenta, of slaked lime, of frozen clay, the newborn unleashed its first scream and began to grow impetuously. The rafters and walls were raised with the rapidity of bamboo, and together with them grew a youth of rare breed and beauty—the hope of the Crown, the heir of Catholic thought vertically restored to the sky. The pulsing heart of the altar, the blasting lungs of an organ, the bronchi and rows of balconies, windows, open wide along the entire wall, prepared for the transference of heavenly visions, the pulpit, raised, as though a barrel on the mast of a caravel, alcoves of confessionals—similar to internal organs, they detached themselves and developed in its body, and, the immediately arched roof closed above its mighty, breathing Gothic ribs, without slowing down they undertook the service of the Christian God, the exaltation of the prayers of parishioners, the transfusion of crimson Christian blood.

But there was some kind of defect from the very beginning, some kind of fateful consequence of the immeasurable number of cross-marriages, a prolapse of either a chromosome, still undiscovered by a nonexistent science, or something still more absurd yet unprovable, as though getting up on the wrong side of the bed, from century to century, disgracing the computations of the wise ones and the knowing. Was not the tsar's hemophilia—in this world—just the hopeless attempt at localization of an unstoppable flow of blood in mankind? The cathedral was named with a woman's name in honor of the empress stabbed by a Swiss anarchist at a spa. Perhaps with the name a drop of poison from the murdering stiletto skipped and penetrated into its blood?

It was divinely complex, with a nobleness of bearing, a stateliness in everything recalling those first paladins, warriors for the tomb of the Lord, it was like a wrathful archangel, an immaterial sword in hands defeating the eternal Enemy—if anyone saw this. But the years passed in a day, and while the cathedral was being built, a thousand years unnoticeably flew past, and a tank crawled along the fields, and a machine gun rattled from the trenches as though it prayed, and above the earth an airplane traced out loop-the-loops addressed to the sky. For some reason the parishioners could smell mustard gas from the censer.

Europe changed its outlines for the next time. The dead turned out to be inveterate and atoned for by prayer, and then buried and forgotten. The plan, to the idea of which the cathedral was erected, was accomplished by the inscrutable paths of Providence. The silhouette of the city changed with the appearance of a new accent. Novy Svet Street was now called Sapiegi Street. And the nearby alley was named Novy Svet. Later it was renamed twice. During the Soviets it would be called Democratic Street.

The *Église* by the Station matured and was now in the bloom of its youthful strength—in a country grown younger. There just weren't any masters, enraptured in the heavens, to set out their colored visions in the hectares of its stained-glass windows. And on the ledges of the roof instead of chimeras hewn of stone there gained a firm foothold little empty-bodied tin pyramids, covered over "in stone" with recently invented concrete. But very few paid any attention to it.

The city grew, and the cathedral labored together by the sweat of its brow, rolling up its sleeves, it baptized and gave communion, listened to confession, performed marriage rites and held burial services, and glorified the name of God, constantly finding itself in contact—with the antennae of crosses capturing the rustles in the ether in the bell-shaped spires, capturing and strengthening them, retranslating the whisper of prayers, the drone of the liturgy, the breaking-off, lonely voice of a man—all a single great internal ear, a single diaphragm, caving in from breathing in and out—it was impossible to figure out, is it from that or this side? . . .

But there was no one, however, who would listen to the earth. And the children baptized by the cathedral had immediately grown up to be lapped by a wave of one more crushing war—from which it itself, while not being summoned to it, will emerge a cripple.

One time they came with a swastika, and when on the seventeenth day of the war the garrison beneath white eagles came out to surrender, they left, to allow the army of Reds to fraternize. Two years later they returned again and for some reason bombarded the city, leaving it in the deep rear front for three more years. A machine gun, dragged up one of the spires of the cathedral, rattled at the retreating detachments of the Red Army, at the railways and cattle cars. The Reds answered back. The new masters without any consultations renamed the former Novy Svet, the former Sapiegi, the former—for a short time—Stalin Street, in their own style: Führstenstrasse. Or perhaps it was Führerstrasse. But the Russians dislodged them after three years and later renamed it back to Stalin Street. Back then they closed the cathedral, because they said there was no God. And they tried hard to prove this in action. If only the cathedral had been smaller, they would have razed it, as they did with its kin, if there were willingness to do that and they had had time for it: A tank unscrewed its tower, like a cap turned front to back; and for several days in a row with its chest assaulted the red-hot superdurable brick, the secret of which turned out to be lost over an astoundingly short time. The tank bounced back from the wall like a nut. The tank drivers got incredible headaches from it. Despite their helmets. Maybe this is what stopped them.

The cathedral lay empty, like the distracted body of an imbecile, bereft of reasoning, shell-shockedly smiling to pigeons, children, drunkards, gaping with broken windows, a roof with holes, with bullet holes in the spires and towers, laying bare its internal structure—the construction of beams and ceilings, fragments of stairways with missing spinal disks, leading now to nowhere. Its body, caught by chilly drafts, wheezed and whistled, as though it were a clay cyclop's whistle, remaining intact for some reason from past epochs, the purpose of which was unclear. Last year's snow lay beneath the walls inside the cathedral until late spring, the sunlight didn't reach there, the confessionals turned out to be broken, their fine wooden bars were torn out with chunks of wood, on the patterned stone floor were scattered fragments of childrens' bodies with broken noses and wings. In the choir loft lead organ pipes were knocked over in a pile and crumpled, like cigarette butts—an angel's trench ironed flat by an enemy tank.

They didn't keep horses in it.

Later in it they kept cement. They turned the cathedral into a warehouse. Dried-up Polish women in drooping stockings prayed, kneeling on the wide steps of the main entrance, behind the closed doors of which cement and chalk were heaped in piles, barrels stained with patches of linseed oil stood in these man-made dunes, the wind pranced. The iron metal binding of the doors was stuck all over with half-dried bouquets of flowers, among which several fresh ones always stood out. Like a meadow rising up vertically. In the expectation of snow.

Next to the praying old woman a coarse leather satchel stood with a bottle of milk and a loaf of bread. A few bread crumbs from the satchel went then to the pigeons in the square that made themselves at home on the empty body of the cathedral—the only ones who still resisted its disintegration, healing the wounds and fissures of the building with encrustations of petrified guano, settling the hollowness of the cathedral with the so appropriate fluttering of wings here, with muffled bird voices.

Courageous roof makers hunted for the pigeons, cooking the free bird bouillon for their lunch. They covered roofs in other parts of the city. Here, banging with their hammers, they riveted the gutters, warming themselves at the rough handmade wooden spools, winding around in an electric spiral, sending couriers for vodka. The vodka store was across the street. And the Crucified One, nailed high on the facade above a plicated Gothic rose—as though He were turned to stone, gazed from beneath closed eyelids at the eternal line at the store and at the crowded tram stop before it. Did *they* remind Him, made smaller by the height, of anything—with their eternal load of satchels, dolls, baby carriages, in short bounds scurrying from arriving tram cars toward the doors of stores and to the street stands and back? It's possible that He, like the cathedral, firmly merged with His fate, was in a profound anabiosis, losing His mind, twice a year alternating with short-lived minutes of illuminating dementia.

Time flooded memory. Horodetsky Street, the longest in the city, long ago had become—and it looked like, forever—May First Street, Stalin Street, and had suddenly turned into Peace Street. But not for the cathedral. Precisely at that time they began to castrate its desecrated, half-dead body. With difficulty it recalled how during the night like a thief a crossbreaker crawled along its body in the scaffolding. Saddling the highest of its spires, he lifted up a saw on a rope and started to cut. Nearly up in the cosmos, in immediate proximity to the stars, uplifted high by his profession above the sleeping city, above Privokzalny Square, above the roof of the cathedral left far below, half-flooded in moonlight, he leaned with his whole body to the cold metal of the cross, fusing with it in this single undertaking, what did this guy think and feel—finding room that night on the tip of a needle?

The job turned out to be not the easiest. Toward dawn he barely succeeded in cutting through half of it. The tram cars started up. From the train station stretched innumerable unskilled laborers arriving in the city on diesels and electric commuter trains. Toward eight in the morning the square turned out to be overflowing with a crowd of people cursing and sending fulminations to the impious one, simply idlers, praying old ladies, children. The hypnosis of the crowd unexpectedly exceeded a critical mass. The enormous cross broke in two and carried along behind it the crossbreaker clasping it with his final—froglike, torpid—love embrace.

They decided to leave the violated, castrated cathedral in peace for a while. Peace, however, was not foreseen.

With the next government stability and loyalty were especially valued. Especially during that government they banned drinking in the streets. The cathedral was situated right at the entrance into the city, at the first tram car turn—a periodontal fang of a Roman Catholic cathedral sticking out, "raped, plundered, and dishonored,"—everyone knew this—as before all the same maintaining in proportions the nobleness and grandeur of its design, at one time a Polish dandy, later a four-time spy, it was "loyal," accessible, and scientifically undistinguished, as though a castle of apparitions, crying like a homeless guy on the parquet floors of the regional housing committee waiting room.

This government went mad over the clearing of the giant squares and its mania for grandiosity, cross-eyed with obvious agitation—so that from the cosmos one could see the advantages of order and so that science became such that it was possible to send off sunny jumping mirror reflections to the moon and other heavenly bodies.

Two projects were nurtured by the city powers: to knock down the cathedral into bits and carry it outside the city, or—to restore it, for prophylaxis.

The first project, as they figured, would have cost two million, the second, presumably, four. Fortunately, there turned out to be no money in the city at all.

At that time they designated the city the homeland of Automatic Control Systems (one of the then-names for a panacea), and, having cut down the crosses on another much smaller church, they set up a House of Quality. On the facade they tacked on a magic pentagram of quality—the church was, by the way, on a hill, and they put a model of the philosopher's stone inside. Having thrown out the caskets, they stuffed the catacombs with bottles of lab samples of the double-distilled water of life. They picked the kind of music that made people enjoy life, and played it day and night.

They liked the undertaking.

That was the time of qualitative illusions—a time of bigwigs. The streets were watered. On the issue of exhibition matches of the soccer team, a bureau even met somewhere. They read writers as they never did anywhere, but they didn't publish them. Loyalty was encouraged, from occasion to occasion, with a stick of cooked kielbasa. Even when the last of the once-powerful dynasty of great sovereigns arrived—a nice pinkish little chubbo with a star on his forehead, the colors already running, losing its outlines—the powers of law and order, gathered from the entire region, stood every twenty paces with a stick of cooked kielbasa under the armpit of an unoccupied arm. It had to have been that then the bright idea came to someone to arm them in advance with inedible sticks. The last names of *the first in* their places changed according to the laws of eighteenth-century school drama: Kutsevol, Dobryk, Pohrebniak, Sekretariuk. If the second had been an authentic prince—every week a cistern of sea water for his swimming pool was delivered to his home (people surely fabricate: a cistern on a rail line? maybe an automobile line?)—and the third tore the human face measuring it—and the last, following the dynamic of the process, declared himself to be illegal and dissolved without a trace like a lump of sugar. But this happened much later.

For the time being the question of the cathedral as before urgently demanded resolution. A small war began somewhere, and in order to take attention away from it, all efforts were thrown into preparation for the Olympiad. All the whores were carted off from the capital cities to parts unknown and new ones were trucked in.

In Kyiv from the cathedral on Red Army Street—a brother-in-law of the one by the Lviv station—they decided to set up an organ hall for sportsmen and dug up giant holes all around it. The *Église* by the Station in Lviv was already surrounded by a fence, and the fence during one of the voluntary unpaid work Saturdays was painted—to explain from this day on to passing travelers that the restoration was already in progress. The drunkards of Station Square were overjoyed and moved behind the fence to drink. They erected furniture made from empty boxes. Then on the gate they hung a lock and obliged everyone. But soon the alcohol deficit began, and this part of the problem was resolved by itself—people started to drink in their homes.

The Ascension never took place for the Crucified One, who was disgusted to the last degree, and His stone legs broke off—as though it were the third degree, but this time no one was killed. This fact remained almost unnoticed, passing though the consciousness of the population—decoders for it couldn't be found—since everything had already driven off, sailed away, or been lost.

A woman with a child, crossing the street at this spot in front of the cathedral, took a misstep into an open sewer hatch and, flying, exchanging years for meters, like a little girl was plumped down into the sewer and ended up carried off by the rushing flow—a light rain was falling—into a collector beneath the neighboring bazaar square—where she dried off and from where five hours later she was dragged out alive, unharmed, and once again grown old.

The names of the streets for the time being continued to glimmer deceptively, like magic inscriptions on swords given by a genie.

They returned Horodetsky Street, slightly distorting it, its name, the Street of Peace—Novy Svet—Sapiegi, see above, now began to be called Stepan Bandera Street. The envelopes began to sparkle with new colors: St. Petersburg—St. Bandera—poste restante. The rusted color of rags yielded to their place to the coloration of hard-boiled eggs from a train station stand. They carted off the fence near the cathedral. They moved the storehouse down Horodetsky Street. They also evicted the suddenly discovered cache of children's sleds in the cellars—judging by everything, a strategic reserve.

The cathedral awakened for the first time when an alpine cooperative, descending on it from God knows where, briskly patched its roof.

The Uniates, who had been given the chapel beneath the cathedral, put glass in the windows. It shuddered again, as though it suddenly had been awakened, recalling something, recognizing but not admitting its symbol of faith in some kind of distorted, not completely understandable dialect. A warm discord of recollections gushed onto it, watering its scalped head. How sweet was this deathbed dream so similar to an awakening—hasn't death really come at last along its bricks, designed for not just one life and a single empire?

And there was yet one more insanity: about the understanding of God in measures, something troubling about acupuncture, by which the nature of an Orthodox Greek is repulsed with a shudder, and about a simple onion dome, bringing him to tears—O lachrymose! we'll remove these spires; and the word PROJECT, spread out with colored tiles at the bottom of a bathing place, where face-down the body of an old woman in white clothes sways, with a bleeding wound in the side, and Baden-Baden, bu-bu-bu, honor et gloria sole Deo, bu-bu-bu: in a sickly, lime-slaked skull struck by a hereditary illness.

There is in Lviv a comfortably erected house, on the floor of which in the entryway is chiseled the date of completion, and which evidently was built for itself—"1938." In a quiet alley.

Who—and in which language—will speak the sorrow of buildings?

Of course houses are lasting, but hardly are they happier than people.

■　❑　■

P.S. Today I was asked how to get to Lincoln Street.
I don't know.

INTRODUCTION TO
THE GALICIAN CONTEXT

THE GEOGRAPHIC CENTER OF EUROPE IS A PLACE WHERE THE SINES and cosines of forces merge, where the tables of square roots slumber, and where the border guards of five states are vigilant, where the borders become hardened and people become softer and are torn off from their own fates, where all the contours double and are stacked one atop the other like a pile of slides, where they are seen and shine through each other, where epochs and ethnicities reveal one another—it is the sluggish pith of the European tree, which, like every pith, is useful just for making pencils and matches.

This is a land over which the foreboding sign of Sacher-Masoch has hung as a razor-sharp half-moon—flooding nations with anemic light (from Munich to Dikanka). This is a land, the fate of which seems to be more infinitesimal than its own longing.

From here lies the path to the "regions of a great heresy," where events that do not fit in time are located—into the blind back streets, into its dead end, and offshoots, a path to a "Second Spring," laid out once by a teacher of drawing of the Drohobych Polish Gymnasium—Bruno Schultz.

Somewhere here he got stuck in the yearly concentric rings of Europe, those hardened circles, which continue their motion, where, like a needle from an interwar record player, he came sliding with everyone—a man with a face that looked like a woman's shoe—the odd writer Bruno Schultz.

You can say straight away that as a writer he is the third missing link that connects Kafka to Babel, but it would be the greatest untruth for all three of them. It would be more appropriate to place him in a line with two other preeminent writers of his time, his close friends who were, just like he, failures (the former hanged himself, the second became an émigré)—Witkacy and Gombrowicz—but the problem is that their names say almost nothing to readers in the USSR (but that's almost exclusively just in the USSR).

Specific to all three of them was a belated Secessionism, which, paradoxically, bore unexpected fruits, saturating the creative work of each—although to varying degrees—with the spirit of metaphysical parody and making each of them artistic radicals.

They all, vaguely and with anxiety, felt what no one around them did—the bankruptcy of reality, that irrational doom that dragged Europe, which was becoming more and more dysfunctional, from world war to something now totally inhuman, attracting the present like a magnet—and they tried to investigate, each in his own way, this landslide, this paralysis of will, to enter into the very heart of masochism.

The only thing they knew: it was already too late. Man can live in some conditions only to a certain limit. This limitation is, generally, a completely concrete minimum of freedom. This is an aside.

By its series of external signs of capitulation, Schultz's situation in many respects is similar to Kafka's (up to repeating time after time a stalemate situation in the sphere of matrimony, documented in an extended and anguished correspondence). Schultz, by the way, is the first translator of *The Trial* in Poland (as it became known later—the literary editor). Following the bankruptcy and death of his father, as well as a series of internal family dramas, his mother, two sisters, and nephew ended up in Shultz's actual care, which all the more bound him with a dead knot to work in a school, all the more hated by virtue of the instability of his situation (because of his incomplete professional education in Lviv and Vienna) and his progressive fascination with literature.

All this was redoubled by the necessity of living in a province, in a low-temperature environment, in cultural isolation. A provincial city, as a matter of fact, is the reduction of a city as such. These kinds of cities are a perfect object for description, but not for life. You can only be born and die in them.

He began as a graphic artist and even achieved a certain renown (famous after the photopublication of *Ksiega balwochwalcza* [*The Book of Idolatry*]), a fame that after several decades all the same would have not become European, if not for his literary activities.

Something most important did not fit him in these drawn pictures. Conducting an expansive and tense correspondence, in the beginning of the 1930s, he finally groped that turn of phrase that would allow him to extract his theme out of the poverty of the surrounding matter, out of the cheapness of its overdeveloped, lush, but ontologically precarious forms, out of the unarticulated mishmash in his mouth, which grows in stylistic papillomas—to extract and tighten like a lady's corset—not so much as to construct something as to sew it, reversing the ratty "wardrobe" of the Secession, the circle of ideas of the fin de siècle. In the mid-1930s, two little books of prose put out by him, *The Street of Crocodiles* (*Sklepy cynomonowe*) and *A Sanatorium under the Sign of the Hourglass* (*Sanatorium pod klepsydra*), became an artistic scandal, that is, a success, and brought him a mass of true friends (as he has noted in his letters—"unjustly").

At first no one understood anything. Without a doubt, this was a magic literature, intelligently magic, which brought the metaphor of a new time into Polish literature—a metaphor that freed it in an unheard-of way, but also tied it to a new convention, because magic is captivity.

Shultz himself, it seemed, didn't completely understand the meaning of what he had done, quite scrupulously and . . . nearsightedly evaluating the innovative nature of his writing. Without a doubt, cultural isolation, the psychology of the backwoods, defined a certain diffused nature of his artistic self-perception.

For example, he worshiped Thomas Mann (as others had done, by the way, before Gorky and Rolland), valued his correspondence with him, Thomas Mann, with the thought about whom for some reason there comes to mind the late, the very late Goethe in Eckermann's *Conversations with Goethe,* who dreamed about living until the completion of the building of the Suez and Panama Canals. For some reason, it seemed to him that the world would really change as a result of these earthworks.

Writing didn't come easy to Shultz. He received a literary prize for his first book, took an extended leave of absence, went to Paris, arrived during the dead cultural season of summer. Europe didn't need him very much. He, by the way, was sure that it would be that way.

Shortly before World War II he started work on his third book, *The Messiah,* which he allowed to ripen in his mind for a long time, which gave him no peace and did not come out right for him— gravitating toward becoming a novel in the process of rewriting. The manuscript disappeared during the war, just as almost all of his manuscripts and most drawings and letters (it's somewhat uncomfortable to read the extant letters—the majority of the correspondents and those mentioned in the letters have also died). He apparently guessed the vector—of the end of time—but he didn't guess the quality of the impending apocalypse, written with a small *a,* because it was deprived of its main character, in whom long ago (transferring his name to belt buckles) the people of his time had stopped putting their trust—God.

In 1939 the division of Poland according to the Molotov-Ribbentrop Pact occurs. In the first days of the war Witkacy puts on a backpack and begins to move to the east with a wave of refugees. On the eighteenth of September he gets off a train to nowhere and opens up his veins in the forests of Volynia. He doesn't want to endure all this just to once again live after the war.

Several weeks before that Gombrowicz gets on a transatlantic liner as a tourist and in the middle of the ocean finds out that, in fact, he has nowhere to return to.

Shultz honestly struggled to become a Soviet writer.

But the Lviv journal *Nove widnokragi* (*New Horizons*), edited by Wanda Wasilewska, returns the manuscript of a story to him under the pretext of its low ideological-artistic level. He sends his only German-language story to the German editorial office of the Foreign Languages Publishing House in Moscow. Fortunately it disappears without a trace somewhere in the bowels of the editorial offices, otherwise, it's quite possible that poor Bruno would have been forced to experience our labor camps.

He draws new heathen illuminations for a local newspaper and, at the assignment of the city leaders, of the greatest "father of peoples" in Drohobych—for demonstrations.

In 1940 he undergoes two operations on his kidneys—the sheerest of psychosoma. By the time of the occupation of Drohobych by the Germans he was a complete ruin, just a shadow of himself. An Austrian officer, who was serving in the Gestapo, took him under his protection. He was a former carpenter who passed himself off as an architect—for whom Shultz painted a villa in the Secessionist spirit in exchange for bread and leftovers.

He was shot on the sidewalk in the course of the most fascinating of hunts—the hunt for people—by another Gestapo man, who was getting even with Shultz's patron according to the principle "You killed my Jew, now I'll kill yours." There is testimony that he specially sought him out. Shultz stepped out onto the street himself.

This happened on the nineteenth of November 1942. Shultz was fifty years old that year. Several snapshots give me no peace, several imagined photographs from his life, with which I feel like ending this work . . .

In one he's standing in Drohobych in his room in front of the mirror of his wardrobe, which had begun to develop golden cavities, in women's clothing, in silk stockings, having raised the hem with one hand, with a woman's shoe pressed to his chest, cutting his skin with the dirty heel, with an ecstatically screaming groin, preparing to reign in his phantasmal world.

The year 1940, on the stone floor of the high school he's drawing a Big Stalin, one that would cover the windows of a two-story house on the square; the ant of humanity crawls across, rolling along the floor—a pygmy with elbows tied behind his back, like a thinking plankton he's swaying on the waves of the ebb and the high tides of empires—he's rubbing in the whale's mustache of the Father of Peoples with charcoal. A cleaning lady, having put aside her pails filled with lye, leaning on a mop, is looking, as though she were a piece of raw meat, at the creative act being completed before her eyes.

There with big suitcases he's boarding a steamship that will take him to Paris—an entire month in Paris! The gangway squeaks. The scent of the sea, of the heads, of disinfectant. The low clouds are moving past him. It's beginning to drizzle. Lord, how unpredictable life is! What strange turns it stored up for you—Bruno Shultz! Right into your hands. Sign here. Mecca and Babylon: A magical, celestial tower of distillation of all the provinces, of all the arts!—They won't find room for you in it, can it be that in a month, in an entire month, it will not reveal its mysteries before you? It will not pierce all of you with its nerve, as though the funny bone in your elbow, it will spin you till you're seasick, it will shout: "Here! You are it!"

Nineteen thirty-eight. An icy wind chases the passengers from the deck. It rocks in the cabins. Prince Hamlet is going by sea to England so they can chop off his head.

. . . He went to Paris by train—so as not to travel through Germany—through Italy, staying for two days in Venice.

Here in occupied Drohobych the Jews trade white bands with six-ended painted signs. The ones covered in celluloid cost more—they have more amulet power, they repel bullets and defend against gas chambers—in which no one believes anyway. This is the way a gardener marks tree trunks with lime—the ones in the orchard that are doomed to be felled.

Bruno Shultz is grafted on the boundary between two cultures, in the border, where transmutations of primal matter, which nowhere else can be found—a link between Kafka and Babel, between Babka and Kafel, Shuno Brultz from now on ceases to understand anything at all. But soon they will explain it all to him.

The streets filled with agate insects with waxed protruding backsides—with ovipositors inexhaustible, sharp as stings, deaths in holsters. Here they began to run about from one courtyard and entryway to another, dragging out onto the sidewalks their catch, which was weakly resisting only by their weight, stinging and paralyzing it with their saliva, a blind-deaf-and-dumb and active force, gathering fodder for its pupae and queen bees, for the birthing factories of the Reich hive, stuffing the railroad trains with organisms soft to the touch, like caterpillars, and delicate, like moths, to send them off to the depths of the anthill of swastikas.

Having done the deed, they smoked, contentedly stroking each other's hard heads with their feelers, these chitinous head visors. Soldiers in helmets.

A TRANSFORMATION took place. But not entirely the way, not entirely in the direction, that prognosticators would have imagined and predicted. Roughly speaking, this time it wasn't Shultz changing, but the world.

But both of them were forced to pay for this in full.

CARPATHIAN NARRATIVES

■ □ ▪ □ ■

A TINY FARMSTEAD
IN THE UNIVERSE

1. On Bears

The tiny farmstead sprawled right below the sky—in the saddle of a mountain range, ironed by clouds crawling across here from dale to dale. Here they always looked like patches of torn mist, of vapor left by a poison gas attack of moisture, moving from the cicatrized Austro-Hungarian trenches on the slopes—from above you could read their line distinctly. You lay down at their bottom as though into a suture, sheltering yourself from the wind, at sunset—but more on the capturing of sunsets separately.

The confluence of circumstances, which roused you here, is absurd. But not any more absurd than all the rest.

Why are you lying here, getting sick, in the middle of the winter—when below it's still fall, as though in a preoperative tranquility, on a bench in someone else's Hutsul hut? Its first owners have long ago lain down in the church cemetery, burial service sung and forgotten; they were lowered with their bones into the earth and seized there with an inhuman cold, which just waits for you to find out for yourself.

You wrap yourself in sheepskin blankets and drink icy moonshine with Nikola, and Nikola hasn't had time to look back for ten years, since he's already on *penzion,* he kept to the slopes, walking along the orbits inside his household cosmos, as though he were inside a wooden clock, until the weight pulls, and the chain hasn't unwound to the end, and the earth turns, for the time being holding him up on itself. And there—*it will tug at its paws.* The day before yesterday they *went out* to hire him for two hundred coupons to kill a blind cat, to make a sled, to stick a boar. Sunday is the day for guests, the day for visits, for negotiations, everyone brings a bottle. A day later Nikola set off alone to the nearest village by the mountain to make a deal for slate, for gasoline, at the same time to buy some alcohol—but had not returned by evening. That means there's hope. Having gotten up late that morning, you could see only the deep tracks on the snow and far below among the beechnut stalks, the unsteady back of a bear dancing, moving off into the distance—stepping softly, leaning on a stick—with a sack over his shoulder.

A bear—that's a topic that turns a Hutsul into a child.

Each one of them wouldn't think about trifles if he had just one *paw like that,* and he'd become master of the mountains. Your hair stands on end and freezes at its roots, when, at the table, in the circle of the light of a kerosene lamp, in the glimmering semidarkness of the hut, Nikola leaned over to you confidentially and spoke like something that stands to reason but is not subject to disclosure.

"A bear—that's half a *liudyná,* a person."

The accent on the last *a* of the word.

Each one of them had seen a bear as a child, and the magic of the Master of the House entered into him when it was impossible to run, and one can only await the decision of their life in the sharp mixture of rapture, terror, and paralysis. This isn't what happens later between you and a woman . . .

You have to unwind them on these stones. They have no sense. They're something else.

Here, rising on his back paws, the bear tosses a cow slaughtered by him across a fallen fir tree, four hundred kilos in weight—in the pose of a weight-lifting press, with the elegance of a basketball player; he hides it so it would rot, beforehand drinking up blood from the nape, he has a sweet tooth. A really thick tongue in pimples, lascivious and slow moving, in the winter it sucks its paw, which had been breaking cows' backbones and the trunks of young pine trees.

"They's not the kind like in a circus—there, on the mountain meadow. Those kind're undersized, tiny ones. That one, straightening up, he'd reach the ceiling with his shoulders." And the shepherds, bolting after the cow's violator and nearly reaching him—seeing how he was tossing up the cow's carcass in the air, so as not to walk around a fallen tree—unexpectedly for themselves, without discussing it among themselves, they *walk backward,* move away, because in the face of such might a herdsman should retreat.

The faceted shot glasses move in a circle more joyfully.

A dusty chunk of dried meat is taken out, God knows how long it's been hanging on a nail. With a palm's-width-wide Hutsul knife you will cut thin strips of meat reddening in shafts of light—and once again you shift the conversation to bears.

The young, merciless chief of the house flashes his ramlike closely set eyes and the gold of his jaws, wonderment moves through him, he's experiencing his rendezvous again, all the advantage of which, perhaps, was only in the fact that he had remained alive. His agitation at that moment was absolutely dispassionate.

His horses stopped still as a clock, not being able to cross the bear's tracks. Along the Romanian border the bear walked along *their* territory, along the plowed strip, carrying a goat under his arm; and when it began to squeal, he squeezed it slightly like bagpipes— just in the opposite way, the wrong way around—to keep it silent. The bear passed twenty paces away and looked back over his shoulder.

"He glanced. Didn't say anything. And left."

Already having clinked glasses and in turn having knocked down your gullet the next shot of moonshine, you begin, with difficulty at first, to understand and you ask: "Listen, how did he carry it beneath his arm? Did he drag it? Did he walk on three paws?"

The story had already been told. He chews.

"Why on three? On two."

2. *The Sacrifice of the Ramkiller*

My throat began to hurt after the fourth night in the *oborih*—the hayloft—when, shuffling up all the cards of the full moon, a blizzard swept at us during the night, it began to flail us painfully with icy kernels, moving in circles from grove to grove, howling beneath the overturned black goblet of the heavenly stadium.

On the first evening Nikola made an opening in the hay for you with his body, throwing himself into it with all his might, twisting himself, loosening it along the sides, like a shrew, and ramming it down. It turned out to be cozy and fresh there, though a little bit dusty like in the summer. You could drink the mountain air like water, especially at night. It rinses out our lungs, the way a caisson blows the veins clean with oxygen, making hangovers imperceptible. By morning the body smells like wash dried on a clothesline. That first night you slept for fourteen hours—till noon—so that Nikola even began to fear that you might have died, but out of politeness, didn't rouse you, but just walked around, listening, waiting.

That night, though, even the walls of the hay tunnel turned out to be incapable of holding back the gusts of wind. Its narrow frozen knives, passing through the hay dust, penetrated right through to the body of an enormous worm, convulsing in the cocoon of a sleeping bag, wanting only to be left alone, struggling to fall asleep, covering his head, trying to take away the chill, to the howling of the empty sky.

By morning—groping in the dawn—you tried to press your mouth to a flagon of spring water. It was heavy, but not even a drop poured out of it. Just shaking it and chasing away either your drowsiness or numbness, you figured out that the water in it had frozen overnight.

Where did it come from, this tiny farmstead?

It would have been simpler to tell about all of life. You can reckon that it always has been and at some point you just climbed up here. This, by the way, was the way it was. You remember, was a friend there too? Yes, a great friend. Nowadays they don't make these kinds of friends anymore.

You climbed up—and found yourself left without time. It flowed away down the slopes, bounding along the stones, accumulating in ravines, somewhere at the foothills of mountains it flowed and gurgled, like a mountain spring. Here there was the domain of space. Romania, Mt. Hoverla, the city of Kolomiya forty kilometers away—all were visible from here. The range crawled away to the Cheremosh River to drink water, where the distant Kuty and Vizhnitsa, like Las Vegas, flickered at night with their lights reflecting in the turbulent water of the river. Then you thought about a night flight on a hang-glider with a Chinese lantern—above the bald ridge, so that flapping a vampire bat's wing above a gas torch by the Cheremosh, you return to the tiny farmstead, sliding like a giant black shadow on the slopes of the hills. You just needed a small detail—a hang glider.

You sent off two of your friends to classes then, so they could carry it out for you in pieces. One of them long ago incited you to fly across the state border on a chainsaw, on a motorized hang glider, on a broom, on a demon . . . He got into the plane at the beginning of perestroika, exchanged dollars for sixty-five kopecks apiece, and managed to send three letters with photographs, before disappearing somewhere in California. On one of the photographs of Independence Day, he was shown raising the American flag. In the last letter he wrote about how in the morning on the way to work, at a gas station, he stretched, coming out of his car, and . . . he finally felt at home. There were three exclamation points.

> Coconuts fly away, they are new-birds! . . .
> They fly away like wasps, the new-birds!

Pebbles of the surf rumble in the throats of the Anglo-Saxons: "I drink 'seventy-seven' in the church bar."

It was he with whom you cut the throat of a ram. This was his eleventh ram, not counting a certain poacher's dark deeds and the experience of a butcher. As well as of a leather tailor, a bartender, duty in special military service, etc.; and he was anxious all the same.

He asked you to blow smoke in his face while he'll be carving up the ram, especially the belly. They drank coffee, and he stretched, although he should have done this a bit earlier before the children had gotten up and were romping about the house, two girls and a boy—they wove braids, fooled around. By agreement the third adult should have kept them busy with something. Suddenly he left his coffee, lustily becoming somewhat agitated, he said: "Let's go!" And, grabbing the ram, started to drag it awkwardly, while the ram was digging his feet in the ground, along the path. Then he spat and tossed your way: "Hold it by the hind legs!"—instead of a skillful blow to the heart or some kind of a stroke, he suddenly fell on it from the side and began in the most trivial way to saw its throat with a knife—he was crazy about knives! There was no limit to the surprise, to the repulsion—for you and the ram. As it was explained later, the ram—a tender six-month-old soul—died from a rupture of the heart. When from the ram, hanging by the hind leg from a tree, skinned and split open like a suitcase, its sensitive executioners threw out the entrails—two rolling stomach bladders full of grass—and tore out the heart, it turned out to have burst in two places, so that fingers passed right through it like two small horns as though it were a child's toy.

It turned out, too, that the children had seen everything—organizing a conspiracy and without giving away any appearance, they observed everything from the window, animatedly discussing what was happening. For several more days they pitied the poor ram, ate its meat with gusto, went out for mushrooms and berries, and learned to toss a knife into the wall of the barn.

Nikola, without uttering a word, dug up the innards buried by you, and washed the ram's stomach and entrails from the ground and grass in numerous buckets of water, and carried them off to the master's farmstead to prepare the most tender of Hutsulian delicacies.

3. The Theory of Sunsets

You have to catch them sitting in the gash of an Austrian trench.

When there is no wind, you can sit on the very crown of a mountain, resting your folding chair against the soot-covered stones of someone's campfire or, if you are drunk, launch the chair by kicking it with your foot into the sky like a biplane. Those who didn't manage to make airplanes made chairs. Back then.

The barbed wire of the First World War deserves respect.

The Austrian differs from the Russian. Two schools of needle knitting. The Austrians stretched it into three threads, weaving three-faceted tiny metallic clasps between them. Having rusted through a hundred times, once it ended up in the circle of housekeeping, it still hasn't gone out of use at all. This time—at the entrance to the tiny farmstead—noticing its interwoven braids at the level of your eyes, you forget. And you asked only on the third day. Nikola stretched it along the top of the fence so that wild boars wouldn't bound into the potato field.

If catching sunsets isn't an art, then it demands a certain skill. This is a hunt during which you shouldn't miss. One out of ten sunsets comes out right. It's the same as in the Professional-Technical School.

You can meet some talented angels there, but the majority are pip-squeaks. With them it's like course work. Or a lab assignment.

You also have to know the dynamic of a sunset. You should omit all preparatory work, like they do in some kind of provincial art factory. Having warmly dressed and picked your cigarettes—you can take liquor as well—you should step out onto the crest when the sun just barely touches the outline of the horizon. You can see in all directions, to the very Transcarpathians, to Bessarabia, to Podolia. The distant dales, villages on the hills, the tree-lined slopes turn slightly and swim, bathed with sunlight, as though they were islands in the South China Sea, wrapped in a tender rose-colored celestial pulp, as though in the mantle of a mollusk.

In the meantime the sun begins to draw the rays not quite dispersed over the course of the day into itself, to quietly rake up the landscape, trying to pull it to that hole into which it is preparing to dive. Its contour is becoming hard and sharp, like the top of a tin can, now reflecting someone's borrowed, someone else's, light. Opposite the sky begins to light up, displaying itself into the depths to the bottom, to the last infinitesimal and meaningless details.

You could now see each tree, as though on a laboratory table under a microscope, minutely notched, like some eyelash shadow, on the background of the peak of that mountain, beyond which the sun will set. Half a minute—and the steep view closes. Patience. This is all nonsense. The main part will begin in two to three minutes, and here you shouldn't miss your chance.

The first stroke of a reagent, with a wide brush—and above the horizon there appears, there swims up, an underwater-airy-flotilla of clouds. Their spindlelike, gray-on-pale-yellow bodies stand like moored dirigibles above the terrain, which has sunk to the bottom. Several of the slopes are still shining—with a light that seemingly emerges from the earth itself, from the root stalks; but the shadows approach. Just a few more sobs—and nothing is left for the earth but to observe what will be happening in the sky.

Strokes with a brush follow one after the other. The clouds on the horizon glow like brimstone, and in the sky more—till now invisible—objects begin to spontaneously ignite. The sky turns out to be populated by a moving, cloudy substance on all levels, going askance, changing outlines—the color floats, and its shades change second to second. The front of cold fire moves right at you, stopping suddenly somewhere above your head.

And here it is—the apotheosis—a grandiose luxurious curtain of dried tobacco leaves, which cover the bottom of a stream, bunches and clusters—the loose piles barely stir in the streams of the current, hang covering half the sky. Their brown, ochre, rusty color is so edible that you unexpectedly begin to feel all your entrails and your heart lost in it as though in seaweed.

Here you have to turn and leave. The sunset should be killed like a blind cat by Nikola, at the most unexpected and at the same time most appropriate moment. Because the finale of the sunset is always, I repeat—*always* shameful, always sustained in celebratory, posterlike tones. Somewhere the cinders of some docufilm smolder away, the slag cools down near the multiperforated slag hole of socialist realism. Deception floats up to the surface, a gray oily rag unraveling *row after row*—the combings of fur, onto which slides prepared in the heavens' studios were projected. Wisps of clouds, torn away by the wind, dissolve.

With ears full of wind—home.

The sky empties. The wind quiets down. From afar the noise of a new night wind is coming.

Far below the swaying treetops pass it from hand to hand, lifting it up the mountain.

You must wait for half an hour before the dreary dawn—and begin to drink.

In the household a cat has priority over a dog. Its duty is to lick out cans of food. A dog can rattle its chain on its platform built out of piles, it can befoul over the edge, stick its muzzle into a pot, into pickles and potato peels frozen into ice. A cat has an opening made under the door. It's supposed to catch mice in order to protect the winter reserves of the master—potatoes under the floor, corn flour in bags, sugar at the head of the bed—and during the empty, dismal night to warm the heart of a lonely old man, preparing to shake out the last of his day and to exit beneath the ground.

Nikola, however, outlived his cat. A she-cat. A sore appeared on her ear. Someone said that it might be contagious. One of her eyes became filled with blood. She went to the valley to seek death. But, not finding it, she returned toward evening of the second day. Nikola was chopping wood. He pitied her and, without any kind of transition, grabbed a cudgel, which he had intended to chop up, and with two blows broke the cat's spine and smashed her head. Then he buried her.

Now he has a fat-heeled kitten—also a she-cat—who most likely will outlive him and who, having sat the entire night at the head of the master's bed, had already caught her first mouse.

4. The Literary Machine and Roll-Your-Own Cigarettes

One can already compare two empires that at one time rolled to these mountains. It's like a stroll through a shoal during a low tide. Some kind of Austro-Hungarian rubbish: bricks with trademarks; bottles; coils of rusted wire; glazed earthenware handles of a chest of drawers with pale blue inscriptions; viaducts on the Dnister River and the piers of bridges, attenuated in the direction of an ice floe; the roof of the Lviv train station; the narrow railroad tracks in the forest overgrown with grass; roads, hewn in bedrock, leading to abandoned quarries; Dutch-tiled stoves; bronze faucets—the most enduring of everything. This was an ample and dependable material culture, from which only isolated objects have remained.

From the Bolsheviks just the names were left, just a priori forms in consciousness. Their material culture is insignificant, it's all sculpted from *saman*—bricks made out of unfired clay with an admixture of straw. In actuality, the Soviet empire was just a colossal literary machine, giving birth to literary plots. And this is difficult to value too highly. All the plots were well known and cataloged from the moment of the writing of the *Thousand and One Nights*. The only one who didn't know this was the one who didn't want to know that from his very birth he had been placed inside a labyrinth.

The blind palace peacock Borges loitered along the endless corridors of this model of hell, building the tiers of the library of Babylon in his sleepless imagination, leaning over in utter exhaustion to the damp walls, covered with condensation, listening for whether the spring of death had made its way through somewhere.

The Soviets managed to give birth to a codex of fantastic new plots—unfathomable, absurd, refreshing. It was given to him by virtue of the fact that they didn't like, didn't have faith in, despised materialism, reckoning with its demands just in the minimally necessary degree—so as not to fly off into space or not to fall through the abyss of the earth immediately.

It was difficult not to understand this, one time having seen—for the nth time—how the students of the Polytechnic Institute painted the fence of their institute with green paint every spring. Standing two meters apart above the spring dirt, they animatedly smear on fresh oil paint, dripping it abundantly on the parapet. In spots the many-yeared layers of paint had peeled off to the very core, and it was evident that there was no wire beneath the scales that had grown on it, the metal had rusted through and rotted away long ago, and that this entire hollow fence was nothing more than a decoration executed in the technique of papier mâché and made of paint and dirt. And the fact of the matter wasn't in the students and, probably, not even in the Soviets. It looks like the Eastern Slavs do not like materialism for sure and, in the best case, just tolerate it. Materialism here is bad insulation. It sparks eternally, smells of being burnt, gives off smoke. People break like glasses.

Below in the Carpathians it's the same thing. And only there where time has stopped, things still mean something and diligently serve their maker—their master.

You never know, having come here with a person you've known for a long time, whether he has a bottom and what depth it's at. Most often the jingling sound of an empty tin can, into which a pebble has fallen, reverberates. You have to leave those in peace, return them at first chance to the city from which they were taken. They loiter about the farmstead with an unuttered question in their eyes: And what are we going to do now? The crumbling slyness of this question gradually decreases, but they can't believe what life is here till the very end—and that's it. The most profound of them, having the courage to test the ideas in their solitude, having loitered about here for two days and on the third day having clambered through all the sheds, workshops, and closets of the household, said—*orthographically* pronouncing all the *o* vowels with a long *o,* as he always spoke, being satisfied with the achieved exactitude of the formulation, that he finally saw here with his own eyes and has definitively become convinced of what he always affirmed: of the "wOrthlessness of cOntempOrary civilization." The question was closed. He began to get ready to go home.

Sometimes it seems that people here don't need anything from the larger world that surrounds them other than batteries—and they can even manage without them. When Nikola was young he dreamed of having a pair of binoculars so that sitting on a mountain he would be in the know about events in the world: what they brought to the village store below, who's being buried, who's coming home from far away, what's showing black over there, in which direction he should search for a missing sheep. The desire was fulfilled, but for the tenth year the binoculars have been gathering dust on a nail next to a spyglass telescope in a tied-up bag, taken apart by the children to the last lens, screws, and hollow tubes.

Your Belgian apparatus for roll-your-own cigarettes was the latest sensation here. People from far away came to look at it. That fall a half-liter jar of Hutsul homegrown tobacco cost a hundred coupons at the Kosiv market. There they also sold cut cigarette paper for self-made cigarettes called "goat legs." With coarse, just at first glance clumsy fingers, they carefully touched the delicate Belgian cylinders. Disbelief turned into excitement, artless delight, before the roguish resourcefulness of human genius. The appearance of a neat, label-like self-rolled cigarette—spread out on a raspberry-colored bed like a hard-currency roll-in-the-steep-hay prostitute—would have elicited an ovation if they knew how to extract applause from their palms. With performances you could make enough for a glass of moonshine and a dinner, if not enough for living expenses, performing as a wandering artiste with a pocket street organ. Until one of them would cut out, rivet, and glue together one just like it, until the time that they start making the same thing in all the Hutsul houses and selling them wholesale and retail, and until the news of the season of the folk trades would squeeze out of the market the automobile massage seat covers made of finely molded beech *beads,* the same way that in their time they in turn squeezed out wooden ball-point pens, and until something just as new and popular would be invented and brought here—by the Germans, Jews, or Muscovites.

5. Sheep and Pochards

From the very first day you turn out here to be under observation. A small flock of sheep, it seems, follows after you persistently. You trip over them wherever you walk. Every time they end up right in the spot you move toward. They aren't obstinate. They're just looking. When you walk right at them, it plunges them into a panic (perhaps affected). They run disgracefully, falling and jumping over each other, but ten steps away they stop in the same cramped group and continue to observe. When you leave the farmstead, they follow you with their eyes without regret, like a chorus that knows the plot, they know you'll return. When you return, the first thing you see are the sheep faces rising above the nearest hill, turned toward you. They don't blink and don't take away their gaze. If you knew how to stare in the same way—it's not clear how this would have ended. A part of them does not stop chewing, a fact which they, apparently, already no longer notice about themselves. This is the coldest and the most moderate interest you've ever subjected yourself to. This is the way one parallel line would look at another, if the psyche of mathematical quantities suddenly began to generate spontaneously. It was about a dozen sheep. Precisely: about. Because they do not yield to exact count. There are always one more or one less of them. Like those pochards in the Dead Bay near Koktebel.

For hours on end you used to lie on the high shore, striving—like a UN observer—to count them up. But because they periodically disappeared—roughly for a minute—from the surface of the water and swam beneath the water for God knows how long, this turned out to have been a task beyond your strength. You couldn't even say if it were the same duckie that had come to the surface some fifty meters from that spot where she had dived, or whether it were some other one. Perhaps on the surface there, generally less than a third of the total number was rocking gently, leading an intense and hidden life in the bowels of the bay. Going head over heels in turn, but without any order, in the end showing you their feathered anus, they were simply making fun of you without being aware of it. When you've gotten completely tense, as though you're a grandmaster during the course of a simultaneous match, and you've counted them with reserves, after a minute it turned out that exactly two more of them are now floating on the water and more of them are surfacing, and half of those that had been counted right at that moment dove down.

Sheep are more static. When they rise up in a faille, they're similar to shepherds in cloaks. Perhaps these reorganizations of theirs mean something, sounding like code: 4-2-4, 3-3-3-5, 6-3-2?

Small groups of puzzling ellipses—unctuous telegraph signs of sheep Morse code—they leave them on the grass next to their cigarette stubs.

Yes. You are under surveillance.

A certain young brown-eyed little fool has stopped fearing you after several days. That is, overcoming her fear, she remains standing in place, when the last, knocking over each other, run disorderedly in various directions. In her own way she is beautiful—with a tenderly pink bridge of her nose and fine fleece curls around her face. And, apparently, she already knows about this. Her hooves are covered with clay. A sheep.

6. The Ukraine of Dreams

On the second day, when you made your way from your childhood spot in the hayloft, with eyelids glued together from mother's milk, it rained and snivels of the night snow lay on the grass.

A nearby grove stood in fog as though in a turbid developer, just the drenched tree trunks showing black. The sound of the rain reaching the earth fused into a general rustle, and only the nearby droplets tearing off the edge of the roof slightly intoned this generally monotonous noise. The wind grazing the treetops at times added the scraping of trunks to these sounds. Here everyone has osteochondrosis.

The sheep shave the slope. The shepherds shave the sheep. Osteochondrosis cuts down the shepherds. Your hands freeze.

Vova began to run along his platform, clacking his nails and whimpering, glancing into your eyes.

The previous one was Vova. And this one is Vova. He'll sit away his lifetime on a chain.

Finally shaking yourself from sleep, you catch on yet to the edge of another dream.

How tactful these apparitions are!—On interpretation, they immediately lose their power and melt, clearing the place for the next attempt. Nothing but that. It's useless to make the sign of the cross to them. When it's done without faith, they're not afraid.

And you never did that.

The next night there will be more of them. And the third—the werewolves will retreat and worries will come; the city you left will take you by the throat and will not let you sleep till morning. It's some kind of a law for the third night. If only you're not deadly tired. Which you don't always manage to accomplish. The Ukraine of dreams.

But even in the cruelest nightmares there is a certain sweetness all the same. When you don't feel like waking up anymore. When you can rest from materialism. The sleepless drowsiness is worse, a weak-willed dull imagination, compelling you to conduct routine work—to clear cups with dirty plates from the table, for an eternally long time to fill up an enormous welded cistern from the spout of a teapot, to sweep up the floor in an imaginary room crammed with furniture.

The cups—on the floor, overturn the table! Blow up the tank, grab the room like a sheet of paper, crumple it up and toss it into the corner. There you have it!

To endure. To lie and think: What good fortune that all this will end sometime! . . .

To wash up. To chop wood. To kindle the stove. But first—coffee.

7. On Levitation and Little Transistor Men

A pillar of shit rose. Allied with the strengthening frost you grew something similar to a salt crystal—or a spire. It became clear that this time it will define the term of your stay at the farmstead. When its needle reaches the bull's-eye of the outhouse's seat, you won't have any other choice—other than gathering your things and starting off down toward the road. You're not such a shitbag that you'd violate the Gothic style of predestination with a stick.

The place on a steep slope where Nikola had chopped off the out-house for visitors displayed strange activity. Some kind of chakra of the mountain manifested itself on the surface in that spot. Each person had his own mark. More than one Russian man of letters coming into his own has walked out of there with traces of shock—and avoided conversations for a certain amount of time. The *outhouse arranged* a demonstration of levitation to a prose writer when a piece of paper, sent off into the bull's-eye, obstinately returned and floated there in midair, fluttering a meter above the roost the writer had just abandoned, and it was impossible to chase it back with any kind of conjuring. For a poet—it was something else. A terrifying place.

Until guests stopped traveling here.

Since morning Nikola asked you to cut out glass for a completed window frame. The hut smelled of wood shavings. The table was cleared off, and on it a newspaper from 1959 had been laid down, pulled out from under the tabletop trunk. The name Khrushchev flashed out from under the glass, some strange, as though deliberate, headlines.

Like a tongue twister—as though above a grave—the glass cutter droned its mosquito song. The glass crackled. Nikola picked up a burr from a bough with a chisel. He seemed satisfied. It was a lesson for his wife. He'll cost her a *magarych*. Gathering himself quickly, he threw on his quilted jacket and hat with ear flaps, and, tossing the frame on a strap on his back, he rushed off to visit his wife. In a quarter of an hour his turtlelike figure with a walking stick, reflecting the low-hanging sky with his glass back, appeared on the peak of the neighboring mountain and quickly vanished behind it.

At last you could take up with your text, lying in your imagination like a male Sleeping Beauty. First you had to let your cares dry up—to let them drink their fill of you like leeches and fall off, then—to return the power of perception, to warm up and to soften, to be like wax in heated water—to rise up in it and lower into it together with your text. It'll take several days. And all the same— here is a hayloft, here is a pen in freezing fingers, here are clouds, barely letting through friable, gray light, enough anyway to discern the letters emerging from under your hand; loneliness, taken in its most piercing register—in all its uniqueness and mortality of everything, which is alive.

Nikola brought the moonshine toward late evening. His brother-in-law came with him. His muscles had hardened to stone over the numerous years of hard work, from which his gestures became sharp, choppy, and his body froze for a long time in a single pose and it took a great effort each time for him to change position.

The stove heated up in just a minute, filling the chilled hut with a sense of abode from its yawning mouth, and potatoes began to bubble in the pot, shadows moved back and forth along the ceiling and walls. Having constructed a machine-gun sight out of the darkening crisscross of the window frame and the bottom of your drinking glass, you opened fire. A stutter of the machine gun, one more—and the attack of the darkness chokes. The dank darkness has entrenched itself for a time but refuses to go. There are no casualties. No wounded either. The abstract opponent is invulnerable. It looks like it's unconquerable until dawn.

When the table is already crammed with the already-sliced golden flat cornbread, steaming potatoes, a bowl of last year's sweating feta cheese, and, finally, a deep three-legged brazier with crisply fried bits of cracklings, while glasses of the moonshine are poured out of a liter jar—you, already having turned the little dial, turn on the Russian cultural program from New York in an undertone. The deal is done: a little demon jumps out of the transistor—a dancing little man, a cunning Moscow playosopher, and, sweeping the table with his tail, he scurries about between the dishes, *kicking up his feet in a* learned culturological dance, sticking out his tongue and raising a snowstorm on the table in a way well known to all devils—looking out from between his legs and grabbing whatever he comes across with all four of his extremities. Nikola and his brother-in-law continued to discuss something of their own, in a strange way without noticing his tricks, drinking and chasing the drinks with food. You also did not fail to do either the former or the latter, meanwhile ending up in some kind of shifted dimension, more accurately, between two dimensions, like a man stuck in a wall—sharply experiencing the comical nature of his situation and taking pleasure in it alone. There was no one with whom to share this sensation.

The fact of the matter was that the Muscovite was your friend, and from a long time ago you've followed after his—always sad— cheerful inventions with interest. This was a quite strange feast, in one of the strangest companies that ever gathered at one table— without having met before or even having known each other.

8. A Kinokephalos

Only a southern man could have thought up Cocytus—and prop up the funnel of hell against it. An Italian. A writer.

The moon had already torn away from the pines and stood above the mountain like an illuminated piece of ice. An invisible power pulled it to the zenith—and wouldn't release it. All this had some kind of strange relationship to your heart.

With a sleeping bag over your shoulder you descend to the hayloft. You pissed moving to the side. Already preparing yourself to step onto the little bridge leading beneath the roof of the hayloft, you looked back once again—glanced at the saddle of the mountain flooded by the light of the moon, hanging above the hay barn. There was no dog-headed creature there. Some kind of insuperable superstition—not serious in a grown man—roused you to wait, each time as it grew dark, for its appearance on the slope of the nearest mountain.

A three- or even five-meter-tall *kinokephalos,* having grown on the background of the sky, without a neck, with some kind of sack over its shoulder—should have chased you with a quick pace, cutting you off from the tiny farmstead, along the steep ashen slope in the direction of the forest darkening below. From there in a broad wave the scent of needles rose. It seems it was a pine forest.

And the fact of the matter wasn't that he didn't come again during that night, but in the fact that today again you were shamefully unprepared for death.

Something jumped and scampered about the hayloft till daybreak, wreaking such havoc that the ceilings shook, quieting down only when you turned your flashlight on. Judging by everything, it could have been a big cat. Maybe a stray. By morning it had left.

Once a rat had come up from the valley and wolfed down two ground squirrels—binocularlike fluffy animals with tiny humanlike swarthy hands. It ruined half of Nikola's supplies until he caught it with a specially made rat trap of his own construction. "It turned out to be a huge one," Nikola told everyone, "the size of a three-liter jar."

That night you slept for only twelve hours, tumbling from dream to dream as though from one hole to another. They were about friends who stood surrounding you as if you were sick and requesting that you no longer do this; about a cat saying: "Daddy dear . . ."—and almost making its mouth in the shape of a Cupid bow arching toward your neck; about a certain woman with made-up eyes, who had died seven years ago and who was now understood immediately in the dream without any superfluous conversations; about the spine of a bear, treating himself to a maiden's shame, torn and quickly glued back together with its tongue, like an envelope . . .

God, what a dream, ugh! . . .

9. A Campfire and a Flashlight

Be more careful when they begin to give you knives—this means you'll soon be left all alone.

. . . Why did she say that he'd betray you fifteen years ago? Where did she know it from? After all everything began not so long ago when things were just beginning to work out for you. At that time a certain color left him.

Is it really "angina"—is it really so simple? And as many times as Khekmatiar enters Kabul, as many times—to the end of the ages— he will have an opportunity to do this?

The *apofatikos* and the *katafatikos.*

He always tried to live authentically, not to be indebted to anyone in anything; he hated advances, which you preferred to all other forms of payments. The life of each one of them is a process, but this means nothing, blood of course is only a convention, one of them. And life without a Jew is like bread without holes in it.

All of this is nothing more than accident.

But why did everything that was a blessing become bitter?

Going away from the surface of life so as not to cast a shadow, to make yourself invincible, he screwed into this conflict all the more deeply. What a strange petrifaction it had as its result: a screw, squeezed by the wooden suit. With what passion to the good news: "You are free!" He shouted out the words of the Old Testament Law: "I am NOT free! . . ."

Now only those words come from those that were spoken at one time. Life, it seems, really turned the page. Let it go. The word "we," several more words, remained on that, life's, side.

Several years ago a little tent made by your friend for your back-packs was rusting on the ascent from the road. You lived here at that time on the bank of a forest stream. Then there was a certain refined craze to seek freedom in natural things. That was a time of qualita-tive illusions.

At that time he wrote a remarkable text marked by noble old-fashioned manners. He already loved to cook back then. His passion was campfires, tending the fire. He could sit half the night over a smoldering campfire, leaning his elbows on a long stick as though on a shepherd's staff. An even warmth emanated from the coals. Flowing spots of heat ceaselessly ran along the crackling, smolder-ing pieces of wood like magical inscriptions. They flashed and died out, casting a spell over your gaze. In the sky an unimaginable quan-tity of stars winked, which you could see only in the mountains— or from the depth of a cave.

And there was one moment. A certain frivolous sacral game pushing aside everything, repeating impudently. From time to time one of you turned on a flashlight, directing its ray into the campfire, and the world suddenly became turned inside out: the living sky breathing just a moment ago above our heads seemingly became covered with some turbid, barely permeable coating, and the coals winking just a second ago turned out to be just a pile of grayed ashes, of barely stirring oily soot.

10. Bathing Day, Impure Thoughts

The third day turned out to be dry. The sun peeped out. The wind cleared the sky of clouds. Butterflies and moths appeared from somewhere and were fluttering in the full glare of the sunshine, weakened by autumn, deceived, mentally retarded. They sit them-selves down on the cleaned and dried-up tatters of a meadow as though on the edge of a tucked-in hospital bed. They don't under-stand anything. You, too, don't want to understand anything. And what's there to understand?

The sun. Warmth. Bathing day.

Haul some water from a spring-fed well, warm up a bucket of it on the stove, put a tub on a stool, stand up in a second, tin one, wash your head to the roots of your hair with shampoo, scrub your skin with a rough glove, shave in front of a tiny mirror on the windowsill, and then, sitting on a bench in front of the hut, leaning your back against the fence, allow the wind to stir your light, washed hair, allow the sun to warm you, allow yourself to smoke, make coffee on a kerosene camp stove brought along for some reason—let it be of service at least once—drink a glass of the moonshine, chatting with the dog Vova, who is going crazy from the smoked sausage skins—he lost his voice, his jaws are in spasm—and only a quiet whimpering that sounds like a love moan emerges from his bowels; he loves you like no one ever in your life has loved you.

One-two—you've corrupted the dog.

Below you've left these shallow abysses.

These artlessly arranged trapping pits.

You put the little man in your groin, a Cyclops, an imbecile, jabbing its blinded eyes into an equally blind nipple—sight is transmitted by periscopes in those bodies.

A lewd alarm clock in trousers.

Sperm, wicked from a hangover, like digestive juice.

Her orgasms rolling and slipping in female lard.

Once here on the slope he had taken possession of her like a swineherd—holding her by her pleated braid as though by her backbone raised to the surface of her skin.

M. is the guide of F.

Distinguished from the F. perhaps by the fact that he does not know what in reality he wants.

11. Cards

Cards appear here as a natural thing.

That was when nearly everyone here was friends. Then there were no enemies.

The three of you somehow got up here on skis at Christmastime.

The sun, puddles in Kolomiya—silly. On the train you devoured somebody's duck and with a fellow traveler drank up a slew of moonshine. Drunk as skunks you climbed up the mountain. You threw away the skis.

The next day you were invited for Christmas Eve to the neighboring farmstead three kilometers away—a rocky little village on piles, five households. They had promised a manger scene, but the children had gotten drunk themselves while they were still in the huts below, and the snow started to fall hard—and they didn't climb up the mountain. You loitered about the new wooden hut, about the chilly, resonant rooms, lined, like ship cabins, from wall to ceiling with freshly planed planks and numbingly smelling of pine, and, pushing ourselves away from the table, sat down toward morning to play preference. You tried hard to make preference with one condition—every no-trick hand, successful or unsuccessful, should have been marked by the players post factum with a shot glass of moonshine. It turned out that eleven no-trick hands were played. You had good cards. Over the course of the night, a half-meter of the lightest angel-down snow fell. The sun broke through.

It was already toward dinnertime that you got up to go home. You forgot your carbide flashlight, and, leaving your friends on the top of the cyclopic cliff, were forced to return. The hut was already empty. The owner had moved into the old one. You found him there. This was a tiny structure, the size of a stationmaster's stall, or a switchman's. In the narrow little room with a single window fit just two iron beds and a little table squeezed in so tightly that there was nowhere to put your feet. The little table was covered by a newspaper with dried bread crumbs. The owner, who sometimes, to complete the illusion, looked like an unshaven Vysotsky, went for your carbide flashlight and picked up one more bottle of potato-based moonshine. In a businesslike way you drank it up in five minutes sitting opposite one another on the iron bunks and glancing in turn through the cloudy glass at the landscape of intolerable, never-beforeseen beauty—a snow-covered and sunlight-bathed canyon that ended right beneath the window, with deep shadows, a thick pine forest at the opposite, nearly vertical slope, and a stream making its way on the bottom of a stone bed.

"I've had enough of these mountains," the owner said and spat on the floor. When I was already at the door, having looked into my eyes, he asked me next time to bring some round batteries. "I'll pay for them," he said.

From the slope your friends waved to you, dancing in the snow from the cold.

You clambered up in a rush.

A *carbide* is a flashlight. A wild rose is *sverbivus*.

Athens are blackberries. *To go to Athens* is to go to pick blackberries.

Gas is kerosene. Aspen mushrooms are trump cards.

For healing: *dzindziura, zmievon, pidoima*.

Telenka is the same thing as *fuyara*—a shepherd's flute.

Nikola's teeth had fallen out, and he no longer plays the shepherd's flute, no sound comes out. "Go-o-one," he says about his teeth and points where they went with his hand.

At some point, such a long time ago that he no longer remembers—he had a wedding trip to Mt. Pope John, to the ruins of an Austrian observatory, where he spent three days with his wife . . .

In several years they'll again invite you to this farmstead. Nikola's son-in-law will carry the master of the house in his arms out of the hut—his father—and will put him on a horse so you could click a picture of him with your "soap-box" camera on a string. The master of the house no longer walks. Osteoarthritis has cut him down, he got it working in the field, where, sometimes even during a snowstorm, falling down up to his chest in snow, he, together with his kolkhoz workers, used to drive his fifty or so sheep and where in summer months he used to make up to three hundred rubles a month.

That autumn a furniture suite in Kosiv cost a million.

Time is shredded and put into barrels to be marinated.

Time's sauerkraut is acidic.

Brine. Russia. Osteoarthritis.

Once a year, on a clear Christmas night, from here, from the farmstead, you can see beyond the Dnipro River and nearly all the way to Dikanka, where trains rush like cockroaches along the badly lit expanses of Ukraine.

12. Night

Here your night has come. Get prepared. Cry.

Your psychological organization turned out not to be any more complicated than a small battery.

It's as though someone turned on a lamp in a room in which you've lived in the dark for forty years and where you knew everything only by groping. The light was turned on, and all the familiar objects of your surroundings, the creaking floorboards, the ceiling and walls— everything suddenly stood before your very eyes, immediately and totally, in its real scale and interrelations, when at four in the morning you suddenly sat up, awakened from your sleep like a pillar on your cot, blinded by a pitiless flash, which, as though by an electrode, cut out the contours of shadows gathered at the head of the bed, surrounding your sickbed like an anatomic table in the soft darkness.

Tears streamed out of your eyes even before words had come, before you understood anything. Here it is, the darkness-cutting, wandering graphic of the temperature curve, which had carried you to that mountain.

How blatant, monstrous, humiliatingly simple and seemingly so inevitable everything is. In childhood you simply weren't loved enough!

Not simply—this was always so much before your eyes—habitually, naturally, and openly—that it wasn't perceived by sight, the way the eyelids that cover and uncover eyes are not taken into account.

They went off somewhere to Siberia, to the virgin lands, to the other side of the moon—to the devil's grandmother's! They've abandoned you after all!

That's where it's from, like a plague, this memory of early childhood. You regained consciousness from the trauma among strange people: A parasite who was not your mother—she didn't give birth to you—and a granny, a slovenly, swollen Catholic woman with a rosary, a birthing machine, immensely tired from her own dozen children, from wars and famine, from famine and wars. But the father—a youth, a Stalinist, experimenting with bodies and ideas, a man, a builder, and whom after all God Himself willed to be a he-man, well she loved him; but how could she, how could she have dared? When at the age of three to four you're soft as wax, completely nourished still with milk, like an ear of corn at milky-wax ripeness, and just when the nearby lying world begins to mature into the depth—these voids, this vinegar, this aftertaste of the silver spoon in your mouth—it was then that you guessed that you were infected with death, that this is incurable, that everyone will die, yes; and twenty-five years later you poked into your memory, as though into the electrical live wiring with your bare fingers, because you, disgusted with everything, couldn't find a place for yourself. You tightened up something there and did something—knowing everything and understanding nothing. And you lived still to forty. And gave birth to a son in order to understand something.

Nothing, perhaps, would change on the grand scale of things.

But, perhaps, it wouldn't have been as difficult, you wouldn't have fallen through up to your knee, to your belt, to your upper lip in that spot where others pass as if walking on dry land, as though they were walking along a bridge, not noticing anything. "We had such a great time at your place yesterday!" And it's as if you have a dog's *snout on your neck,* the brain is squeezed by lengthwise stocks, there's nowhere to run. To endure and wait. You'd kill the viper! . . .

Anesthesia of the family. Like an incantation: Homeward! But there is no home in the universe. Orphanages. Night lodgings. A farmstead lost in the mountains. Night.

There's no strain either. The children of course will not get angry—something else is happening.

It's as if something is being frozen in them, some kind of strange insensitivity, some kind of piece of ice in their chest, which doesn't bother them, it's imperceptible, and only when it melts and comes out with tears is it painful. Sometimes it doesn't come out. It, after all, doesn't bother you. Almost.

Until then, it's as though a lantern is burning in his head, even pouring forth from his eyes, he is created for the sake of joy and for the joy of people—a wooden boy, a cardboard trick, a tumbling doll. Before sleep: "Pop, calm me down, because I can't calm down by myself . . ."

"Don't stamp in puddles!"—"But I feel like stamping and stamping."

How simple everything is. When the impulse is gone, it becomes visible from a single glance—who is live-wired, and who is switched off.

The Varangians came and left. God is waiting somewhere.

All is irrevocable. They are old people already. You've forgiven them long ago. And they would hardly have understood. For this you have to have a specific early experience. Sometime in childhood.

Let it even be worth less than a kopeck.

And then in Nikopol, about forty years ago, you scooted away into a coal bin in the yard and, having made a spiral from aluminum wire and having pushed it through in the gap between the boards, you glumly rotated it for days on end—in order to fly away.

Then your dad came to take you to Siberia. He's here.

What did you have to say to him? As the most cherished, of which you secretly were proud, you said awkwardly that you and your friends can throw round sharpened tin cans all the way to the highest voltage wires. He said that he'd yank your ears and your friends' ears too, and he'd do this if he sees it.

And there is nothing else in that story. A state-thinking man.

And whatever the parents would do to make you love them, you couldn't. Until they became your children.

But sometimes things happened. The most poignant one happened once in Slavyansk. When he came in the summer on an overnight train and chatted the entire night till dawn with his granddad and grandma—young, cheerful, free, and strong; you weren't sleeping on the veranda till dawn, catching the noise of their voices, the senseless energy of some kind of stories and opinions, the clanking of teaspoons, absolutely happy, contented, numb from love, and if you had known that you could cry, you would have.

13. Game Pieces on the Slope

By morning Nikola came back tired, having circled three villages on foot in search of a compliant driver—finally he was promised that in a week they'll bring roofing slate to his mountain if they have gas.

Beneath his jersey a liter of shpirits turned up, bought at your request.

He reached into a hollowed-out log filled with spring water and from the bottom of it pulled out a three-liter jar of meat salted from last spring, covered with a plastic lid. His son-in-law, as it was explained, had distilled his own home vodka and had ordered shish kebabs for the evening. And while you soaked the meat and cut the onions, Nikola sat down before the stove to load the five-barreled mousetrap, with his three undamaged fingers artfully setting the spring-loaded catches of the steel loops, generously sprinkling flour like gunpowder onto the bottom of the cylindrical openings. Sometimes up to five tails hung out of the hollowed-out wood block on successful days.

Nikola paid with his fingers for his love of cigarette holders (*dzegarnychky*). One of the retreating armies had tossed onto the field of battle for the perdition of the enemy's smokers a miniature mine— *dzegarnychka*—a cigarette holder with a piece of a thread hanging from the bit. To his misfortune the shepherd lad had picked it up.

Nikola chopped off his fingers, dangling on scraps of skin and, whimpering, didn't say anything to his mother, he clambered above the stove—this one, under which he is sitting now.

His head and the stove survived. From that time on while playing on his shepherd's flute, he stuffed up one ear with the stump of his finger so that his shattered eardrum wouldn't be so drafty and wouldn't keep him from hearing.

Having picked at the floorboard with his ax, Nikola shoved the mousetrap into the crawl space onto a pile of potatoes, played with a kitten on his way, and crawled onto the sleeping shelf of the stove to rest. He laid down on his side, placing his hands under his cheek, with his paunch hanging at an angle, as if it were one of those bags that were standing by the legs of the stove. He dozed off and sighed heavily in his sleep.

What does an old man dream of?

Of the leakage of strength, of sugar and flour from a ripped bag, of the wasting away of the clan—all three brothers had only daughters, God hadn't given them a son; one lived for two days, the wife miscarried the second one on the grass at the seventh month; of a *penzion;* of an *insuranze* policy on a baby bull that had fallen down a precipice; of a bear sleeping in raspberry canes; of open-marriage lovers, and here they're making their way to his paws—getting ready to drag him somewhere beneath the ground . . .

Nikola grapples, moans, turns onto his other side.

You step out onto the mountain to smoke, to take a breath of fresh air.

The sky is covered, as if it were a throat, with gray dampness. It smells of cold steam, like a laundry. Tufts of fog crawl. You lie down chest-first onto the smooth, bone-polished cross-tie of a fence. You lift up your collar. Far off below a swollen hill breaks through a solid swaddling cloth of fog, as though it were an island, with an isosceles triangle of a graveyard landing. It was quite visible from above. Several times someone strikes a church bell in the fog. The pealing unexpectedly turns out to be not muffled, but somehow tinkling, screeching, as if a ship's bells were being struck. The disquieting sound of them is carried far along the winding valley, squeezed by the mountain ridges.

Shish kebab is a metric rhymed abacus of food, it's a threading of the stories of a thousand and one nights, it's mountains stretching their curving backbones toward Munich, it's a historical homeland and the formula of the cuisine of nomad encampments. Did a man climb into the mountains or did he hatch at a spot where the earth had peeled and heaved—was it somewhere close by? "Nothing to it," the Hutsuls say about everything that doesn't have a definite purpose.

In 1945 Nikola was plopped into a heated freight car and carried off to Kharkiv—to restore a defense plant. He saw an enormous world turned upside down by the war. And that world crushed him. But it turned out that one could live anywhere. In exchange for the *magarych,* a milled iron paw was carried out for him from a factory shop—for this they could have executed everyone—and at night he sewed footwear on the sly—the war had unshod everyone. Money showed up. Feta cheese, cornbread, lover-girls, what else? Buying himself off from the foreman, Nikola would now sit for hours on a cot in the barracks, playing on his shepherd's flute made from the end of selected steel pipe; someone kept looking in: "There the

Hutsul . . . fuck your mother, is banging out a tune!" The Hutsuls didn't know this awful curse.

But he began to get depressed after half a year. And, having just told his countryman, having left the iron paw, his food, and his thread behind, got into a heated freight car empty-handed, rode off following the setting sun, climbed onto the mountain—and never again left it for anything. And even in the times of Khrushchev and after—he didn't go down the mountain to be closer to the people, the store, the office.

One time he went to Kishinev for feta cheese, another to Chernivtsi.

And then in '47 people trekked here to the mountains to die from hunger—from Moldova, Bukovina, Podolia. They lay about beneath the fences like dogs and stared into your eyes. There wasn't enough food for all of them.

Having fallen into a dazed state from unaccustomed, delectable sat-edness, from the strength of the alcohol, from the spiciness of the sauce, from these manly preserves, amid the table festivities, Nikola suddenly ended up sleeping on the stove, and you with his son-in-law, having drunk *to the horse*—O this all-conquering Slavic part-ing drink to the horse!—they decided to walk immediately to the proprietor's farmstead to pass to the crown of the *evening—numero uno,* that is, the twice-distilled 140-proof moonshine in a three-liter jar, on the farmstead flooded with electric light with a junky black-and-white television and winter stockpiles of marinated mush-rooms, fried canned beef with fried cracklings, blackberries sprin-kled with sugar, with crumbly feta cheese, cooling in milk, thick as cream.

. . . In the summer it smelled of wild strawberries. Alpine cows. The left legs of them slightly shorter than the right. Their milk doesn't go sour for weeks . . .

It was sometime between two and three o'clock in the morning. You've forgotten about weather and time sitting in the house. Outside in the meantime a *snowstorm* had broken out, clouds were carried by the wind with a furious rapidity, protuberances of snow rose up from beneath your feet, swirling like a pack of wolves, they jarred you in the neck, got caked under your raised collar, plastered the left side of your face with wet snow—no stars, no moon, it was all just white whiteness.

Stopping up the opened bottle with your finger, you stepped onto the path going along the top of the slope—and things started to move. This was the only moment when you were located on the path at the same time—at the start. And one more time at the finish—two hundred meters afterward, when you crossed onto the other side of the mountain. In an hour. Or perhaps even in two.

Wet snow, having fallen onto the dry grass, made the path invisible and turned the slope into a high-speed downhill track. When your traveling companion suddenly had slid down along the steepest slope, disappeared, and called to you from somewhere below, some fifty meters away, you, without managing to be surprised at this, sledded off a hundred or so meters in the direction of the nearest forest. And no spreading of feet, grabbing at stalks, descent on all fours and backside forward could violate the rules of the game, to which you turned out to be drawn. That is, in turn and together, flying head over heels like two circus clowns, knocking each other off their feet and helping each other to get back up, coming close and separating from each other on the slope, swept up by a snowstorm, in the clouds of snowy dust shining with an unknown illumination, you jerked as though you were tied on rubber bands in a children's board game with game pieces, dice, and numbers, where, ending up in a penalty square, you, your game piece, as if your playing body, was losing its turn for several moves and was even moved several squares back on the difficult path, leading to the high right corner of the board.

In this game your partner was stubborn and venturesome like a wild boar, and didn't, by the way, spill a single drop of alcohol on the ground, the entire time holding his thumb on the throat of the bottle, but this had zero result.

Still enraptured with a play of chthonic forces, with the brocade curtain of the blizzard hanging in the sky, still, on leaving the farmstead you immediately understood that rapture gripped your heart, that they were playing with you. Lord! What undeserved happiness! For some two hundred years, and maybe never at all, these mountains had not heard such joyful, such healthy, such unconstrained, such *natural* laughter.

You didn't come out from there until they released you.

A TINY FARMSTEAD IN THE UNIVERSE

It is here that you caught up to him—that circling of prose, tearing away like a bird above the jot in the word "Ukraine."

Nikola ran about the house and thought: Where? Sonny! There's no *carbide*! There's no roll-your-own-cigarette roller. He had frozen on the mountain covered with blown snow. Where can I run? What can be simpler—there the neighbor doesn't remember stabbing his wife to death—he had gotten drunk and lost his head. Where? It's night. A blizzard. Maybe he's still alive!

He lit the kerosene wick on a bench by the stove. Consciousness quietly returned.
    "Aha, two of them. He won't get lost with Vasyl."
    He walked around till morning. Started up the stove. Calmed himself.
    He burst into tears the next evening.
    The knife getting blunt without a whetstone.

He'll die if you don't *come to the mountain* in the summer.

The wooden farmstead grew emptier with each year but tried to stand firm—and for the time being was holding together. The same way as the empty shell of Easter eggs, placed with the wide end down on the horns of a roe deer in Nikola's house above the table. Between two darkened, badly colored oleographs behind glass—of the Mother of God and of St. Nicholas, as though between two cards drawn out of a gigantic playing card deck, nobly worn out from time.
    On the same wall there were: a photomontage of Nikola's parents at different ages—a strong young man and a retouched high-cheek-boned old woman—ordered by Nikola from a traveling photographer not long before the death of his mother, and an empty packet of Yugoslavian bouillon with a painted rooster, with a tail bent in an arc in the form of a bright rainbow; or as they call it here a *raiduga,* an Arch of Paradise, or a *veselka,* Joy, which was also hung by Nikola.
    Slightly below there was a row of nails, on which there hung by the handles—facing back to back—a dozen and a half porcelain

teacups bought at various times—with multicolored dots on the sides—covered with a thick layer of oily soot and dust.

14. *Untitled*

On the slope.

The earth burns behind us—and smokes underfoot.

Who'll pay for all this?

Snow up to your knee. Your knapsack pulls you down.

Legs shoot out by themselves. In a quick step—almost at a run.

The cutting in the tree felling leads dizzyingly down—to a bus stop that's on the other side of a swollen mountain stream.

A run-down jeep rushes off somewhere along the mountain road to pick you up at the appointed place, once again winding the slackened spring of time. The road will lull and shake. Drowsiness will cover up the end of the plot with a chicken's eyelid. Your leg muscles will sweetly ache the next day.

. . . A moth at the tree felling when the wind had grown quiet. A white mealy idiot, with a feeble-minded gaze, looking at the exposed light and unrecognizably changed landscape. It doesn't lose hope. It was glad to see you.

It mechanically flaps its wings, moving in snatches, suspended in the air as though in a silent film reeled in slow motion.

It's quiet. The snow has melted a little here. It's dripping from the branches. The water from the melted snow trickles down along the wet stones, flowing into a ravine.

Press *your kisser* to the trunk of a fir tree—frozen, fully prepared for winter. Turn back, prop up your knapsack against it. Have a smoke.

In the most interminable of all labyrinths.

Because—it has no walls.

■ □ ■ □ ■

THE DEATH OF THE FORESTER

AGE FORCED HIM NOW TO CONSIDER THE POSSIBILITY OF DEATH. NOT his own yet—but nevertheless. It forced him to include *the noseless one* as an error in all life's calculations. That was why the day before on the phone he answered: "Yes, yes, of course I'll come," without taking a minute to ponder whether he had enough time for the trip. Now he had to find it, postponing the forthcoming departure for a much more distant and longer "business trip" to "forever." There was the sensation that he hadn't completed something in this land which he was leaving, but which had some strange, not-quite-understood right to his heart. "My haart in zee mountains: my haa-at in zee hi-land, my haa-at eez not hee-er," as a schoolboy again and again he recited the poem assigned for the next day, the poem that was exhaled, together with the smell of alcohol, by the Scottish boozer poet about two hundred years ago. The poems quickly disappeared from his memory, but years, decades passed, and everything they spoke about had come true. How can they teach children these kinds of things in schools?

It's probably because of all that, early next morning—still not quite clearly understanding why—he was sitting with his young wife, as though in a waiting room, on a hard bench in an unheated commuter train, just so that after three hours of a tiring trip he could find himself in that village in the mountains—in which he had not been—when he counted he couldn't believe it—for twenty five years. It just happened that in all those years he was carried past and through it. It wasn't because he was prohibited from entering this village—you could say there wasn't a need in him for that. If he got off at the railroad station, let the handle of the railroad car go, the familiar places—the quiet mill pond where time would catch you on live bait—would surround him. But more urgent business was constantly at hand—he also made trips to new, still-untested places. There was also some hindrance—just now sitting in the commuter train when the bare groves and snowy fields had started to fly in the window, and he felt like napping—he was suddenly confused by the suspicion that there was that hindrance. Together with a displacement.

The perspiration of embarrassment had appeared on the back of his neck when he unexpectedly realized that it was precisely in this place marked only on the largest-scale maps that he, for the first time, as they say, had "known a woman," but it had happened so long ago and had disappeared without a trace. Besides, is it proper to call in earnest an ordinary deflowering the knowing of a woman or the loss of innocence—hell, no. It can rather be called the deliverance from innocence as though from a shameful deficiency: mother's milk still fresh on your lips, the youthful peach fuzz on your chin and cheeks, and a milky coating, film stuck between your legs. The grown-up children hurrying to mature do it in a freezing "jeep" with a tarpaulin top, the icy leatherette of the back seat crunching in the darkness like a crust of snow—numb, unfeeling sex lips, shamelessness, fear, guilt, tenderness. All the while the inebriated parents at the top of their lungs were mangling the pliable Ukrainian songs in the lighted windows of the second floor. When she finally lost her virginity, his girlfriend all of a sudden became tangibly older than he. They of course made *her* catch cold then. He brought her a cup of warm water in the morning and then waited for her, stamping his feet under the plank wall of the outhouse. Next day they left for a neighboring region, for a town in the plains where mountain rivers flow together, reducing themselves to a common denominator in the outskirts. Soon after he had left for another town, suddenly then he found himself in a third one, well and so forth.

The matter, however, was not in that nonmellifluous story, which was being kept in the storage of memory. The story had, by the way, at some time in the past all the signs of madness and was accompanied by inevitable excesses, which go together with first love: environmental resistance, isolation together, the symptoms of asphyxia, escape, the realization of freedom through betrayal, etc. The matter wasn't in his young friend whose sexual blossoming after the deflowering dumbfounded him and many others like the stifling smell of the bird cherry or a broken lilac bush in a familiar backyard. All these had to do more with the sprouting of savage souls and bodies than with what's sometimes happening with a person later on in life. His problem consisted of the fact that his relationships were entangled with the impersonal power that decided everything for him beforehand. In amazement he understood that he had been caught, being still on the threshold of independent life, like a fly in a sticky trap hanging in a kitchen with an open window where women cook jam. Then, calling things by their names, the hero made tracks—saving himself by escaping.

Warmed up by the recollection, memory itself now offered him an unexpected branching of the plot. With hindsight, he thought that the much more important thing was the fact that still before the above-mentioned story took place, in the environs of the same location, he had accidentally lost another kind of innocence. With a throaty company of teenagers, he wandered the mountain roads and paths carrying backpacks and tents, crossing rivers at fords and in turn carrying, like a prize, their classmate whom they took along and in whom every one of them was a little in love, keeping a wary eye over each other at that. Until she, soon after the beginning of the trip, got her period. Then they took her to the closest bus station and, supplying her with the cotton they had procured somewhere, sent her home to her grandma. They continued their journey in empty freight trains, riding past junction stations and jumping off the moving trains, sitting after that with scratched knees and bruises in the station cafés and recently opened bars with "jukeboxes" made in Czechoslovakia in which the voice of Czeslav Nemen was called forth by a coin, breaking into a scream and becoming ultrasoundlike, a diamond saw in reciprocating motion, cutting the generation's music with anthracite disks. It was the summer of '68. Loaded trains moved intensively as never before through the Carpathian Mountains to and from Czechoslovakia. Inscribed in red letters on the lower part of the white corrugated walls of the Czech railroad cars, the word POZOR! attracted attention and intrigued them. As they found out later, it had a technical meaning and meant exactly that—"attention."

Meanwhile the expectation of invasion was hanging in the air. Nobody doubted its inevitability, differences in opinion in conversations concerned only when. Fathers were called to enlistment offices and taken to training camps for the whole summer. There were a lot of problems with summer vacations. Even schoolchildren knew that back in the spring a tank brigade was relocated to near Mukachevo, and city hospitals and clinics in the neighboring areas were quietly but hurriedly preparing to receive a large number of the wounded. At newsstands, however, you could still as before buy from under the counter, paying extra or taking something as an "overload," almost a dozen intoxicatingly risqué, unfamiliar Czech and Polish newspapers and journals. It was exhilarating to scrutinize the caricatures in them sitting at a table in a café and passing them around, getting tipsy from light white wines from neighboring countries, from the first drags on cigarettes and tar-black coffee in tiny cups, melting in the objectlessness of desires, the readiness to defend our sovereignty and uniqueness in an immediate brawl—in the feeling of long-awaited liberation from the control of our fathers; marveling at the unreality of what was happening, with our heads spinning from first dates with "guys with holes" or "double barrels" as Uncle, the forester, called the girls they *took,* making fun of the unskillful conspiracy of his nephew and his friends. All this was taking place at the very foot of the mountains—by the way there were songs on that occasion.

By that time, one cold morning, Uncle's nephew managed to climb a pine tree at the top of a neighboring mountain. It wasn't clear what drove him upward. We had to think it was the general constraint of the organism by depraved virginity. But it was precisely from there and at that time that he saw ALL THE MOUNTAINS above the thick woods for the first time.

Begrimed with pine tar and scratched all over, he finally punctured the pine covering that was saturated with moisture with his head and became glued to the trunk, slightly swaying together with the treetop, moaning and creaking along with it above the steaming surface of the universe. The night rain ended at dawn and the sky gradually started to clear. Above the distant mountain ranges several pockets of rain still could be seen. You could guess the presence of the sun in the haze. It was still hidden by the clouds but it already had begun to burn light tunnels and mine shafts here and there in the sky, chaotically shifting them from one slope to another as though asserting itself on gigantic stilts. He wasn't able to tell below what he saw that was *so special* up there. And still that accidental foreshortening—the view from above the martial mystery of creation—was imprinted in him deeper than anything else he had experienced before that time. The sensation of the absence of any supports, of openness along all axes and in all directions, more than once visited him in his dreams, forcing him to wake up with his heart at times not beating, at times pounding madly, at times feeling unhappy, at times crying from happiness.

He was a teenager who had climbed to the very top of the tree of omnipotence and remembered this ordinary case of phallocracy. It would be an easy answer and therefore wrong. There was no militancy in that experience, there wasn't the conquering of a summit and the thirst for supremacy. But there was something like a discovery of the orientation in the world based on the vestibular organs to the call of which all swimmers and fliers are attracted—all childhood bed wetters, all sailors and pilots, all dreamers and some mountaineers, all who cannot sit still and grow in one place. This experience begs for description and on this earth it should be in all earnestness immediately forgotten, otherwise you could not move, you could not walk.

On another occasion, his friend climbed the tree after him. He shouted from the top encouraging himself during his ascent and apparently he had climbed higher than Yuriev because he came down from the top with a trophy—a red linen necktie soaked with pine tar like a handkerchief—and then tiresomely teased Yuriev with it: Wasn't it our hero the discoverer who had tied it at the very top of the pine tree? Did he use it because he didn't happen to have the panties of his lady of the heart? And shouldn't he give this rag to the young pioneers' council when they return to transfer it to the school museum? In their school it was considered especially cool to clean your shoes with a young pioneer's tie during recess and then carry it crammed in a pants pocket, answering your teachers' pestering that you didn't have time to iron it or you left it at home. Back during last summer they left the rank of pioneers because of their age and didn't hurry to become members of the Komsomol. They still had time before getting their high-school diplomas and applying to colleges.

In order to understand the further development of events, it's important to know that another sky was stretched out like a blanket cover over the land where all of them lived because of different reasons. Many years later Yuriev would learn how the character of the sky could strikingly change depending on location and especially a country. The sky of the Carpathian Mountains and the area beneath them was a special one—resonant and empty inside, it isolated the area even from its closest neighbors. The mountains attracted and held clouds close to them, they were what created that special sky, that wet atmospheric pocket that turned the entire population of the area into potential patients of otolaryngologists. The wetness was drawn in by the stones which had cooled down in the process, passing its coolness along further—returning it to the subterranean springs and infertile and treacherous graveyard land. You'll bitterly regret if you decide to sit on a stone or lie down on this lean lime soil overgrown with grass. The clearer and louder all the sounds sound here even in the distance, the more unintelligible they are. The pauses are drawn out unbearably long, the echo wanders reflecting off obstacles like a ball from the sides of a billiard table. The local landscapes, comprehensible only by their appearance, wear out any person who arrives here from the great plains.

Yuriev's uncle the forester lived in these mountains for more than thirty years. And all this time he dreamed about leaving—to settle on the plain, to change climate, to buy a house somewhere in his native Proskuro district across the river so that the house would have a meadow and a garden and the river—crayfish. He was a respected man in his village and went to work every day in a uniform jacket like a public prosecutor's. During the decades he spent here, the village underwent drastic changes. Under the Soviets, it was first transformed into a skiing sports center and then into a winter resort. Hotels, tourist hostels, and restaurants grew in it like mushrooms during a good season. In the summer it also remained quite a busy vacation place, hotels were overbooked for the bigger part of a year. But not so long ago, everything suddenly stopped and subsided. There is nothing more melancholy and dreary than an off-season resort, which in addition to that gradually begins to lose its characteristics of the season until it becomes the final norm of the village's life.

Hunting by the members of the Central Party Committee ended a long time ago—that golden time of stability when a crowned Soviet Hetman was followed everywhere by his favorite milking cow in a special attached railroad car, and two weeks before the arrival of the guests, huntsmen would begin to feed a bear, teaching him to come exactly at noon to a feeder at a forest clearing. A bullet in the forehead, dispatched by a dignitary's hand, testified to his successful completion of the lumbering science. At that time in the forestry industry, they gave out bonus pay, apportioned the coarse, hard meat of the killed game, distributed the surplus of the deer's antlers and goat's horns without which no self-respected common citizen, and it goes for a forestry worker without saying, couldn't imagine his existence.

There was enough game in the Carpathian Mountains, despite the fact that the local mountains had become quite bald right after World War II. The timber of their forests went to the restoration of the damaged factories and mines in the east. That was why later, in the 1960s and 1970s, construction timber had to be transported here from Siberia or even from North Korea, which couldn't help but rouse suspicions about a conspiracy and sabotage in particularly zealous heads.

During those years, Uncle traveled to all the socialist countries on forestry-paid tickets, including transatlantic trips, tropical Cuba, and once he even visited capitalist, wooded Finland as a member of a delegation. Yuriev himself remembered well, partially thanks to a photograph from the family album, as a preschooler holding the huge hand of the imposing Uncle, the boss of the forest, at a clearing in a city arboretum park, studded everywhere with plaques with the names of trees and trimmed bushes. Uncle was distinguished by a natural, exceptional curiosity. He treated the systematic acquisition of knowledge with a special respect, praising thoroughness in any kind of activity and organically unable to bear hurriedness. He was a perfect representative of the postwar charmer with a large-featured face and wavy hair combed back, with that unhurriedness of movement which attracted women so much and could pass did pass for either the testament of his closeness to the authorities or for the sign of a pedigree.

In his adult life, Yuriev rarely had an occasion to meet his uncle who, by the way, maintained rather vast family ties. That's why when he visited his uncle in the district hospital a couple of years ago during his regular visit to his parents, Yuriev was quite surprised when

Uncle started to talk to him about his personal life. He had never before seen his uncle in such a way. After he pulled up the flap of his hospital gown, showed Yuriev his immeasurable, almost wild boar's side of his body, covered with indentations from leeches, and talked a little about illnesses and surgeries, Uncle suddenly got agitated for no apparent reason. That day vexed and discouraged him. His naturally slightly slow mind began to lose its bearings in the impetuosity of changes, and Uncle himself was ready to bring action against Time, addressing it for some reason to him—his nephew. Being always a bit cunning, avoiding open confrontations and arguments, being used to maintaining even-keeled relationships with people and watching his manners in the folk Ukrainian way, he suddenly felt himself robbed blind and twisted around a little finger. Now at every step he was cut short in his own family. Not making any allowances for him, his own sister and her husband pushed him directly from the opposite side, and some *plucked up* people, who had come from nowhere, divvied up power and grabbed all the good positions, openly snubbed him, depriving him of the right to judge anything in the world. The air rushed out of his lungs with dry elderly drooling through his teeth, forcing him to spit all the time and catch his breath, which made his speech incoherent:

—I'll tell you everything as it was in reality—the collectivization, famine, war, people—and after the war! I know one thing—I never talked to anyone about it. Come visit me, and I'll tell you all about it.

Yuriev didn't try in the least to find out something new about people in general, the political truth of events interested him even less. The only thing he wouldn't mind doing was to dig a bit in his own root system on his mother's side—to look deeper into the history of the family, to find out some details about his relatives' survival in the extreme circumstances in which many people didn't survive. That's why two years later, believing right away in the predestination of the totally nonessential telephone call and the telephone conversation, which had taken place almost out of some misunderstanding, he was going now to the meeting in a commuter train, testing his chronic fatalism by madcap behavior as it was supposed to be done with this spiritual gout. The poacher's fervor and hunter's tremor which awakened in him told him that the pit traps and snares of the past couldn't be empty, that someone's life was already twitching and rushing about in them.

In the past few years, the railroads had fallen into total decay. Rails, which from time to time nevertheless were received from the east, were immediately resold to western neighbors, and by them—to someone still further west. The ties had become worn out and flimsy, embankments had turned into steep slopes. Dangerously listing then stretching then contracting in length, the train drew its rumbling chain of cars along bridges over never-freezing, often-growing shallow rivers, which milled pebbles and gnawed at the banks. The banks where the rivers overflowed were no longer lined with checkered cement tiles. Not only lifeless earth and timber and cement pillboxes guarding the bridges, but even the guard booths were now empty. Although the zones around them were, as before, surrounded by barbed wire. Occasional sentries started to be met only in the mountains at the entrances to tunnels. The windows in the railroad cars though had been gone for a long time, therefore you could only guess about the existence or nonexistence of a large number of things in the world beyond the windows. Yuriev went several times to smoke at the car platform with broken windows and snow-drifts in the corners. The encrustations of dried-out paint flaked and peeled on the car's back wall. This was an involuntary imitation of autumn, the inside and outside of the paint scales and scabs differed not only by hues but also by color here and there. The corridor was drafty. The freezing air burned his lungs in a deep breath and pleasantly invigorated him. Yuriev already had traveled once at night in a sleeping car where the side bunks were taken down—there weren't just compartment cars in that train. The sensation was sharp and wonderful, and that's why he remembered it. "Halfway to a cattle car, the comfort of a cattle shed," he thought, having recovered from the first impression by resorting to the tested means of melancholy, and after that he wasn't amused at anything, except, perhaps, the residual presence of doors in the destroyed train toilets, which you couldn't use anyway. They said that the railroad workers themselves disemboweled the cars and pulled them apart while the trains were standing in the depots. There was nothing out of the ordinary in that. He remembered during the extremely cold winter of 1975 just the blackened skeletons of trucks and buses which had driven off the beltway into the field and had overturned. That was a legitimate tro-phy for the neighboring villages, the not-particularly-safe hunting expeditions of the handy and thrifty peasants.

In the Carpathian Mountains, a young Hutsul once admitted: "If anyone encroaches on my sheep, I'll kill him, no matter who he might be. Drop him in a ravine so that the brook will wash his bones clean by spring."

"No matter who he might be, even a relative?"

"A relative wouldn't do that."

"You'd kill a man for a sheep?"

"Yes."

"Kill for stealing it?"

"Yes."

"But you're a churchgoer?"

"I'd kill him."

This is what maintained and kept the relative order of things in the villages—the self-righteous sense of justice of the chieftains. The rackets, which quickly became the norm, blossomed luxuriantly at the district marketplaces, but there was no robbery in the villages. Still during the time of the boom of the cooperatives, in Kosiv, a frail old grandpa climbed to the attic, supposedly to get his savings he had hidden there, but instead got a *Schmeisser* kept there since World War II or guerrilla times and killed the entire band of rack-eteers who through beating and torture had extorted money from him and his old lady. The instructive story spread like lightning all over the Carpathian Mountains. People were left alone. It turned out sooner or later that everyone, whom Yuriev got to know close enough, had a barrel hidden somewhere. Sometimes it was a First World War item that brought to mind the weapons of James Fenimore Cooper's hunters with its absurd length; more often than not it was a sawed-off shotgun or a smooth-bore rifle—Yuriev hap-pened to shoot one like that, anything for which they could find cartridges.

The train crawled deeper and deeper into the mountains. Tunnels began.

In the past decades, Yuriev had passed this station so many times without stopping that even this time, despite waiting for it, he had almost missed it again. When he and his wife got off the train onto the platform, he looked around. People who had poured out of the railroad cars quickly dispersed, disappearing in the narrow, crevice-like passages, snowy streets, and wicket gates. Several five- and even nine-story apartment buildings, placed haphazardly any which way, could be seen at a certain distance. In one of them, about ten years ago, his uncle had received an apartment with a phone. It soon became clear that nobody knew the numbering of the houses, and he didn't feel like answering the question "Who did you come to visit?" That was why Yuriev and his wife walked past the house they needed twice until Uncle's wife rushed out from behind one of them and ran toward them across the street. The embarrassed uncle showed up at the opposite end of the street. He had gone to the station to meet them but didn't recognize them in the quickly dispersed crowd. So now his wife shamed him with might and main. Yuriev and the uncle embraced. Yuriev, himself, probably wouldn't recognize himself immediately, if, in his youthful years, he were shown his present-day photograph. It was as though several people who didn't resemble each other lived too much during that time under his last name, changing photographs and addresses, observing the rules of secrecy and starting from scratch every time around. Different mustaches landed on his upper lip, a beard clung to his chin, changed its shape, disappeared without a trace. He could be identified only by checking his documents, and, perhaps, his gait, the most betraying thing in a person, gave him away.

In the past years his uncle had grayed completely, like an albino, he had become even bigger in circumference, and his usual collected composure acquired the character of an old man's economical unhurriedness. His pushy, spry wife, who was many years younger than he, looked, to the contrary, as though she had been pulled out of a deck of cards, the Galician queen of spades, beautiful like witches and strongly resistant to aging. She continued to work as a vice-principal at an orphanage located on the same street just a few steps from their house.

His quite urban apartment, up to which they climbed the stairs, made a rather strange impression because of the countryside views from the windows. City conveniences were imitated quite skillfully in the apartment, but there was no water in the faucets, the radiators were barely warm, the bathroom and the toilet were separated from the corridor to the kitchen only by draperies, and large transparent panels of glass without any draperies had been inserted in all the doors of all the rooms so that the entire apartment, excluding some distant corners, could be seen from the entrance hall. As the guests, who were not without pride, explained, for two years now in his spare time, the uncle's son had unhurriedly been lining the walls of the kitchen, bathroom, and toilet with tiles, carefully measuring and replacing the domestic conveniences with imported ones, and ordering new doors. Apparently, the labor and efforts on the improvement of the apartment brought tranquility to the souls of its inhabitants— so was it worth it to sacrifice the comfort which was brought to them by the sense of purposefulness for the sake of quicker completion of the remodeling? It didn't really look like remodeling. By profession the uncle's son was a dentist who recently graduated from a dentistry institute and maintained his practice in one of the neighboring villages. That day he turned out to be at home and immediately, right at the threshold, by the right of kinship, started to use the familiar form of address with the guests.

Yuriev barely managed to free himself of the presents from the city—the sack of oranges, the loaf of bologna, obligatory like an "Our Father . . . ," something else sweet to go with tea—as he and his wife were sitting at the table. Everything turned out to be excessively hearty and too substantial—accompanied by chilled vodka with marinated white mushrooms and other homemade marinated delicacies. The common conversation was carried in the "Ukrainian tongue," which the uncle's relatives were able to value. Yuriev addressed his wife in Russian as she did him. At first, the uncle spoke to him first in Russian, then in Ukrainian—their visit presented a problem for him. After dinner, the uncle, who had drunk several shot glasses of vodka, lay down on the sofa in the same room. His wife, after she had fulfilled her duties as a hostess, hurriedly threw a shawl over her shoulders and ran across the street to her round-the-clock school to the children she had left there. Yuriev and his wife went outside for a walk.

The motionless overcast sky above their heads resembled an unmade bed. The entangled little streets, barely marked in this part of the town, looked more like laid-out paths and were almost empty. Seldom passersby moved and rolled down along the trajectories which were indiscernible from afar, either following the local relief or obeying the call of some different, unclear logic, and when they approached, they disappeared as if they had fallen through the earth. When they walked in several open stores on the main street, Yuriev and his wife were stunned by the neglect that reigned there. It reminded them of the recent past with the only difference being that now not only were the goods absent, but also the customers scouring for them with thick wallets. The store windows and shelves were empty in the direct meaning of the word, and with that, they were not apparently embarrassed by their underscored nakedness and braved their demonstrative, grocery-store nudism. But to make up for it, everywhere in the town, wooden, glass-lined kiosks grew, crammed with imported alcohol, which accommodated no more than three drinking buddies at the same time. By their size and proportions they strongly resembled roadside chapels of the Mother of God, which were plentiful in this area. The "imported" alcohol, as you could easily surmise, was almost entirely produced in the closest district center, and the "Amaretto," favored by highlanders on holidays—right there in the villages, in the huts from pure grain alcohol and contraband extract. Life in the town was acquiring more and more chimerical dimensions. The uncle's son managed to tell them during dinner that one of the prospering merchants somewhere had bought and installed a Swiss elevator in his house, which cruised between the cellar and the attic with stops on two floors. The past spring some apparently bankrupt circus or zoo released a few mature bears from a helicopter onto a nearby mountain, and those bewildered beasts roamed for a long time in the district looking for food and scaring the population until migrating further south. One of the uncle's former coworkers took one of them for a passerby on a night road and was even heartened to have a fellow traveler, but pulled back just in time, having remembered the bears. Meanwhile, it was possible to buy something to eat only from the Transcarpathians, for whom a tiny, two-row market under an unpainted board roof had been built near the train station. The Transcarpathian farmers, whose climate was milder and on whose garden beds everything grew, made their way here by riding completely broken trains four times a week. During the remaining days, music was screaming, sellers, hired by local trade bosses, sold vodka, syrup soda, and whatever small stuff they could find, and gypsies wandered all over. The prices were approximately the same everywhere, slightly higher than in the regional cities and district centers—the difference in price covered the approximate cost of travel to their place. If you wanted, it was possible to economize only on the expenditure of muscular effort and time, and there was, as previously, an excess of both, as well as of the inveterate habit of surviving, here.

At the edge of the town the road dove under the open overpass along which rails were laid out. They led to a small bridge thrown over a small mountain river not far from there. The mysterious word SHCHEK painstakingly drawn in white letters across one of the overpass's supports leaped at their eyes. Here for the first time they met several skiers who, one after another, were gliding with a careless skating step along the road in the direction of the town center. The fiberglass skis rattled at the turns and loudly knocked against the beaten, and in some places icy, crust over the thoroughfare. The lodges at the outskirts of the place were empty, most of them now were no longer heated, but nevertheless someone still came here to ski. Judging by a grocery bag swinging in the hands of one of the skiers, this group of visitors was headed for a store to get the next portion of "fuel" for warming. Like some kind of searchers for mysterious life flickering somewhere, they stirred up the deadened landscape. Right away, a heavily loaded timber truck chased after them, rattling and ringing the chains that were wound around its tires, leaving behind itself frozen clouds of exhaust hanging over the road like wash. A locomotive immediately responded with a whistle from behind a nearby mountain and a few minutes later rumbled across the bridge over the river and along the completely unfenced scaffoldings above the highway, having been imprinted for a moment against the sky, an oily belly of a herbivorous colossus crossing a path. When it passed the scaffoldings, it whistled again and again, informing those like itself at the station about its arrival.

They didn't feel like going back, so Yuriev and his wife walked down from the highway and went along the river's bank, deciding to return home in a roundabout way. The same unrelentingly and incomprehensibly clicking word SHCHEK-SHCHEK-SHCHEK caught their eyes several times. It was painted with the same white oil paint on objects that were noticeable but not quite suited for writing: on the cement beams unloaded by the side of the road, the picket fences, and the railings of the pedestrian bridge over the river, it was written like a slogan: SHCHEK FOR PRESIDENT! So that's what the fact of the matter was—apparently a serious political fight had been in full swing in the town not very long ago. "Was it maybe the election to the local council?" Yuriev lazily thought. Although something jabbed him at that moment, he couldn't figure out, no matter how hard he tried—from what side and in connection with what?

Yuriev and his wife crossed the bridge and ascended the hillock, from where they could see the entire town stretched along the railroad track. At two opposite ends the exits from the mountain gorge were shining brightly. One of the summits on the opposite side for a brief moment perforated the fog. The tear crawled along the slope, revealing a cable lift for skiers with a wheel on top like in mines, which, it seemed, could be picked up only with a clockmaker's tweezers. A slalom course led almost perpendicularly down from it, barely noticeable, on the scale of an ant. But the unsupported, uncoordinated efforts of the weather couldn't, no matter how hard they tried, prevent the fog from quickly covering the formed break.

Yuriev clicked his soap box camera several times, taking pictures of his wife under the branchy fir trees. Her face flushed during the walk, from the light frost the skin on her cheeks became applelike, perhaps, only a frozen tear or the hot trace of a kiss was missing on it. Having clicked once or twice—now with the lighter—he inhaled the smoke to his heart's content. The path that rose upward led up against the fence of the local graveyard. Below the churchyard it sprawled under the precipitous slope, the cross above the church's cupola reached the foot of the fir trees. A shopping center towered on the riverbank under a peaked wooden roof, with a restaurant that occupied the entire second floor. Drinking stands made of wooden planks and kiosks with handmade garlands of coarsely painted electric bulbs stretched between the roofs crowded in front of it. This place, with a well-trodden path to the shopping center, could even be called populous if you took into consideration the neglect reigning in town. The local inhabitants amused themselves by observing a few visitors recognized from a distance and without skis—by the details of the skiing clothing and, even more, by their manner of behavior. No big deal, a man!

Yuriev got a bit cold and then chilled to the bones and suggested to his wife that they warm up with something at the restaurant's bar. They carefully started to walk down the hillock holding hands—it was slippery. In the past quarter of the century, the town had changed drastically, but at the same time in a completely superficial—not to say, false—way. The external modifications were not suited for altering the environment of the location, its acoustics and atmosphere—and that meant the people, too. During the entire walk, Yuriev, when he knew how, would move his ears like a horse, or sniff like a dog remembering smells. The sounds and smells remained the same, only their meaning had disappeared somewhere. The experience of these involuntary sensations did not trouble him so much as they slightly intrigued him, and if he wanted to concretize his feeling, they troubled him not more than, let's say, the end of a typical movie, that is, a device by which the viewers' satisfaction could be achieved. In the morning he intended with his uncle's help to record something on a Dictaphone just to clarify certain things for himself. After all, he caught a little bit of that time of oaths in the gloomily frivolous country where every child couldn't help but ask himself this serious question: Would he withstand the tortures inflicted upon him by an enemy, like the heroic young pioneer so-and-so? No unequivocal and, it goes without saying, satisfactory answers to that rancorous question had come to him since those times.

Meanwhile, dusk was falling. The sky over the mountains still remained bright, the thick clouds transmitted the light of the body of the luminary hidden behind them. Diluted inky shadows had already started to crawl along the bottom of the valley, their spots merged into sleeves. Having recolored the snow, they climbed the walls. Along a path trodden in the snow shining with the phantasmagoric blue, Yuriev and his wife came to a half-open gigantic double door, which was hiding an entrance, it must be supposed, to a drinking establishment. The bar on the first floor was locked, a padlock of an impressive size didn't leave any doubts on that account. A wide stairway led to the second floor from where not a sound could be heard. They walked up the steps and, pushing open a bulky carved door, found themselves to their surprise in an absolutely empty, chilly, unlit restaurant dining hall big enough to seat several hundred people. After they wandered for a while in the darkness, they found people gathered in the kitchen next to a homemade "billy-goat" heater wrapped with a spiral glowing red in the dusk. They were told that there were only cold snacks and drinks—since there were no customers, the kitchen wasn't open, and no one would heat or even light such a huge space for the sake of a couple or even a dozen customers, and it would be better for them if they went to find another place for themselves. Without squabbling, Yuriev asked for a drink. Only then several women reluctantly stirred. Yuriev was amazed by their persistence, not to say their selflessness—of which he soon made certain, having spent the first quarter of the hour in the restaurant dining hall. They sat by the window on the western, brighter side. The volume of darkness on both sides of the glass, however, soon equalized. A waitress turned kinder and lit a chandelier above them, which looked like a cartwheel, but the light of its dim bulbs was barely enough to cast the shadows of the ceiling beams up onto the gigantic tavern's dome, disappearing in the darkness. Their hands were frozen, their behinds were mercilessly benumbed on the wooden seats of the two-ton chairs. In five minutes of sitting like this, if not for the cognac, their teeth would be chattering. There was, however, something somberly attractive in the enchanting uselessness of this ark, abandoned by people and raised above the town. It became pitch dark beyond the window. Meanwhile the waitress was reacquiring professional skills. She said that she would ask the barmaid not only to prepare hot coffee but also to make a mulled wine for them—in any case, it was much more than what they could count on. While awaiting what was promised to them, Yuriev asked his wife: "By the way, did you noticed all those slogans everywhere, 'Shchek,' 'Shchek for President?' It's highly unlikely for it to be what I think it is, but, you know, that year when I worked on assignment after university in a village near Lviv, I told you a little about it, do you remember? Marusya's fiancé, a shell-shocked forty-year-old carpenter, once signed a letter to a school principal with 'the Prince Shchek.' It's too improbable for him to turn out to be that one. I couldn't even imagine that that could be a nickname or a last name and not just a joke. That guy was also from somewhere here, from the Carpathian Mountains. When we get home, I have to ask my uncle—after all, they must know each other here. And what is it we'll find out here, how that story ended?"

His wife calmly answered that while still back at the station she had noticed this word or a nickname coarsely painted with meter-high letters on the platform, and, of course, she had noticed that, appearing in different places, it had followed them during their entire walk. She had thought teenagers had written it, but it looked like a much more interesting story was behind it.

In proportion to warming up with their drink, the possibility of such an impossible coincidence seemed less and less impossible to both of them, and Yuriev's assumption appeared to him more and more justified, and, if he were lucky, hitting the very bull's-eye of his unformed expectations—the desire to tie with a single knot and try to lift from the ground the life he had lived in this area. Yuriev didn't want to make a hash of his participation in that story, and he post-poned a detailed exposition of it for later. Meanwhile, the waitress, in a last gesture of magnanimity, took Yuriev's wife to the staff's toilet, the only still-working one in the entire establishment. After paying, Yuriev went down and waited outside, where he, too, having gone around the corner, coped without anyone's help with his need, which had become unbearable because of the cold. The time was evening, not very late, but it seemed that a dead polar night fell for thousands of kilometers all around them. The sky was covered with shaggy clouds from which snow started to fall. In the blaze of light, a streetlight on a pole hissed like a sunny-side-up egg. The oily body of the river was iridescent, reflecting the light in the breaks in the ice. At the thought of the chilly river water, goosebumps covered his rib cage and his head was involuntarily drawn into his chest below his shoulders. Sand, which someone had generously poured from a bucket at the entrance to the wooden bridge, happily crunched underfoot like beetles. Windows of houses shone in the distance, and the one central street leading to the train station was dimly lit.

The darkness washed away the borders of bodies and objects, increasing their mutual interpenetration. The remains of indoor air completely vacated the lungs in the outside cold. The troubles of the city, which were abandoned for a day and which were waiting for him to return to in order to leave them in another day for good, from time to time came, as soon as he would stop paying attention, up to his heart, throat, stomach, confusing his thoughts and feelings. Did his wife feel the same? Had she decided for herself what she was supposed to decide?

They half slid, half ran down into the resemblance of a shallow ravine behind the rear entrances of the main street. Passing by the barely lit warehouses, and the frequent barns and gardens, they finally came to the back end of a five-story box, which showed up darkly on the hill. Something began to move noisily and grunt anxiously in the shed closest to the entrance, past which they had come along the path. After all, it still was a village, not a town. Yuriev remembered his uncle's trained chicken, which used to climb a narrow plank the height of a man, to their chicken coop, clucking loudly at that, and how they out of habit exaggerated their giddiness and affected fear of the rooster. Every evening his uncle slammed the door of the day behind them. He still had to saw and split wood in the yard, to bring buckets of water from the well to the second floor of a two-family house by the river, where in the evenings, when the electricity was for some reason cut off, his wife, kneeling, corrected piles of schoolchildren's copybooks by the open door of a tiled stove.

Some time ago, Uncle's wife used to sing in a teachers' choir. The forestry office allotted a bus to the choir that drove the local artists on tours all over the district and, most important, to the amateur art festivals and official concerts at the district's capital. That was a wonderful, Golden Age time when you felt like singing, a time of merriment, adventures, youth slipping away, expectations, flirtation, and even some success. They met at one such concert: a thorough and respectable forester with a wonderful deep singing voice, as it turned out, still on the way back home in the bus, and a spry geography teacher with dimples on her cheeks (with years—with little apples of paradise on her cheekbones) and with eyes hot like the roasted chestnuts that were sold in the early spring only in the streets of Mukachevo and Uzhorod in the neighboring Transcarpathian Region. For him, she gave birth to quick-witted children, like herself, who caught everything on the uptake. He had to fix both of them up to enter a medical institute at a central district city, finding connections and disregarding the amount of money it cost, and he supported them both, one after another, for all ten years of their studies while they lived away from home. His problem, though, consisted of the fact that he himself belonged to those who didn't comprehend things too quickly, and because during the war he had defended and fought for the country he had considered to be his homeland, in his old age, when his strength had started to wane, he got all the knocks and bumps—for everything—all at once. He was deprived of his voice in his family, and he in fact almost lost it. His voice began to break, as it happened, once when he was a teenager, and it was at times high like a woman's, at times hoarse and barely audible because of the heaving and shortness of breath. At moments of weakness of the body and soul, he even thought of leaving that place on his own, abandoning the house and the family, the members of which got along perfectly among themselves without him, without realizing that the husband and father was for all of them precisely what united them. Several times a year he went to visit different places where, thank God, he still had relatives. He returned always in a more oppressed mood than the one in which he left. That peasant's reckoning which is deposited, lies, and grows in the back of the head of every mature person told him that he had missed a right turn; that, speeding up, he had overshot a highway exit to a country road leading to his native land; that the traffic rules and signs would not allow him to turn around; and that he had no determination or strength left to violate the rules. He also thought that it was left for him either to die as a dependent at someone's house, which is unworthy for a master of the house, or to decide to dissolve away among his own family, having surrounded himself with the cotton of deafness, submersing into senile incomprehension when facing the family's reproaches and tweaks that were felt ever more strongly. And it was time to think not about the cotton for his ears—and where would he gather up so much cotton?—but about making a wooden suite and finding a place for the pit on a wooded slope where several decades later only the forest would be able to say a kind word about the forester who some time ago climbed all over these mounds and gorges and whose bones were still left in the captivity of the Carpathian Mountains and whose name had been erased.

■   ❑   ■

Yuriev's guess was confirmed. As was found out during dinner, "Shchek" turned out to be the same person about whom Yuriev had thought. To the accompaniment of cognac with lemon and tea with sweet-smelling jam, the relatives willingly and interruptingly poured out for Yuriev a heap of everything that was known about the town's madman and what they had managed to remember about him. The year before last he in fact had conceived the idea to become the president of Ukraine, and at the same time as other candidates, he unfurled an election campaign on his own in the town. "Shchek" was his passport name, it wasn't a nickname or some bad-taste mystification as Yuriev had once thought. That was the reason why the word he saw painted on the cement support didn't immediately connect in his mind with that ancient history. About twenty years ago he had squeezed everything he could out of it and thereafter lost the connection and trace and became disinterested in it. Today he got the preamble and the denouement, he got witnesses and the texture that he hadn't had for the epilogue.

The prehistory, despite the apparent sound mind of the witnesses, smacked of the credulity of myth and of the superficial beauty of superstition—*zabobon* in Ukrainian. Thickset and wide-shouldered Boikos also lived in these mountains between the Lemkos in the northwest and the Eastern Orthodox Hutsuls in the southeast. The inhuman strength of their ancestors, the born lumbermen and shepherds, came from what they drank—as few people drink nowadays here—beer with sour cream. The lungs of these people were of monstrous size, and, if there were a sea with pearls in these mountains, they would become the best pearl divers in the world. Two brothers Shchek lived their eccentric lives, played pranks, competing with one another, in the time between the wars. Both were unmarried. If one on a wager managed to lift a church bell from the ground, then the other not only would lift it, but would also swing it, because the Boikos know that it is not strength that determines everything, but the *traction*. The older was a self-taught mechanic and inventor. What happens to a person once in these mountains is doomed to haunt him to the end of his days, and even further—until the last witnesses die out. The older Shchek hadn't been alive for half a century already, but the Boikos still proudly recollected in detail how he on a wager managed to start up the motor of a sports car which he had seen for the first time in his life and which had broken down on a mountain road, stupefying the rich Polish gentlemen who was traveling in it. It was said that he had been a prisoner of war in Italy during the First World War. On the way back, he saw Rome, Florence, and Venice and came home along the Carpathian range on foot. When in the 1930s he made an airplane out of a barrel and flew several kilometers in it over a mountain valley, the younger brother understood that he could not surpass him in that feat and took a different path. By the way, the barrel was the most plausible detail of this story. In a Polish magazine from the time between the wars, Yuriev once came across an article and the schematic of an airplane assembled by an English (actually, probably Scottish) inventor out of disassembled empty barrels. Meanwhile, the older Shchek couldn't, perhaps, wait to fly up, or, perhaps, he didn't intend to land—to such a degree that he totally disregarded this part of the flight. After landing he could no longer walk. Death couldn't take him for a long time as well, because, as people who visited him at his house said, he built a rotating bed for himself and, as soon as Death came to take him and stood at the head of his bed, he, sensing it, immediately turned with his feet toward him, and Death would leave in disgrace. At that time he very much wanted to live. He took *for himself,* as it is accustomed to say here, a young left-handed maiden from a village below. She gave birth to that son of his with his feet turned front to back, who, toward the end of the century, would want to become the Ukrainian president. When he was still an infant, before the very beginning of the war in Lviv, a Polish professor performed surgery on him, turning his feet to the right direction. That surgery left only scars and stitches on the back of his ankles, which looked like shoe lacing. Pops Shchek paid for the surgery with gold ducats, the news of which quickly became known and agitated the entire area right on the eve of establishment of the *first* Soviets. The NKVD, as it got a feel for the new surroundings, soon pulled the old Shchek out of his rotating bed, and he never returned to it. The Polish professor of medicine was shot two years later by the Nazis when they came to Lviv for the second time—he turned out to have been a Jew.

The younger Shchek not long before the war became a preacher-athlete: he walked along the railings of bridges over gorges and rivers, learned the technique of running with a hatchet on his shoulders, in one night covering in dancing leaps the distance to the Transcarpathian valleys where the Boikos tended sheep and returning home at dawn. He wanted to communicate something to his compatriots in this way. Once he sawed off a fir tree at the edge of the village so that the stump would have room for his two feet and, standing there for half a day, prophesied to the gathered inhabitants of the village: not about God, not about the devil, not about politics—but it looked like it wasn't for fun either. Nobody understood anything in his speech and afterward they wondered about it for a bit, laughed a little, wondered again, everyone little by little dispersing, returning to their own affairs. For this type of people, there was a succinct word with a not quite defined meaning—a "character-*nik*," not a buffoon, not a sorcerer, but something like a magician. During the first Soviets, the younger Shchek joined a team of painters who painted churches. He wasn't a part of the guerrilla movement. After the war he was sent, accompanying the timber, to restore the Don Basin mines. He never came back from there. In the middle of the 1950s, his grown-up nephew came to him there in search of work. In the early 1960s, one nephew alone came back from the east. He was the last of the Shcheks, who resembled the two brothers with the breadth of his chest but had lungs littered with coal dust since his youth and poisoned by methane. He was paid a small pension as an invalid. His mother had died by that time. He locked the hut on the slope of the mountain above the river and began traveling through villages doing carpentry work. As it recently became known to his fellow villagers, during those years he was preparing himself for crossing the state border—not here, but somewhere in Central Asia or the Transcaucasus. From somewhere he found out, or, perhaps, guessed, that the real border was in fact kept secret and was located five kilometers beyond what was marked. The main traps are located between them, and that is what their treachery consists of—let's say you have just crossed the footprint-checking line, you've overcome the crafty obstacles of the Stepanov system, and you've relaxed, thinking that you are now in the free world, as suddenly the border guards appear from out of the blue in their familiar peaked caps, with dogs, and pounce on you, grab you, and send you to a labor camp till the end of your days.

No, you won't fool Shchek with this kind of simpletons' trick! To defend himself against the dogs, he bought a foil in a sporting goods store, making a special trip for this purpose to the regional center. He broke off the tip of the foil and sharpened the remaining part on both ends so the foil could fit into a small suitcase that was supposed to contain everything he might need during his crossing. To strengthen his organism once a week he loaded his knapsack with cobblestones and set out carrying it on foot from village to village, refusing offers from cars traveling in his direction, because "drivers" sent undercover by the secret service might be sitting behind the wheels. He had a plan: in the West he was going to make public his project of building a five-hundred-meter-high pyramid with an oasis on top, a symbolic pantheon mountain that would glorify the heroes fighting for the freedom of Ukraine. He had, it's true, ciphered a principal schematic and also a great number of drawings of various fragments of the structure-to-be, each detail of which signified and symbolized something. The span of the steps would be calculated, it would be defined what would be located at each of the tiers, the number of plates that would be put at the very top, and how many and what kind of trees would be planted. In order to deliver huge stone blocks to the top, he would need special devices that he had to invent along the way, drawing them in checkered school arithmetic notebooks. He was cunning, persistent, and circumspect: if he were arrested, what kind of evidence can school arithmetic notebooks provide with pictures of whimsical mechanisms and columns of calculations with coefficients taken out of the blue, with drawings of an installation of *nets for wind-dampening* and with drawings of some SCWs, which simply meant "special configuration windows"? In reality, it was the model of a Heavenly Ukraine, with the construction of which the establishment of a Ukraine on earth should begin. When independence suddenly fell out of the sky on the country in the early 1990s, he published a pamphlet about his life's work in which he finally put into words and presented for the judgment of the society his plan, which he bore in him for decades, with explanations, calculations, and drawings, the plan for which he wouldn't be able to escape imprisonment or at least a nuthouse during the previous regime. He published his work with his own money at a regional press in five thousand copies the size of approximately two school copybooks, placing his photograph at the back cover. On that photograph he was shown in full height wearing a checkered jacket, which was a bit too big for him, leaning on the back of a Tonet chair from the props of the regional center's photo studio. Soon a great multitude of similar such books was released and his was forgotten, and it's doubtful that it ever sold out, but luckily one copy was kept on Uncle's glass bookshelf. It was the one Yuriev took to leafing through before going to sleep.

So that was who had shown up two decades ago in that village near Lviv where Yuriev happened to be assigned after his graduation from university and where he had worked for a year as a teacher at the local school. In bed before falling asleep, he told his wife, a person the same age as the main heroine of those events, about his part in the story, which was played out then and there, to which he, himself, was related somewhat indirectly. In the course of his narration, he had to remember many things that then took the somewhat wild story beyond the borders of a dark anecdote, beyond the limits of the competence of the criminal code, applying the coarse makeup of characters from an archaic drama (which the specialists in philology considered lost for a long time) to its participants.

■　❏　■

Everything at that school was disposed and inclined to playing a blasphemous joke, especially if you consider the age of the young teacher. The former four-year and later Soviet middle school occupied a building of a neglected dairy farm, a primitive milk processing plant during the time of Polish occupation, with cement floors that had strange ledges and troughs, inviting you to stumble at every step. From its porch, where Yuriev usually went to have a smoke, on clear days he could distinctly see the curly hills of the Keiserwald and, towering above it, the High Castle Mountain with a TV tower blocking the entrance to the city, so close and unapproachable from this side. When he ended up here, a novice teacher of Russian language and literature, he found himself taken out of not only the physical outskirts of the city but also with a minus sign, an invisible parenthesis. In that area, he felt about himself approximately as an imaginary negative number, protected only by its temporary exclusion from the conditions of a mathematical problem, would itself feel, landing into a sequence of natural numbers. The circumference, corresponding approximately to the beltway, was also the axis of coordinates at the intersection of which some kind of numerical transformation took place, and what had appeared unconditionally valuable within the circumference was perceived as nonsense outside of it, the white tuned out to be the black, the black looked like the white, and vice versa. It was a kind of a spatial dislocation. Time also behaved differently here. It stood still, and no one bore a grudge against it for this. An intercity bus was waiting with doomed patience as though for an execution or for Godot, whose name didn't say anything to anyone here. The dusty, humpbacked LAZ sooner or later appeared from behind the corner, always causing some animation at the stop, promising those who waited till its appearance the happiness of conversation during the trip. Any four-wheel transportation was for the locals a variant of a movable club: you want to communicate, you need to go somewhere. The inside of the bus was excitedly and bone-crushingly packed with passengers, especially during market days. Piglets, which sullied themselves in tied bags, squealing, wriggled under the seats, bumped against and got entangled in the passengers' feet. A young stout woman, leaning with her bosom on those who were sitting and turning back over her shoulder, moaned, not without pleasure: "Buddy, where are you climbing? You'll crush us gals!"

Because of the crowd and the odd bus schedule, Yuriev soon adapted himself to hitchhiking. In his school he belonged to that small segment of teachers who, in the teachers' lounge and at meetings, were contemptuously called "last minuters." In addition to that, as it was found out, he was the only male teacher who didn't physically terrorize his pupils on the sly, in the upper-level classes he addressed them exclusively in the polite, plural "you," inciting the students at first to lose their already meager gift of speech. Discipline in his classes was maintained primarily on account of that childish curiosity the students felt in regard to the intriguing mystery of their new teacher, who came to them from afar, from a different life about which they knew only by hearsay. Everything about which he was talking and which for him stood to reason *there,* within the circle, they heard as though through water, coming to them dressed in the clothes of foreign, incomprehensible speech. The principal hung on him the supervision of the most troublesome of the graduating tenth graders, but after Yuriev brought the bound-to-burn-your-hands-if-you-hold-it magazine *America* to one of the lessons, the principal immediately removed him from this duty, having become seriously fearful for his own position. The teachers' lounge resembled an exemplary chicken coop with hens whom the principal, also the chairman of the Party Committee at the local Soviet collective farm, reigning here indivisibly, squashed beneath him as a result of his purposeful efforts. He used to croon at weekly meetings and teachers' conferences like a wooden platypus, rolling his eyeballs in inspiration and gurgling out the sounds: "Nowadays we live in a hi-hi-highly organized society!"—drawing a semblance of the Marxist-Leninist spiral in midair with his index finger and at the same time using it to make a threatening gesture to Yuriev's still-unknown, high-placed patrons who got him the assignment at the school located just a half-hour drive from the city. Very soon, just at the sight of the young teacher, disregarding his lasting habit of maintaining self-control in the presence of his subordinates, the director broke into a shaking fit—his breathing would be cut short, his palms would get sweaty, the knuckles of his involuntarily closing and opening fists would become white, his fingers would begin to jerk. It was quite understandable: the young man was asocial, wore shoulder-length hair, behaved arrogantly, not like everybody else; at a meeting with Latin American students, which later grew into a banquet in the school cafeteria, he gave a toast without coordinating it with anyone, forcing everyone to drink to the health of the presently thriving "great Latin American writers,"—naming several names, but how can you know who they were—isn't it a provocation? The director's favorite word was "oR-R-der"—pronounced precisely in that way—and he wasn't going to tolerate any violation of it. But he had to tolerate it until the situation was clarified. The director was an old fox who at first faced such an insolent, semiconscious, and, because of it, still more scandalous and shameless bluff. The subordination in the chicken coop had been shaken up—also in connection with the appearance of another new teacher at the school, who at forty had left a job at the regional television station. From her waist tightly squeezed by a belt and her bust aimed at you like two warheads, it was obvious to the naked eye that she had been so hungry for men that the director's jaws cramped and his voice became husky when he talked to her. But no-o-o! She grabbed the young one, made eyes at him, didn't let him leave her side, *arrived* together with him. They were just about to unbridle the immoral affair. In regards to the director, she took the position that he couldn't get to her; whether he called her in for disciplining or not, he could do nothing.

The school, like the village on the whole, could be observed throughout from any point. The director's wife and his daughter-in-law were confidants of female pupils burdened by the burning secrets of sexual maturation. Gym and shop teachers also divulged the information they had gotten. On the very first day a young geography teacher, not quite realizing whom he was talking to, shared his inhumanly strong desire to join the Communist Party with Yuriev. As he put it, the Party was a fortress he had been storming for three years, intending even to join the army for a few years after the Institute to penetrate it at least through that entrance. In less than half a year, the gates of that fortress would open before him by themselves, thanks to the director's patronage, and after that the gates of many others because there were no fortresses, as it had been said, . . . well and so on and so forth. Nobody could guess then how unbelievably close the expiration date of these words would be.

All teachers, and in fact all students, were obligated to carry out the so-called social extracurricular activities. When Yuriev expressed a desire to lead an additional seminar, he was immediately offered a fixed program. He offered to organize a literary club but was informed of the detailed program for a literary club approved by the Ministry. He refused. Then he was sent to deliver a morning lecture to mechanics, and in a week to milkmaids. One of the mechanics asked him how much grain the Soviet Union bought yearly from the Americans. He didn't know. The satisfied mechanic confirmed: "Nobody knows." Yuriev left the stifling meeting room, which was crammed with the village men in dirty quilted jackets who knew perfectly well that the teacher had been sent to them. He didn't even go to the milkmaids. He began to miss weekly political information meetings, didn't make notes on the materials of the last Party plenum or even Congress. Not paying attention to the director's warning that a deviation from the approved program for each subject is criminally punishable and persecuted by law, Yuriev began to do what he deemed necessary for his lessons. The task was greatly simplified because the pupils had no place to get the books they were supposed to read. That was why the lessons were mainly reduced to reading aloud, retelling the plots, and his attempt to elicit from his pupils the answer to what they thought about what they had read. Strictly speaking, the story of Marusya Bohuslavsky began.

Approximately at that time, disoriented by the change in her circumstances, the romantically inclined TV worker began to complain to him about her female students. She returned home from her classes in a state of bewilderment and hysterical excitement. Everything connected to the world of feelings, motivations, the notorious "dialectics of the soul," which made the classical Russian literature of the nineteenth century famous, was completely inaccessible to the Galician village kids, as if the very soul possessed for them exclusively bodily tangible parameters and was strictly limited to physiology. The teacher, who had entered the dangerous age, as it could be guessed, was clearly enticed by the possibility of adultery with "psychology," the lack of which for two decades had repelled her from romantic involvement with the powdered anchormen and clammy editors of the regional television station.

Yuriev didn't rush to his own conclusions. Recently, for half of the period, he read books aloud, books he had brought with him, and for the other half asked questions and talked. By the end of the class, his throat was scratchy and it hurt when he swallowed. Four or five hours of talking every day—his saliva glands and throat were not suited for emitting such a quantity of words.

The children were lying in wait. They were listening. As a rule, there were five or six smart female students in each class. As it turned out later, they became city saleswomen. But the well-to-do parents fixed the F students up as salespeople in the city, although they more often became shipping clerks or longshoremen. It wasn't clear why they remembered their teacher, and even ten years later called him by his first name and patronymic from behind their counters and stands—they adapted somewhat to life in the city, gave birth to a lot of children, and grew inconceivable faces—offering him something from under the counter, asking him God knows what, something like: "Well, how are You?" He had to give higher grades to the diligent students, give them A's and B's so as not to extinguish their barely smoldering interest in knowledge and barely glimmering ability to learn. Each class also had several dolts and sometimes complete imbeciles whose parents tearfully asked that their mentally retarded children not be sent to special schools, it was easy to understand their request. These kids sat at the front desks in all grades, were well behaved and even made efforts to learn. Accidental praise from a teacher, it seemed, was capable of performing a miracle on them—how their hands shot up!—if only God, nature, or heredity hadn't hopelessly warped something in their poor heads. But you couldn't resort to this too often, in order not to turn them into a laughingstock, allowing them to disgrace themselves in front of the entire class. It was enough simply to allow them to be present in class with other children, to listen to something, from time to time even to write down something in their notebooks. There were several students in the entire school whom it was absolutely hopeless to ask to stand up and answer questions. Teachers quietly gave them C's for trimesters and for the year, and passed them to the next grade. The rest of the students knew that they were born to shovel manure at a state collective farm and sell fresh produce at the city markets—that was the profession and main source of income of the villages adjacent to the city. You had to try very hard or be a totally unlucky lazy bum to be poor in those villages, although such types were known. That was why everyone in the upper and lower grades, the relative "go-getters" and the worst F students, in all the classes and from all the desks, beamed and shined their golden teeth—the water in Galicia is very bad—they did it also because the desire to "bare teeth," to laugh, to make fun of yourself was so total and uncontrollable in youth, this cheap joy of the happy guffaw never ended.

Parallel to the road, a few hundred meters from the school, the Poltva flowed, a tiny sewer-river with drainage waste from the city, its factories and plants, which tirelessly refined oil and slaughtered cattle, produced soap and tricycles, bulky TV sets and heavy buses, hulls of submarines and bombsights for strategic bombers—about which very few knew at that time. Right at outlet from beneath the ground, contentious gulls intercepted from rats the contents of the city sewers. The river emitted fog in the mornings, especially on cloudy days, and its stench was a part of the concept of the land-scape. Yuriev imagined an ecological canoe trip: torsos in gas masks, raising and lowering oars, would silently glide like targets along the groove of the ditch in the field. Further downstream, the fetid river arrived at another big village, at the railroad station. From there almost half the students made their way to school by bus. Many of them were spirited pigeon-fanciers, which, since the postwar years, for some reason had become a local business.

Yuriev, however, was occupied with something else. The head-quarters of the First Cavalry was located in that village by the rail-road in 1920. Posted to it, Babel spent three months there, going insane from boredom and idleness and keeping a diary in the expec-tation of the storming of Lviv. The situation was such that everyone turned out to be more or less a madman at that time. A few years before that, in Zakopane, the future Nobel laureate in literature Stefan Zeromsky caught lodger Juzef Pilsudsky wearing nothing but long johns (he had given his only pants to be mended), caught him playing a difficult solitaire, on which he guessed his fortune— whether or not he would be the dictator of Poland, that country which wasn't on the map yet! That was why he strove for Kyiv at any possibility. Answering it, Tukhachevsky moved his army to an unprotected Warsaw and demanded support from Stalin. Stalin, however, after success at Tsaritsyn, thought too much of himself and became obstinate, insisting that Lviv should be the target of the main strike, and moved Budeny there. They both couldn't make up their minds for three months to unleash the cavalry avalanche onto the city, where it would undoubtedly get stuck, dispersing in the canals of winding streets and alleys, which promised the Red Cavalry huge losses, if not a glorious end. Meanwhile Tukhachevsky got whacked badly at Warsaw and then Budeny got the same, and all in a bunch they were driven back to Kyiv, so that the border came out precisely along the Zbruch.

Yuriev was nevertheless preoccupied with the exclusively literary aspect of the geopolitical turbulences. Simply put, it was not so much bolshevism but rather the Bolshevik Party policy in the area of art that didn't suit him. And he asked himself: Would the hypo-thetical capture or noncapture of Lviv by Budeny's cavalry be paid off by the Red Army man Babel writing a novella about this event a few years later? The city and the cavalry—what a beautiful antithesis! They annihilate each other upon contact, and as a proof of their meeting, only a short novella is left. That novella was not and could not be written because the event did not take place, and a testimony to that impulse was the destroyed Polish memorial at Lychakivsky Cemetery in Lviv and a belated Soviet monument at the descent from Pidhoretsky Castle to Olesky Castle, which could compete in its size with the castles—the raging cavalry drew its petrified hooves and maws into the tender sky of the west, where pink, naked women, indistinguishable from the clouds, wander along the straw-colored heavens. People say that in evening twilight, local girls love to give themselves to local guys on the pedestal of the monument right under the gigantic horse's testicles.

You cannot drop a word in a song—that was young Yuriev's way of thinking half a century later after those exciting events. Yesterday's permanent anarchist or, perhaps, anarchic syndicalist seriously thought that the art of the avant-garde, like a little male dog hand-drawn on a wall, was capable of impregnating the huge, lifelike bitch of the people, of arousing in its inert mass the ability of imagination. That smart young guy, whom he had singled out and had given books by Babel to read—as well as those by Bulgakov, Olesha, Kharms, and Kafka—grew up to be a movie projectionist with a very narrow forehead who scurried about the city in search of additional income, even finding it from time to time. That adolescent reading remained a never-clarified and vague episode of his school years, which he soon forgot as unnecessary. As were forgotten those last classes of the quarter at which there had been Homeric laughter, and the students had died laughing from the short stories of Zoshchenko, Kharms, and Zhvanetsky in turn. The vice-principal and the math teacher, sent by the principal, would run toward the laughter. By the way, she knew how, like no one else, to very skillfully compose the class schedule for an entire half a year, noting and rewarding (the "good") teachers by eliminating "windows" (free periods) in their schedules and censuring and punishing the "unacceptable ones" by giving them a great number of such windows, with an affected naïveté . . . hanging the entire remaining number of them onto the "arrivers," so that life wouldn't be as sweet for them. She would freeze picturesquely in the open door every time—but what was wrong with the children laughing when the teacher was present, and the grades had been already given? She had no choice but to make a not-very-sure semblance of a smile herself and close the door behind her. It would be interesting to know if anything other than that laughing got stuck in the heads of his pupils from the rest of his classes. A famous question ripped out with flesh, a phrase, a line of poetry? Or at least a name—let's say, of the Shaker of Englishmen with a spear across his body? But what are fallen Englishmen to them? Isn't it enough of idle questions?

■   ❑   ■

It went on until late autumn. Something difficult to imagine happened in one of his grades. The winter crop of the young teacher produced unforeseen fruits before the cold set in. Marusya Bohuslavsky, a slow-witted ninth grader, having listened to plenty of plays and novels he had read to them aloud in class, wrote a Russian literature composition. The director's daughter-in-law, who was also the headmistress of Marusya's grade, had warned Yuriev back at the beginning of the school year that he shouldn't waste his time on Marusya trying to get her up to answer questions, because she had not yet answered a single question for anyone. She was a mute orphan living with her grandmother in a hut with an earthen floor. She, like a seedling, was replanted from grade to grade, receiving C's for quarters and years. She was sat in the front row by the wall. Without bothering anyone, it might happen that she would hear something; anyway it was better than to be in the hut with the earthen floor, which was falling apart. You felt pity for Marusya and her grandmother, they had no one, and no one could take care of them.

The girl was indeed retarded, shy, with her gaze pointed down and sliding away, like a shadow crawling over objects that happened to be in sight. Therefore, it was a complete surprise for Yuriev, when once he started to go over the students' compositions, he came across Marusya's thin school notebook. It turned out that Marusya was taking notes! At first they were sluggish: the date, below—"The Class Work," the topic of the lesson, a medley of titles and characters' names in her own orthography, obscure fragments of the teacher's phrases and words. And suddenly—a composition on Ostrovsky's play *The Storm:* the pious and dreamy Katerina surrounded by the morals of the pigsty, the awakening of feelings, the conflict, the river, the suicide. That was a confusing and fragmentary retelling of the plot, or rather an attempt at that—an ecstatic stream of consciousness, where all ties were broken off and rolled without punctuation marks into a single tangle, which fit in the space of one big paragraph. No comparison to the Red Cavalry man from Babel's novella! No comparison to Beckett and Joyce together—no literary modernist could even dream about such an Ionesco. Kharms's refined *Incidents* looked out of Marusya's composition as though reflected in a cracked hand mirror, her writing bared the stylizing nature of Faulkner's narration in the best part of his best novel and brought it back to the source marked by the heavenly Shakespeare, a story told by an idiot, full of . . . "sound and fury."

The very next day Yuriev ran all over the city. That was ovulation time and the ripening of several local artistic schools, which later dissolved, dissipated, or withered away, but perhaps it was a time of the sexual blossoming of the generation in something of hothouse conditions. In the course of a week, Yuriev's friends and acquaintances, one after another, lost their minds over Marusya just as at a different time people had lost their minds over Cherubina de Gabriac. Now what was happening at his school was more important and more interesting than everything taken together that could be offered to him in that respect by the city, which still carried the traces and more often the scars of a specific, eccentric, Central European madness: old Polish ladies wearing hats with veils and knickknacks and an unbelievable number of cats in their apartments, trumpeters, fiddlers, street artists, hippies, kitchen and underground preachers, paupers sobbing poetry in streetcars, the overcrowded asylums—the entire breed of those people was systematically hunted down and exterminated by the Brezhnev police. In that country, picturesque lack of seriousness was regarded as lawbreaking and was persecuted, along with an apolitical attitude, a more serious infraction that goes without saying. That's how it was conceived by someone.

Yuriev, of course, wanted to know more about his pupil. Since it looked quite problematic to find out anything from her, he was left with nothing else to do but to rely on confidential information, or gossip, in common parlance. The class mistress answered Yuriev's questions with an embarrassed laugh. As it turned out, a forty-year-old, shell-shocked carpenter, Ivan, lived in the hut with Marusya and her grandmother. He had come to the village in search of work and had contracted to patch the roof of their hut, which had been leaking for a long time. With this promise the grandmother let him in the house. Already by the end of the summer, the villagers suspected something—the grandmother had no money at all and could settle the account with the carpenter perhaps only with her granddaughter's body. The director's daughter-in-law called on them in the hut before the beginning of the school year. Marusya was sitting sideways on the edge of her bed. The grandmother and Ivan denied everything. To avoid troubles, the director decided to dismiss the retarded pupil, handing her a certificate of graduation from the eight-year school. This way he washed his hands. Nevertheless, as the chairman of the Party Committee of the state collective farm, he sent the local police inspector to their hut. The police inspector also didn't want trouble. The matter was hushed. The inspector threatened Ivan with criminal prosecution and the latter got the hell out of the village, back to the Carpathian Mountains from where he had come, without even starting work on fixing the roof. But before his departure he wrote a partly official letter and brought it to the director on his own. In it he was bringing to the director's notice that, despite the great difference in age, he had fallen in love with the student Marusya Bohuslavsky, who was recently dismissed from the school, and firmly intended to contract matrimony with her upon her coming of age. Till that time and for her benefit, he was leaving her, reserving the right for himself to visit the orphan from time to time. And because he wished his chosen one to be at the peak of a modern high-school education, he asked the school administration, and even insisted, that it provide his future wife the possibility of finishing the ten-year school. The date and signature were at the bottom: "The Prince Shchek." Kiy, Khoriv, Shchek, and their sister Lebed! The carpenter turned out to be not just shell-shocked—as he was saying in a mine pit-face—but shell-shocked, so to speak, completely with his bell rung. Whatever happened, it's not known to what understanding the director and Ivan had come and what assurances Ivan gave him, but he kept his word and didn't show up in the village during the entire first quarter. Before the beginning of classes, Marusya's grandmother cried and wailed a little at the teachers' lounge and then at the director's office, and Marusya was allowed to return to her school desk. That was how she ended up in the ninth grade.

Yuriev's head was spinning from what he found out: underage Marusya and the carpenter who came from afar, down from the mountains to marry her; the imbecile and the "prince"; he definitely wanted to see them and, if he got lucky, photograph this strange couple.

That was, it means, the source of Marusya's writing, that was the state of mind in which she had come into contact with the Russian classics, listening to the retelling of their plots and the reading of separate fragments and chapters! Everything had become confused and tangled up in her poor elongated head. The awakening woman in her agitated her entire nature, awakened her mind out of its sleep, breached the curtain of darkness and apathy in which since childhood her consciousness had been submerged. She tried to fit literary heroes, their emotional experiences, to herself, spiritually selecting only what suited her and could go into the furnace of her troubled feelings. Externally she remained completely unperturbed, her eyes didn't become darker in the least, didn't become filled with animation, or shine, or moisture even of an animal quality; on the contrary her eyes shyly looked downward. Sometimes Yuriev thought he saw a flitting shadow of that smile which doesn't look like anything else and with which women smile to their secret thoughts.

Marusya's next composition simply floored him. With the confident hand of a master, she recast the plot of *Fathers and Sons*. Its main female character became Fenechka, who was close to her socially. It was a story of her tragic love for Bazarov, which was concealed by the Russian writer. To hell with Pavel Petrovich Kirsanov, Odintsova, the nihilists! The history of the love of a maid for her master, perhaps, for a duke, or in any case for a prince, that was what the novel was all about, which she "read into" Turgenev. With complete assurance it could be called *Fenechka:*

A Composition
Bazarov is a person with a clever opinion. Fenechka fell in love with him very much. When she declared her love to him he was very

happy for her. Fenechka is a young woman who fell in love with Bazarov. When he kissed her on her lips she was calm. She liked Bazarov very much. Fenechka came to his house. Bazarov was in the house. She rejoiced very much and put her arms around his neck. She was happy that he loved her and didn't forget about her. Bazarov treated Fenechka well and she—also well. Fenechka loved him very much. Bazarov thought that she didn't love him. There was a disorder in Bazarov's house. Fenechka was very good and that was why Bazarov loved her. Bazarov's look was very calm. Bazarov thought that he will marry her. Bazarov died and she hanged herself. Bazarov was a nihilist and she was a simple woman who was calm about him and very glad. Fenechka thought to get married to him but a thing happened that she didn't marry him. Fenechka loved Bazarov very much. Bazarov gets into a trouble and forgets about her.

Yuriev gave Marusya the first B's in her life for both compositions—this one and one on *The Storm*. When he transferred the grades into the grade book, he was in turn approached by Marusya's class mistress, and then the colorless teacher of Ukrainian language and literature, who was stung by the fact that in her classes Marusya's notebook still remained virginally clean, and, finally, the director's wife, who was well informed in everything that was taking place in the school and its environment and who thought of herself as the rare combination of immense worldly experience and pedagogical talent, and consequently as one who had the right to do as she pleased. Her influence in school, and even more so in the village, had a character rather of a psychic pressure than a real power, because for her husband she long since had been like a bone in the throat. He even tried not to look in her direction, keeping up the appearance of an accentuated correctness in public—in his own way, like everything here—that is, forced to address her, his eyes wandered all over the wall behind her back. He was a Party woodpecker and she—a swelled up, unused Siren—their family duet didn't turn out. And because of that both were voluptuaries of power, martyrs, competitors, who carefully watched over their own rights and territories.

Yuriev let the director's wife's exhortations fly past his ears. The rest of the teachers chose not to interfere for the time being: well, a young, inexperienced teacher gave the imbecile a B for her unexpected diligence; it's fine, the system won't collapse from that. In Yuriev's eyes, Marusya deserved the highest grade, but for the time being he didn't want to tease the beast of public education, entering a conflict with the system over a trifle. He simply wouldn't be allowed to continue his field observations. The B was a temporary compromise on that battlefield, which was represented by Marusya, who didn't even suspect a thing.

Meanwhile Yuriev started to carry a bulky camera with a mirror on a spring, which fell down when released with such a knock that it sounded like the blade of a guillotine. He started to use the camera during breaks and after classes to take pictures of everything, since he didn't doubt for a minute that the setting of an unfolding plot played a very important role.

That area seemed to him to be forsaken by God, too, pushed out of the way, punished, put in a corner to such an extent that he couldn't understand how its inhabitants couldn't help but put their trust into the coming of the Messiah any day now, couldn't help but wait for the coming of at least His angels in their dreams, who would bend over them and whisper in their ears: "We all well know, you must endure a little longer, we are on your side, everything will be all right . . . ," or if not for them then, if worst comes to worst, for a Redeemer from such a life sent by the heavens. Such thoughts to Yuriev could seem ridiculous twenty years later if an ever-present sincerity of feelings had failed to show in them, as they did then. Not very long before the beginning of the last world war, the last case of stigmatization, which also determined the western border of the war's spreading, was noticed somewhere here in one of the nearest districts, near Sadovaya Vishnya. The wounds of Christ opened like rosebuds on the maiden Nastya Voloshin's palms, her feet, and under her heart. Later, at the time of the waning of the Soviet empire, the sensational "Grushevo miracle" took place in another remote, backwoods district—a case of a mass vision of the Mother of God, which was unanimously disproved by the Party press; and the village itself was cordoned off by the police. Somewhere during the interval between those two local sensations, closer to the second one, the story of the imbecile schoolgirl Marusya and the Carpathian carpenter found its place. None of its witnesses, except, perhaps, Yuriev, perceived it providentially.

In the school yard he photographed Marusya with her eyes cast down and a heavy schoolbag in her hand, leaning against the trunk of a leafless tree waiting for the bridegroom who would come for her and take her home. He photographed the cheerless milk processing plant, which pretended to be a school, using coarse-grained black-and-white film. He photographed the drunkard, thievish school cook with a ladle in his hand and wearing a dirty white hat. He made a collection of photo portraits of affable, kind-hearted Down's syndrome kids and of ever-cheerful F students, those empty-headed children of nature whose mood could be spoiled neither by bad grades nor by bad weather. Yuriev photographed the melancholy and naked landscapes around the village; the deserted segment of the highway leading to the beltway; broken, smashed school desks piled up in a heap in the corner of the school yard; a three-legged cupboard in someone's garden among yellow, unharvested pumpkins; himself wearing a tie sticking out with his elbows to the side from a square hatch on the slope of the school roof, for some reason ogling the sky from there. He would photograph the monstrous, hairy, coffee-cup-saucer-sized nipples of the TV hostess if someone didn't get in the way. His memory stumbled at this unphotographed shot, started to slip, and continued to turn over pages of memory without any connection, as though obeying its own hypnotic will and choice.

Like when the explosion thundered in the school building and everyone poured out of the building and crowded in the yard, then a heavy, caustic smell of chemistry, death, and broken glass enveloped both the schoolchildren and teachers. A young lab assistant had tried to dilute sulfuric acid to the necessary concentration in a huge jar but made a mistake, forgetting what should be poured into what. The explosion knocked out the window. Someone passing by the school along the road at that time managed to notice how tongues of flame were licking the window frame and were immediately stifled by white clouds of steam belching out of the window. When an ambulance arrived in approximately an hour, the lab assistant was led by the arms onto the school porch with his head wrapped with a wet, wafflelike towel, his hands eaten by deep sores and one of them missing several fingers. The most desirable marriage prospect in the village was in a state of shock. Chroniclers who

THE DEATH OF THE FORESTER

179
▼

described the connection of events and the arrival of any changes by the "sudden" principle knew their business and understood the nature of living phenomena. In a similar way, Yuriev suddenly and all at once remembered the gloomy little man he had forgotten, barely visible from behind the lectern, who looked forever to be in dismay from his own subject, and who for some reason for the entire semester was teaching a course on safety precautions at the philology department, like a flipped-out Sheherazade with a thousand stories in the style of socialist realist dark humor.

The Christmas manger floated across this row of reminiscences, which he saw by chance from the window of an intercity bus. A stretched-out little group of costumed people was crossing an endless plowed field, dusted with snow, twisting their ankles in the earth frozen into lumps. Death in a white shroud with a scythe in its hand, the Devil with blackened face wearing a black sheepskin coat turned inside out, two angel-girls with gauze wings, King Herod with a crown made out of green foil paper and his armor-clad warriors with thick wooden swords wrapped with silvery foil, Joseph, Mary, and the Magi, behind them a Jew with long side curls, and, finally, a headman with a Christmas star on a pole resembling a starfish and also wrapped with colored foil paper. The Communists fought the mangers mercilessly. The village Party organization tracked down the mangers in huts, trying to render them harmless while they were still being set up—the Party activists burst into huts, broke the props, threatened parents and other adults with arrest. The school principal personally participated in those punitive operations and demanded the same of his subordinates. At the teachers' conferences he related in the style of Icelandic sagas about victories achieved with his participation over shameful obscurantism, especially intolerable in a country where obligatory secondary education had recently been introduced. Then he sat down to scribble reports to the district committee. Little embryos of Judas, informers always were at the disposal of that mighty enemy of primordial Disor-r-rder. It was a strange game played with a very serious appearance. The principal organized teachers' cordons, night posts, and ambushes by the entrance to the church on Christmas and Easter, thereby turning teachers who lived in the village into outcasts and derelicts, interlopers who were living affronts to village life. More than once the principal paid recompense to children carolers from his own pocket so that they would go home and not come to sing. He truly was a strange and, probably, unhappy person. The Party needed him the way he was, and he liked being that way.

The rest of the time there were clouds of dust whipped by trucks to the heavens, or dirt, and puddles ankle-deep or deeper. The process of walking itself took a lot of effort and attention—especially if one tried to do without rubber boots, which were called *gumaki,* from *guma* (rubber), there. Other people were knocking on the door of his memory, and he let two of them in. One was a teacher of the elementary grades. A huge cardboard case with a year's supply of feminine hygiene packets stood in the middle of her room in the unfinished multiapartment teachers' house. The rest of the furniture consisted of a bed and a table with two stools in the kitchen. The teacher interested Yuriev with her advice to spank his pupils; she herself did it and advised others to do the same. Once every quarter she arranged a common flogging in the fifth grade, the class mistress of which she was, and she flogged one and all, the A students along with arrant F students. She assured him that such an undertaking for a period of time raised diligence during studies and, consequently, grades. Parents accepted this pedagogical method with understanding. The teacher had a protector in the district office of public education and one joke which wasn't really funny because it was repeated so often. After the second shot glass she was already disposed to recite it, and with the words "And then Danko tore his heart out of his chest! . . ." She pulled her left breast out of her décolleté and after a pause hid it back with a vulgar laugh—as if saying, It's mine, don't ogle it. She understood things with difficulty, all her reactions were late, and because of that, in communicating with the children, she easily became irritated—they operated at different speeds. But in class, they, we might guess, were worthy of each other. There were times when it seemed to Yuriev that even the blood in this young female was not in a liquid but in a solid state, congealed as in blood sausage. But with all that, she was quite good-hearted. It just happened that her personal, intimate space practically didn't exceed the surface of her skin. Therefore, when she wanted to guarantee that her message would reach an addressee, she was in the habit of lowering her voice and almost pushing her words

into her interlocutor's ear with her tongue. If the interlocutor happened to be of the opposite sex or simply ticklish, all kinds of misunderstanding took place. She herself wasn't ticklish at all. On the
surface at least. Yuriev didn't rule out a possibility that during sex
she was quite capable of humming something or making wreaths
behind her lover's back or cleaning her fingernails, not even thinking that it could traumatize her partner. But it was only a bold
assumption on Yuriev's part, the truthfulness of which he didn't
intend to check.

The second person was a lame old man with his story about the
release from a German concentration camp. The story was totally
absurd. That was why Yuriev didn't doubt its genuineness in the
least.—I told them I can't fight. I tried twice and each time, in exactly a week, ended up captured. And the third time I told them it
would be the same, the school janitor told Yuriev, putting his broom
aside, stretching his lame leg and treating himself to a cigarette from
Yuriev's pack. Yuriev didn't have a class, and they settled down for a
smoke on a pile of broken desks in a corner of the school yard. The
old man wore a blue lab robe. In all schools, cleaning was usually the
women's job, it was the women's position. What old people needed—was to be heard out? He unhurriedly plaited his story. In the
beginning of the summer of 1944, a far-sighted SS officer, after he
found out that one of his prisoners had relatives on the other side of
the ocean, began to persuade him to flee there together with him
after the war. He would help the prisoner survive and for that, the
prisoner would deliver him to the New World. The SS man assured
him that separately they had no chance. The prisoner thought it over
and agreed. He wrote a letter to his relatives in Canada to the SS
man's dictation, and the SS man sent it over. However, after he had
brought himself to the thought of wandering and foggy indetermi-
nacy, the prisoner became melancholic. He hadn't seen his native
home for three years and now he would perhaps never see it. He
made it a condition that he wanted to see his family before leaving.
No matter how hard the SS man tried to talk him out of it, he stood
his ground. The SS man had no choice. Having taken the prisoner's
firmest oath that he would return to the camp in two weeks, the SS
man somehow arranged documents for him, gave him a travel
authorization and money for the trip. He only pleaded with him not

to delay his return because the eastern front was cracking at the seams and was inevitably approaching the prisoner's native home. After he had seen all his relatives, put on a little weight, and breathed in a lungful of the unhealthy Transcarpathian air, the prisoner could not return to the concentration camp. All the oaths he had given disappeared from his head. He crawled into a cellar and crawled out of it only after a cannonade had rolled, like a storm, over his head. He exceeded the two-week leave by just a few days although it didn't matter any longer at all. As soon as he climbed from the cellar to the surface, he landed in the hands of Russian recruiters. These were the ones to whom he pleaded—I cannot, he was saying, be a soldier, even if you cut me into pieces!

"What do you mean, you can't?"

"I can't 'cause I'll end up a prisoner in less than a week—that's my fate. That's how it was in September 1939 when I was drafted into the Polish Army, that was the same in June 1941 when I was drafted into the Red Army, and now there will be no good from me, I swear by the name of our Heavenly Father, I'll be captured again! And every time I'm not alone, I end up a captive with my entire unit every time. It doesn't work for me to fight longer than a week, it's not my destiny, as God is my witness!"

When they finished laughing, the recruiters said: "Since it won't work for you to fight, maybe can you get us some home-brewed vodka? Then get it! You'll tell us everything in order one more time."

Thanks to relatives for their help, he brought in so much moonshine that he had to drink it for three days with the recruiters himself. Before they left they told him: "Listen here, guy. You lie pretty good, but now crawl back into the cellar and stay there quiet as a mouse. Because the front is moving forward, and following it, the SMERSH men will come, and those guys don't like fooling around. So you'd better not get caught by their eyes. Stay in the cellar until it's all over."

So he stayed there till victory day itself, and it seemed that everything had worked out fine. But then, not too long ago, his fellow countrymen, from among those who had been in the same concentration camp with him during the war, began to visit the village. It turned out that the camp ended in the American occupation zone. That was why after the war they found themselves some in Australia, some in Canada, and some in the United States. It turned out that of all of them, only he had returned to his homeland and did that thanks to the SS man. Everyone who visits here started a family back there, got their own houses, became well to do. They asked him: "And how are you?"

"'How, how?' My salary is seventy rubles, but I told them a hundred. They asked: 'A week?' I answered, a week. They shook their head—yeah, they said, kind of small. But it's all right, you can manage on it; you, they said, come visit us.

"But when they began to drink, going from one table to another, from one hut to another, in a couple of days they said: 'You get so little but put out such incredible spreads everywhere that our income would all go up in smoke if we treated our guests this way. We can treat ourselves to something like maybe once a year, and the way you do it—no money would be enough!'

"And they left on that note. And I work as a janitor in the school and as a night watchman. If I only knew beforehand I might've given it a thought then, but now nothing can be done! . . . That's the kind of vacation I happened to have."

"And what's wrong with the leg, is it from the war?" Yuriev inquired.

"What do you mean, from the war! Two years ago I climbed to replace a *bulb* in a classroom and fell down from a table, breaking my leg. I've become old, my head was spinning, my bones have become fragile—since then I've been gimping."

The overwhelming majority of the Galician stories caused in Yuriev an acute attack of an immediate hankering for a drink. But this one turned out to be amusing in its own way. The bell rang. The children ran out into the yard. It was time to get ready for class.

The memory of the bell even now seemingly brought his consciousness out of its drifting state, liberating it from the power of uncontrolled recollections. Other characters were still agitated, noisy, grumbling, and demanding to be admitted, as though they were in front of the door to an office which had closed for a lunch break, understanding that no one would let them in and that this time they had nothing else to do but be resigned to it.

They were both the spectators and the chorus, mute from birth, of that drama which, if it were moved to a slope of a mountain, could sprout the grain of a new Carpathian myth, if not for . . . if not. But better that we do things in order.

By the end of the long and unusually warm autumn of that year, Marusya's fiancé suddenly appeared in the village. He came every day to pick her up from school after the end of classes. Yuriev finally managed to ambush them and photograph them together. The self-styled prince was dressed in a black suit, wide-in-the-back slacks sharply narrowed at the ankles and folded up against patent-leather shoes of an exaggerated size. The strap of a turned-on shortwave radio was flung over his shoulder in the manner of a sword belt. You couldn't say that he gave the impression of an unhealthy man. Somewhat excessive gesticulation and jerky body movements could quite reasonably result from the general steadfast attention which he undoubtedly felt and which was fixed on him and Marusya. He was thickset and looked from afar like an inverted black pyramid. Marusya was stretched vertically—her hands shivering in the wind were sticking out from the short sleeves of her overcoat, under her school uniform she wore simple sweat pants stretched over the knees and tucked into high *gumaki*. She carried her schoolbag herself. They were moving off together down a village street, walking along the edge of a ditch that stretched along fences, without looking back in order not to meet the dozens of curious children's eyes that were following them.

The teachers' lounge became agitated once again. The math teacher–vice-principal with the rabbit lip was sent on a mission, and in the evening he visited Marusya's hut. Ivan was squatting on the table in nothing but his underwear and talking to his guest from that position without any intent to get off the table or to put anything on. He explained his position on the table by the urgency of his business and declared that he himself intended to improve Marusya's knowledge of math and some other subjects. He moved his finger through a notebook laid out on the table, muttered something under his breath, and drew something on the margins of the newspaper page with the stub of a pencil—it was a column of calculations. The grandmother looked at him from the woodstove. Marusya was sitting on the edge of the only bed. Without stepping over the threshold, the vice-principal reminded Ivan about the condition on which Marusya was accepted back to school, then she shamed the grandmother, shaking her head disapprovingly, and quickly left the hut with the earthen floor and a single dim bulb hanging down from the ceiling, under which Ivan was nesting on the table like a spider that had climbed down from the ceiling along the twisted electric cord.

In the morning Ivan left the village, but people said that a few days later he reappeared again. He no longer picked up Marusya after school. People said that supposedly someone had seen him at a bus station—once in the neighboring large village, another time in the city. Marusya was just about to turn sixteen. And everything, perhaps, would work out if you just looked at it from the point of view of a criminal case of sexual relations with the underage.

Thunder thundered in February. After the unusually severe January cold and snowstorms, of which no one could remember comparable ones. Snow was blowing for days. The beltway was covered with ice crust and potholes and became impassable. Abandoned vehicles were lying at the sides of the road like roadkill. The rear axles of trucks were sticking out of the snowdrifts, several potbellied, iced-over intercity buses were lying on their side. The local inhabitants developed a taste for marauding. Dogs came running to gnaw at their stiff brothers frozen in the ice. When the disaster was finally over, the February usual for those parts settled in, already fraught with the March thaw. The snow condensed, changed into a granular state, but the fields were as before, weighed down with its rumpled down blankets under the many-kilometers-long blanket covers. When Yuriev was a student, he was amazed at people sleeping here on the hard plank beds with high sides—often favored by mice—covering themselves with down blankets. You could bring your girlfriend and tumble with her in bed till morning—nobody cared about it—but if in the morning they found out that you were lying on the down blanket instead of covering yourselves with it, your hosts would sternly warn you the first time, and if you attempted to repeat it, they would point you to the door. It's one of those rules not a subject for discussion around here. One February morning when he hitchhiked his way to school, as soon as he entered the teachers' lounge, Yuriev immediately felt that everyone present was wound up. Each did something with an absent air about them—rummaged through the contents of their briefcases or moved things from one place to another on the table, but to the last person they all intently listened to the content of the director's telephone conversation—he was the only one speaking. The former TV host walked up to Yuriev with a sure step and announced in a stage whisper, pointing with her eyes to the rest: "Ivan kidnapped your Marusya!"

Yuriev in principle expected something like that—just as the entire school and the whole village did. Sitting at a table by the window, the director was talking on the phone with the chief of the district police, seemingly saying by this that he had been the first to sound the alarm and had turned to the authorities for help. Yuriev missed neither the subservient notes in the director's intonation nor the coarse flattery to which he resorted: "You have a voice like, God rest his soul, the late Paul Robeson used to have! Which I could have listened to forever! Yes, the black man's bass, yes . . ."

Nobody laughed. Only the TV hostess expressed shortness of breath and hurried to hide her face in the lid of her briefcase on the table.

As it was found out that day from conversations during breaks, Ivan, who had come in the evening the day before yesterday, had promised Marusya's grandmother to take her granddaughter, who had been complaining about pain, to a clinic in the neighboring large village. But people had seen them yesterday getting on a bus going in the opposite direction. Someone suggested that Ivan could take Marusya to the county clinic. But by evening of the same day, neither Marusya nor Ivan had returned to the village. In the morning, right at dawn, Marusya's grandmother was already at school, where, after she had waited for the director and had heard out the director's reprimands and reproaches, readily nodding her head and saying yes, yes, asked for only one thing—to help her have her granddaughter returned. In the morning Yuriev had almost not noticed the hunched old woman in rubber boots a head kerchief wrapped over her padded jacket, perching at the chair by the director's elbow and ingratiatingly and not without alarm listening to the conversation of her defender, who had invisible heavenly powers. The ringing school bell swept the teachers' lounge clean, leaving only the director and the old woman alone with the stern and not-too-polite incognito on the other end of the telephone cord.

The following two days passed in uncertainty. Yuriev's friends, meeting him or talking to him on the phone in the evening, asked him about the fate of the schoolgirl, whom none of them had seen—some with idle curiosity, some with compassion for the drama of rural life and morals, some with a stupid literary delight—demanding either from the life given to them for reading, or from Yuriev, further twists of the plot. At that they allowed that the very existence of Marusya, as well as the texts of her compositions, could be a mystification, a fruit of philological leisure and a game. But by the end of the week, filled with dramatic expectation, the doubters and unbelievers got their hands on a document of such power that their skepticism was at once dispelled and their arrogance disappeared in compassionate attention to the retarded village girl. Everyone, including Yuriev, understood that they had gone too far.

That was the explanatory note of Marusya Bohuslavsky, who was found in the Carpathian Mountains and through the efforts of the police returned to her native village and school—Marusya's report of her kidnapping written under the pressure of the school's principal. In that new composition, one could see and guess the slivers and fragments of the director's crushed logic and demagogy and of the brainwashing he arranged for Marusya. The dark waters of Marusya's mind closed above them and pulled them in deeper than the bottom of her depression.

Yuriev had to admit that the director in collusion with base reality managed to get more out of Marusya's pen than he in union with classical examples of Russian realist literature. Unfortunately, the text of Marusya's "Note" is practically untranslatable, especially into kindred languages, and only the approximate and pale line translation executed by Yuriev can give Russian readers some idea about its contents.

Explanatory Note

I went to the Carpathian Mountains I slept at a train station I thought that he will take me to Borshchovichi to the hospital and he brought me to Slavsk. I was sick. I went to get a radio in the Carpathian Mountains. I now don't want him because he was beating me and Ivan says that he didn't beat me now doesn't say the truth he was beating me for that I didn't want to wash myself and I had already washed he didn't have a right to beat me. I was afraid to sleep with him. Ivan didn't want to come to school because he said that he'll come when I finish school. Ivan taunts me. He writes Love on a newspaper in my hut. Ivan said that there is dampness in our hut and this is bad for my sickness. Ivan brought cognac for the holidays and told me to drink it. I didn't want to drink but he said drink. I won't forgive him that. Let him not pull wool over my eyes. He says that I have to finish ten grades. You he says must finish ten grades. Ivan says that if I won't want him he will grind me to dust. I wouldn't want that. And I don't want that. It is very difficult for me to study there is nobody home to help me. Grandma thought he will fix our hut. He beats me beforehand and what will be later. Ivan tells me not to drink medicine says it's poison. What am I to do? How can you help me. Grandma fought with him a little but he didn't want to hear. Let him not to beat me and not to take to the Carpathian Mountains. Ivan said the other time let's go to the Carpathian Mountains for the radio batteries and I didn't want to listen. Let him leave me alone or he'll get it bad. He said that he is not afraid of anyone. I won't drink cognac anymore I didn't know that it probably harmed me or how it could for sure be different. He doesn't love me and says that he loves. He doesn't want to do anything just to listen to the radio all day. Doesn't want to dig the garden doesn't want to plant potatoes. I'd Ivan says heal you take you to the Carpathian Mountains the climate is different there. Ivan will probably come again because he left his radio with us so that I listen to it. I don't want Ivan. I loved him before and now don't love. Ivan goes to Lviv to eat at a cafeteria every day. Ivan is very irritable. Ivan hit me in the face with his hand I flew all the way to the stove. Grandma says I didn't see. What do I need him for. I don't need him. Ivan said that he must marry me. If Ivan beats and will beat then it's no point to marry him.

Strictly speaking this exhaustive dispassionate statement completed the short period of Marusya's literary development, which turned out to be as impetuous as a spark flying off the striking side of a matchbox. From that time on, no one else's, and concurrently her own, texts interested her any longer. With her explanatory note she completed what the *thunderbird* so feared and what it warned the *seagull*. At that time the Moscow Taganrogian had hacked out and had buried with him Critical Realism. Now Marusya pulled down realism as such, driving an aspen stake into its very foundation. After that she receded completely into herself and in her former manner finished the ninth grade and was passed to the tenth.

In the summer at the end of the school year, with unexpected ease, Yuriev managed to cancel his assignment and left the job. The director let him go with unconcealed relief. For the first time they shook each other's hand. At the moment of parting, Yuriev even became sad at the thought of the director's efforts wasted in vain, of the futility of his power and the ephemerality of his business—even if he had a half century at his disposal.

On leaving, Yuriev picked up the notebook with Marusya's compositions on Russian literature. Still before that, partially in the manner of a spy, he managed to make a copy of Marusya's explanatory note, which the director had left for a little while at the table in the teachers' lounge so they could all read it. The future life of the unemployed teacher moved in a completely different direction, shifting to the inside of the concentric circles of the city from which, as it turned out later, it was difficult to escape. The focus is successful up to the third try, as the Poles maintain. At that time he already didn't care about Marusya's notebooks, or about those acid soils and restrained spaces where time falls into catatonia and is measured by distances.

The last thing that Yuriev happened to find out about Marusya was told to him by one of his former colleagues, a teacher whom he accidentally met on the street. The new information overwhelmed him, but not for long, because it already had an immediate relation to his life and work. Marusya didn't get to the tenth grade. Just before the beginning of the school year, Ivan took Marusya, who had reached legal age, and drove her to his place in the mountains. He took her as his wife, although no one could say for sure whether they were legally registered and married or just lived together. Whatever it was there, he soon declared to Marusya that he had spent too much money while he was courting her and now it was time for her to work for the means spent on her. Ivan's hut stood at the slope of a mountain, and Ivan thought up a job for his wife. Every day she was supposed to roll up the mountain a wheelbarrow full of smooth river stones collected by the foot of the mountain, which are usually used for building house foundations. But even that Sisyphusian reckoning wasn't the crown of Ivan's inventiveness. The main thing she had to do for him was to give birth to a son, but he made a condition that he himself would deliver the baby. In this way Yuriev received the nightmarish echo of the Sub-Carpathian quasi–Holy Virgin myth, which he constructed himself: the retarded woman day after day rolling the wheelbarrow of river stone up the mountain (what structure—could it be a fortress that Ivan thought to build on his mountain?), and her maniac husband who intended to lie in wait—to be on guard and find out the mystery of human birth at the gates of life itself, having slammed the door of his hut before the entire world. It could end with anything you want. Finding out the mystery of life, Ivan could immediately move to examining the mystery of death. Marusya with her future child were left to their own devices, to their fate, to the location of the stars above their heads and the tides of the full moon that split her head. It was pointless to appeal to the human chorus left far behind on the plain, to the law of Caesar and to the still colder and deceptive light of endlessly distant stars. It turned out that no one owed anything to anyone. The teachers, in answer to Yuriev's misgivings, immediately ended the conversation and disappeared in the street crowd.

Now, twenty years later, it turned out that Yuriev, not knowing it himself, rushed to a rendezvous with the epilogue of that forgotten story pushed to the back of his consciousness. From here, from the mountains, from the groom's side—or more precisely, from the point of view of the fellow villagers who knew him—the matter looked as follows:

Shchek had brought a young wife from somewhere and settled with her in his hut on the mountain. They were rarely seen in the village. On those rare occasions when they came down together to do some shopping, it was said that Ivan always led her by the hand. Only Ivan entered conversations with fellow villagers. Nothing definite could be said about his family life, even less was known about any of his particular intentions. A woman pushing a wheelbarrow with stones up the mountain is a normal thing here. People knew something about everything, and only in Marusya's distant school did they say they were horrified—she managed to send a short letter to her grandmother, for whom the last light of day had darkened after her granddaughter's departure. As he promised, Ivan handled his wife's labor himself. Later it was found out that Ivan had kept a separate school notebook in which he described for posterity the essential scheme of the female organism's system, accompanied by his own elucidating drawings, for which he used his wife as a visual aid. Here people found out about the birth of Ivan's child only by the swaddling clothes that were suddenly hung on the mountain like flags, and then from Ivan himself during his regular morning trips to the village for milk. One should think that Marusya's youthful and underdeveloped body could not produce breast milk in the required quantity, if she had it at all. But Ivan's trip didn't last for long. The swaddling clothes on the mountain disappeared as suddenly as they had appeared. While people in the village figured out what was what and had come to the hut with the police, it was too late to establish anything for sure. Ivan explained that the baby bothered him with his yelling and didn't let him sleep, and then it died all of a sudden without any reason at all. He showed the place under a spreading pear tree near the hut where he buried the baby. The police and witnesses suspected that the infant could not leave this world without the assistance of its parent, but it was too bothersome for the police to begin the investigation and order the forensic examination, not to mention that such a case could seriously damage the criminal statistics in the district, even if they succeeded in solving and proving the fact of the infanticide. As a result, someone could lose his post, if not in the police then in the local administration. And because Ivan wasn't confused and firmly stood his ground in his testimony, and it was impossible to get any testimony out of his silent wife, who had sunk into torpor—a flowerpot could've said more—and there weren't any eyewitnesses at all, they didn't open a criminal case. They wrote a report, warned Ivan just in case, and left the hut on the mountain. As soon as they were left in peace, Marusya left Ivan a few days later and returned forever to her native village. Nobody knew if Ivan tried to get her back—in any case from time to time he disappeared somewhere.

After his wife left him, he noticeably aged in his appearance, but his body remained strong as before. Once collecting grass on the

CARPATHIAN NARRATIVES

192
▼

neighboring mountains, Yuriev's uncle met him sunbathing at a forest clearing. Ivan was stark naked but wasn't in the least ashamed of that and easily conversed with the uncle on a quite neutral theme. The uncle was struck at that time by his athletic build.

Soon Ivan dug a pond on the mountain next to his hut and put fish in it. He lined the sides of the pond with the stones which Marusya had brought up the mountain in the beginning of their life together and which had been stacked into small pyramids in his yard. Ivan needed the fish pond for his cats, not less than half a dozen of which, without counting their kittens, he now had. In the winter, the fish that didn't have time to grow to maturity in the summer ended up freezing in the pond, and then he had to go down to the village just as he used to every few days to get milk for his cats.

Once arguing with a guest who just happened to drop in, Ivan stabbed him with a knife—or rather with a filed fragment of a fencing foil, found later in the hut during the search and arrest. This time Ivan was brought to the district police office and later placed in a district psychiatric clinic, but they didn't hold him there for long. A few months later he returned to his empty hut, to his cats, who had become totally emaciated during his absence. After that incident, no takers to visit him and especially to argue with him could be found.

When he came down to the village, Ivan willingly struck up a conversation with his fellow villagers, but he always conducted the arising arguments along a tangent in relation to the theme, so that with a few tricks he confused and befogged the unsophisticated village polemicists, making fun of them in front of the listeners. That contributed to the distant feeling for him in the village, which was kept behind his back.

Those were the strange and quickly forgotten times of the all-inclusive debates, when, it seemed, nature itself began to stir and climb from under the roots of its plants, exhibiting the creature that just had learned to speak yesterday, still with its sides covered, with clods of earth stuck to it and mouths full of stones, persistently demanding participation in the historical life of the people with their lips. There is a point of view that the Carpathian Mountains are young. Perhaps one had to relate to everything that was going on here that way—as though to a geological process.

THE DEATH OF THE FORESTER

After the defeat in the tempestuous presidential election campaign, which, by the way, didn't venture beyond the limits of a small segment of the railroad and the godforsaken spot in the mountains, Ivan Shchek suddenly faded away, realizing that he wasn't fated to possess the throne of Ukraine and its capital city, which had been pounded, it was quite possible, judging by his last name, by some of his glorious ancestors.

He could be now seen every Sunday at the porch of the village church—because among other things they stopped paying his pension. The village women once a week took pity on him and gave him as much as one could, most often food, because in some part of their souls they were nevertheless turned toward their God, regardless of the hardships of life on this barren and unexpectedly festive land, bristling with an ancient disagreement, fertilized by bodies, sown with the bones of their relatives, and redeemed by their compassion.

■   ❏   ■

In the morning, after hearing the early noise in the kitchen, Yuriev and his wife got up in order to say good-bye to their hosts, who were hurrying to work. They themselves were going to leave on the noon train. The uncle's wife led them to the kitchen and pointed to the reciprocal gifts that were standing on the table, which they had neither strength nor the possibility to refuse. Judge for yourself: canned boletus mushrooms with oily reddish spots on the caps submerged in brine and magnified by the jar's glass; jams made of aromatic forest berries; gristly stewed meat drowned in congealed, snow-white lard; and a big plastic bag with a collection of dozens of Carpathian grasses and inflorescences, each of which the uncle picked at its peak. Yuriev, who was making excuses for not taking the gifts, was forcefully pushing his head into the opened bag like a toximaniac and immediately lost his breath from that concentrate of the summer, from the dried meadow crammed into the transparent bag—he was slightly embarrassed and disarmed by this gesture of slightly coarse kindred generosity, which allowed you to give something as a gift for which it was difficult to find a precise name.

The door was slammed loudly and the uncle appeared at the threshold of the entry with a zinc-coated pail in his hand. Wearing a scarf thrown on top of his jacket, his son stood behind him breathing steam from behind his father's shoulders—both invigorated with the injection of the morning frost. They had gone out to the yard to take care of the piglet in the little brick barn, which they had built themselves. That was it, the pig—the support and nearly a member of the uncle's family—that had made noise when Yuriev and his wife were returning from their walk last night. The farewell to the kinfolk went in a speeded-up and somewhat bravura tempo, leaving in his soul a vague, warm, and at the same time guilty feeling, which brought to mind overfermented yeast that had fizzled out. In any case for some reason Yuriev had the sensation of just such an aftertaste.

Having quickly washed themselves, breakfasted, and categorically refused a drink, Yuriev and his wife moved to the living room, where the uncle had invited them. There already were several stacks of photographs laid out on the table with pictures face down, identical as decks of cards. Tourist guides and other typographic productions lay there separately. The uncle walked around the room. He now wore a vest trimmed with fur and white felt boots. He touched the radiator with his hand, it was barely fifteen degrees in the room. Having put on his glasses, he took the reading from the thermometer behind the window and recorded it on a sheet of graph paper fixed on the wall. Yuriev asked him why. Instead of an answer, the uncle extracted several school notebooks filled with yearly notations out of the drawer of a sideboard. For many years now he had been keeping a weather diary in which he recorded the daily temperature data, sometimes accompanying them with brief comments, for example, when it snowed or there was hail or whether it rained and how hard. By this diary it was easy to count the number of pleasant days in a given month or to compare the weather of one year to that of another. But the most important thing was that the synoptic method allowed the retired forester to distinguish days, to grope for their weak pulse, to discover at least a meteorological meaning in their change. The uncle couldn't add anything to the fact that this occupation was interesting to him. Judging by everything, it was a natural physiophilosophy of despair that he had created for his own needs—a practice of tracking

THE DEATH OF THE FORESTER

down the symptoms of that illness which people call time, which somehow helped him to handle the flow of life during the last fifteen years.

The diaries were followed by a series of photographs. Those were heaps of badly focused prints, eaten by chemicals (and coated with the veil of time), made from negatives taken during his tour of the victorious socialist island country. In this way the tropical hunks and beauties, stepping down from the path of multiplication and competition, lose their stripes and bright colors, calming down in the heaving grayness of the alternating high and low tides. The same happens to people whose irises grow dim as their weariness of life increases. But the uncle, looking at the prints, still saw everything that had been photographed in living color! It was Yuriev who turned out to be colorblind by necessity, to which the picture testified objectively.

The conversation didn't get on. At first Yuriev turned on the tape recorder, then turned it off and didn't turn it on again. Already sitting in the train, Yuriev understood that the uncle badly needed his help, the help he had failed to provide for him. And what would it be possible to do? His uncle wanted not to tell something he knew, but rather to find out himself what it was precisely that he knew— what was that heap of impressions he experienced and accumulated and acquired in the course of his long life? Could it be that they had as little meaning as that pile of the amateur black-and-white nine-by-twelve photos summoned to testify to the fact of a tourist trip to the Island of Freedom in the one thousand nine hundred something Soviet year? He desired and strove by all means to avoid one and the same thing—he passionately wanted to receive an explanation and absolution for his sins without judgment and evaluation, while still in the human world. Was it possible to help him solve his insoluble solitaire? Probably no more possible than to help a tree move from the spot where it had grown.

The older brother of his mother sat before Yuriev, the burning knowledge of firearm wounds was buried in his body, the close acquaintance with hunger that makes you insane when the sphincter doesn't hold up any longer and when a touch leaves boggy white indentations that don't intend to straighten out—as if time has stopped for the body. Inside himself, this person still remembered how he, fastened with a belt, dangled on the armor of a tank, trying to sleep and forget himself, fearing death under the tank's caterpillars, during the last marching attack on Vienna when the tanks were ordered not to stop. That was like shell fragments imbedded in his body, like facts deprived of the means of their transmission which the conscious mind tries to hide the way a tree hides the traces of bad weather in its yearly rings. In 1933 their family survived thanks to a cow. Still, in the spring of 1932 their father knew from somewhere that there would be famine next year. Every day he brought waste oil cake from the creamery, as much as he could carry. After the backbreaking work of softening it, the cake was suitable cattle feed. The entire family, obeying the father's iron will, worked on processing the cake for the entire summer—the smallest defect could damage the cow's digestion, and then you could say good-bye to the milk and with it to the life of the family. The entire terrible winter of 1933 the father slept in the cow barn. He stretched ropes with tin cans, bottles, broken tin pails, and other noisemakers, hanging them across the yard. Hearing the noise they made, the entire family was supposed to jump out into the yard with loud yells, armed with whatever they could find, and make an unbearable din. This way all ten children, brothers and sisters, survived on the milk, the youngest of them, Yuriev's mother, turned five that winter—precisely when the first bodies of peasants who had come to the town to die from the nearby villages with their wives and children began to litter the streets.

The intuition of death is never as deaf in a person as it is at forty.

Yuriev was still preoccupied with the question "From where?" His uncle—already only with "Where to?"

His uncle's childishly inconsolable face in the bathroom doorway, washed with tears, which, being ashamed of them, he unsuccessfully tried to hide just before he left home, flickered in the train window before Yuriev's eyes. Only separated from them by the window, already bouncing along on the way back, with his wife sleeping on his shoulder, Yuriev not so much realized as he responded bodily, feeling with his own glandules the consuming meaning of those tears.

■   ❏   ■

THE DEATH OF THE FORESTER

The uncle accompanied them to the train station along the crunching snow. The light frost bit on their cheeks. People were crowded on the platform, some traveling to the district center, some to the regional capital. There was almost no one traveling empty-handed, the majority of them were overloaded with luggage of inhuman size. A small Russian-speaking group of several persons, men and women, with packed downhill skis, stood out—someone was saying good-bye, someone was seen off, vodka was noisily poured into disposable plastic glasses. The dissolving, soaplike grayness of the day, which was pouring down from the sky like sepia, imparted everything with the unreal character of a black-and-white photograph. Yuriev was haunted by the recognizable caustic smell of photo-developing solution.

The train was late. The uncle said that was typical.

Yuriev only then noticed with surprise that the entire station was painted with someone's generous brush, as though it were a campaign center. The eyes couldn't help but notice slogans: SHCHEK FOR PRESIDENT! GODFATHER POPS SHCHEK, SHCHEK IS THE LAW, STRENGTH, ORDER!

. . . DYR, BOOL, SHYL . . . The uncle suddenly pulled Yuriev by the sleeve.

"There he stands."

"Who?"

"Shchek, who else!"

A little peasant in a winter hat with its earflaps sticking out every which way, in a quilted cotton jacket and felt boots, holding a couple of kittens in his hands, with a milk canister standing on the ground by his feet, was distinctly talking to someone on the platform a dozen of steps from them. Yuriev would have never recognized him without his uncle's prompting. Shchek talked about the fish frozen in the pond and about from whom he was getting milk for his kittens and cats. Having met his the drills of his eyes, which were looking at him over some kind of an unkempt, sectarian beard, Yuriev suddenly understood that from the moment of their appearance at the station, Shchek had been observing him and was talking to his acquaintance only for show, making an effort meanwhile to capture with the power of his will the escaping recollection, the slipping connection between the two of them. And it seemed that by

Yuriev's own look, Shchek felt that he wasn't mistaken, that they had met somewhere, and that the alien knew something about him which gave the alien some vague advantage over him. He turned his eyes a little to the side, continuing to observe the alien askance and preparing to rebuke him, whoever he might turn out to be.

Yuriev got agitated for a minute but was soon calmed down by reason, laziness, and something else, finally, by simply the unwillingness to betray his position of tracker, and assumed the pose of a participant, which smacked of the putrid smell of "investigative reporting." The postponement of his departure for, let's say, one more day would cause too many minor difficulties and extravagant inconveniences. And would the story which was approaching its completion, which had practically already ended, need distracting details and rewriting?

Their personal demons sniffed each other, their guardian angels exchanged looks behind their backs. It was time to place the period. It wasn't kept waiting. The train, consisting of a locomotive and four warped cars, showed up between the mountains like a worm cut with a spade. Having picked up their belongings, people poured onto the distant platform 3, where the Transcarpathian train was arriving. Looking back, Yuriev managed to catch a glimpse of the departing back of Shchek, who had come down this day from his mountain carrying kittens and a milk canister so as to rub shoulders with people at the station who still refused to recognize their president in him.

Yuriev and his uncle embraced, Yuriev's wife did the same, and they clambered together with everyone else to storm the nearest entrance to a railroad car. Doing this, Yuriev directed and pushed his wife in front of him, protecting her at the same time from the shoves into her sides and back.

■   ❏   ■

Several events or, more precisely, information about the events, are, meanwhile, missing in this story, which resembles the forked tongue of a snake, for the story to come to its natural completion. Perhaps it would be more appropriate to compare it to the split of the steel tip of a school pen scraping the paper, but such pens had long ago stopped being used, along with inkwells, pen cleaners, stiff white collars, and many other things. People are doomed to die in countries other than the ones they were born in, even if they live their entire lives in the same place.

The first piece of information is so absurd and artificial that you cannot do anything with it but take it into consideration. Cities either squeeze people out of them like remnants of bars of soap or draw them in their dreams, haunting them all over the world. The city which Yuriev was leaving was precisely one of those, imparted with a woman's character, which always sends something after you. On the eve of his departure, on its streets Yuriev bumped into the miniature gym teacher from the same school where Marusya had studied and where both of them worked—someone he had not met even once in the last two dozen years. The gym teacher turned out to be the chair of a trade cooperative which brought goods from Poland and sold them at the stadium, which had been transformed into a clothes market. Yuriev was delighted at the news that despite all the changes of the recent years, the school director had continued to hold his post. The former gym teacher was a little surprised at the interest which Yuriev expressed toward the fate of Marusya Bohuslavsky but didn't show it and, pretending that he remembered, glibly related news of her further fate. After her return to the village and her grandma's death, Marusya lived for a long time alone in the half-ruined hut. Until last year, when an inheritance from America fell on her head. She didn't build a new house, but immediately bought a big furnished house in which she lives now, alone as before, almost never coming out. Her fellow villagers see her rarely. "What crap!" Yuriev thought. "A carrot with a braid, a dungeon, a chamber . . ." Someone higher up gave the red-tape merchants from the heavenly chancellery such a dressing-down that they were forced to send an honorarium for Marusya's compositions down to the earth. It looked like the office had gotten a serious bawling out because, it might be guessed, it was they who had arranged this meeting in the street for Yuriev with the news that the reckoning, they say, with his pupil had been made and the debt, let's say, had been paid off, the atonement hadn't taken place yet, and the entire production had been carried out according to the pay sheet as an "artistic failure." Although it's possible that it could be compensation for the right to a libretto, which would expound the story of a wedding between a village schoolgirl and the descendant of ancient Russian princes, and the subsequent death of the unusual child. Americans.

Yuriev hurried to say good-bye to the gym teacher, who was careful and cautious in his expressions. Yuriev remembered his little hand and his facial expression, like that of a funeral caretaker. Yuriev had just a few hours left before departure and had a host of things to do.

He gleaned the other news about an unexpected flood in the Carpathian Mountains in the heat of the summer from the newspapers half a year later. When he finally got through to his parents on the phone, he found out from them that the central part of that town in the mountains where his uncle lived was flooded, but the water didn't rise higher than the thresholds and windows of the ground floors and didn't stand there for long. The biggest inconvenience was that the uncle and his son had to take the pig up to the apartment for a few days—thank God their apartment was on the second floor. As with everything else, it could be said that it worked out.

In Yuriev this news awakened a recollection of the forgotten flood of 1969 in those parts, the year after the troops were brought into Czechoslovakia. At that time the entire Sub-Carpathian region was flooded, and there were casualties. The city in which he lived then turned into an island. The water entered its streets and the edges of the city sank. As in a dream, the water gushed across the roadway, flowing from the flooded park into the city lake. The girls in his grade who lived on the outskirts in nine-story buildings had to be brought in by boats so they could take exams. When they were getting into the boats from the windows of the ground floors, the girls pulled up their already very short miniskirts, which were in fashion at that time, and demonstratively squealed, attracting the attention of their classmates, who stood shifting from one foot to the other on dry land, waiting to walk them to school. You could see behind the walls of the houses how the brown swelled-up stripe of the river swiftly carried past, playing with them as though with matches in the fingers, uprooted trees, logs, swollen carcasses of cows, empty barrels, and various household bric-a-brac. That was a little river flowing down from the mountains, which at another time could easily be forded in places without taking off your pants. It felt joyous and frightening at the same time. Here and there people were sitting on the roofs. Helicopters flew about. A regiment of paratroopers had been brought from near Kyiv to save people. The water stood for almost a month.

When he called his parents on another occasion at the end of the summer, Yuriev unexpectedly found out that his uncle had died. The parents planned to go to his funeral. It was a heart attack—the dead body was brought to the district hospital. It happened less than a month after the ill-fated flood. The last summer month started with the flood and ended with the death of the forester. The rising water washed out the ground, bared his root, and he fell like a heavy old tree that has nothing to hold on to.

Next night Yuriev had a dream. He dreamed of a boar with gray spots, sinewy, with a light pink snout. The boar in his dream was worried—it was alarmed by the sounds of water gushing somewhere, by the rumble of boulders in the distance, by the increasing and unexplained noise. It was alerted by the appearance of moisture under its feet, which raised the excrement from the floor and tickled its tummy. People think about themselves during floods—they save their families, more often than not forgetting to open the latch of a barn, they simply don't have time for that, and they can be understood. Then pigs, cows, goats rise like people on their hind legs, leaning with the front legs on the barn's walls in a mixture of horror and hope, resembling the pose of worshipers, waiting until, with their last bleating, mooing, and grunting, the persistently rising water takes the last hope away from them.

Yuriev continued to dream of that locked-in, sensitive, well-tended boar with a frivolously coiled tail standing on its hind legs, stretching with all its might its head and split hooves upward. And he felt in the dream how the freezing water lapped, tickling his unshaven throat, which was covered with a three-day bristle, and stroking his raised chin.

■ □ ■ □ ■

NOTES

Kallimakh's Wake

5
Pidzamche
"The City Quarter Below the Castle": a neighborhood in the city of Lviv at the base of Vysokyi Zamok (High Castle Hill).

5
Rynok Square
"Market Square."

5
the capital of Galician Rus
Galicia (Halychyna) is a region in the western part of Ukraine along the Polish border, which, at the time under consideration in the story, was under Polish rule. It includes the city of Lviv. The Rus civilization flourished in the Kyiv area from the ninth through the twelfth centuries until the Mongol invasions.

6
Caffa
Now called Theodosia.

6
Kallimakh Buonaccorsi
Filippo Buonaccorsi (1437–96), humanist, statesman, historian, and poet

who helped found the Roman Academy. Later he took the name of Greek poet Callimachus ("Kallimakh" in Russian) to indicate his desire for the restoration of the old ways. In 1468 he, along with members of the Academy, was accused of immorality, impiety, and a plot against the life of Pope Paul II. He fled to the east and later Poland, where he came under the protection of the Polish archbishop, and later became tutor to the children of Polish king Casimir IV. He was active in affairs of state, concluding a peace treaty with the Turks in 1487, and in promoting humanistic culture in Poland (Catherine B. Avery, ed., *The New Century Italian Renaissance Encyclopedia* [New York: Appleton-Century-Crofts, 1972], 183). For detailed information on Buonaccorsi see Gian Carlo Garfagnini, ed. *Callimaco Esperiente Poeta e Politico del '400* (Florence: Leo S. Olschki Editore, 1985). The name Callimachus means "noble fighting," the fact of which William R. Schmalstieg was kind enough to inform us.

11
Vysokyi Zamok
"High Castle." The highest hill overlooking the city of Lviv, atop which a castle once stood. Only minor ruins of the castle remain. The spot gives the best panoramic view of the city.

12
Ruthenians
Medieval name for Ukrainians.

13
Virmenska Street
"Armenian Street."

16
Vlokh
Old Slavic name for a Wallachian, someone from what is present-day northern Italy and Transylvania.

20
the Hapsburgian lady, Queen Elisabeth
The wife of King Casimir Jagiello.

20

Wawel Hill

Location of the Polish king's palace in Krakow.

21

Varna

The Battle of Varna occurred in 1444. The Turks under Sultan Murad II defeated a Christian army headed by Janos Hunyadi and Ladislas I of Hungary. The city continued to be ruled by the Turks until 1878, at which time it became part of Bulgaria.

25

Grigory of Sanok

Grzegorz of Sanok (ca. 1407–77) was the archbishop of Lviv who gave Callimachus shelter after the latter was exiled from Rome. Callimachus's book *Vita et mores Gregoii Sanocei* is considered by historians to be "an attempt to create the ethos of bishop-humanist rather than an historically faithful biography" (Jerzy Ziomek, *Renesans* [Warsaw: PWN, 1976], 82).

27

Hnyla Lypa

"The Rotted Linden Tree."

28

Sonka Holschanska

The wife of Galician magnate Oleksander Holschansky, who supported a pro-Moscow orientation. Thanks to Maria Zubrytska for informing us of this.

28

Zbigniew Olesnicki

Zbigniew Olesnicki (1389–1455), bishop of Krakow and supporter of the Krakow Academy (Jagiellonian University). He served as secretary to Wladyslaw Jagiello, regent to Wladyslaw III, and mentor to his successor, Kazimierz IV. Adam Zamoyski says the following about him: "Educated, tough, and absolutist in his convictions, a cardinal who was a born statesman, guided by a vision which combined his own advancement with that of Poland and the church, he had no room in his scheme of things for a vociferous seym" (*The Polish Way* [London: John Murray, 1987], 52).

28
Jan Odrowaz
The Odrowaz family was a wealthy gentry family with roots in the eleventh and twelfth centuries. Iwo Odrowaz was a famous bishop of Krakow, who studied in Paris and Bologna and founded several small colleges in Poland in the thirteenth century.

28
Zolota Lypa
"Golden Linden Tree."

30
Kadlubek
Vincenty Kadlubek, chronicler of Polish history. Our gratitude to Paul Bushkovitch for identifying him for us.

40
But what Jupiter can do, the bull can't
A Latin saying ("Quod licet Jovi non licet bovi") that is also a Russian aphorism. We are grateful to William R. Schmalstieg for providing us with the Latin original.

43
Sandomierz
An important Polish trading center between East and West. From the fourteenth century, it became a stronghold for Polish forces attacking various enemies.

46
Privokzalny Square
"Train Station Square."

47
Novy Svet
"New World."

49
Dlugosh
Polish chronicler Jan Dlugosh (1415–80).

An Incident with a Classic

61
Mirgorod
Nikolai Gogol, a great writer of the first half of the nineteenth century, was born in Ukraine but wrote in Russian. One of the collections of his stories was titled *Mirgorod*—the name of the town in which all the stories were set.

61
the not-made-by human-hands puddle
The description of a huge puddle in the center of Mirgorod is a pivotal element in Gogol's collection. This also refers to Pushkin's famous poem "Exegi Monumentum" in which he refers to his poetry as a monument not made by human hands.

61
the small boat of Peter
A reference to the boat that Peter the Great built when he was a young man, which would become the seed from which the Russian fleet would later grow.

The Foreigner

65
Alyosha Parshchikov
Aleksei Parshchikov is one of the leading poets in Russia today. He is author of several books of poetry, among them *Figures of Intuition* (1989) and *Cyrillic Light* (1995). Parshchikov is a personal friend of the author.

65
a new long poem, "Poltava"
"Poltava" is a long narrative poem by Alexander Pushkin about the victory of the Russian army led by Peter the Great over the army of Swedish king Karl IX and the Ukrainian Cossacks led by Hetman Ivan Mazepa at the Ukrainian town of Poltava.

67

Ghel-Giu, brutal, like all port cities

Places mentioned in the novels of the twentieth-century late-Romantic Russian writer Alexander Grin.

68

the outskirts of a Eurasian capital

A reference to Moscow.

68

fifteen-year-old captain

Reference to the character in Jules Verne's novel by the same name—*Un capitaine de quinze ans* (1878).

68

Patagonia

Location to which the fifteen-year-old captain journeyed in Jules Verne's novel.

68

Great Kursk Anomaly

Huge iron-ore deposit near the city of Kursk in the south of Russia.

68

Baykonur

Site of space launches, in Kazakhstan, which was part of the Soviet Union before 1991.

69

The Expert

Klekh seems to have in mind Pieter Brueghel the Elder's painting *The Peasant and the Bird Nester*. The "expert" is the peasant who points his finger at the nest robber.

69

Red Presnia

Presnia is the district in Moscow where, during the first Russian revolution of 1905, the revolutionary workers held their position against the tsarist army for months. In Soviet times Presnia was called "Red," and the "Presnia worker" became the quintessential Soviet worker.

71
echolalia
Psychological illness manifested in obsessive reproduction of fixed lexical forms.

72
the "Fish"
Position in the domino game in which a player closes one end of the row with a piece of the same denomination as is on the other end with no more pieces of that denomination left, thus winning the game.

The Way Home

77
Excuse me, do you have a smoke?
Spoken in Ukrainian.

80
this poor seminarian's body
A reference to Gogol's character Khoma Brut, a seminarian who is tormented by witches and demons in the story "Viy."

The Église by the Station

89
The *Église* by the Station
Privokzal'naia is the adjective for "rail station." The Polish Catholic Cathedral of St. Elizabeth, built in 1903, is located a short distance from the railroad station in Lviv. Our gratitude to Maria Zubrytska for background information on the construction of the cathedral.

90
the empress stabbed by a Swiss anarchist
The fifeteenth-century Polish empress Elizabeth, who became a Polish saint for her help with the poor.

94
raped, plundered, and dishonored
An untranslatable Ukrainian idiom approximately meaning "raped, crushed with an asphalt roller, and subject to an extreme degree of mockery and violation."—AUTHOR

94
housing committee waiting room
BOMZH (*Bez opredelennogo mesta zhitel'stva*), an acronym that literally means "without a determined place of abode." This category during Soviet times included political dissidents and those who somehow threatened the state who, as a form of harassment, were not given official permission to live in cities.

94
Automatic Control Systems
Klekh uses the acronym ASU (*Avtomaticheskie sistemy upravleniia*), a popular term during Brezhnev times signifying the scientific-technical revolution. Thanks to Maria Zubrytska for elucidating this for us.

96
Stepan Bandera
Leader of the Ukrainian Insurgent Army (OUN) during World War II. His troops fought both against the Nazis and the Soviets. After the war he fled to exile in Western Europe. He was assassinated by a Soviet agent in Germany in 1959.

Introduction to the Galician Context

99
Sacher-Masoch
Leopold von Sacher-Masoch (1836–95). Galician writer born in Lemberg (now Lviv), best known for his highly autobiographical novel depicting a masochistic love relationship, *Venus in Furs*. His last name provides the coinage for the term *masochism*.

99
Dikanka
Ukrainian town from Gogol's famous collection of stories *Evenings on a Farm Near Dikanka*.

99
Kafka to Babel
Isaac Babel was a Jewish writer in Soviet Russia. His most famous work is
the book of short stories *Red Cavalry.* Babel was one of the so-called fellow-
traveler writers and was killed during Stalin's purges.

101
before Gorky
Maxim Gorky was the most recognizable Soviet writer, the author of the
novel *Mother,* the first Socialist Realist work.

103
another Gestapo man
Whose last name history has deigned to preserve—Gunter, in which a certain law that has been in effect till recent times can be seen: the killers of writers and, in a broader sense, of people should be named; it has always been
accepted this way—in order to be able to strike a man, a killer should present
his name—I'm not a werewolf, I'm of the same blood as you. Although in
more recent times even the murder itself has learned to deprive the murderer
of his individual significance, making him completely anonymous. The name
of the killer is the last thing that links the death of Schultz with the world of
culture, with the deaths of that long-past and reliable, as it became clear, age,
in which he still had managed to be born.—AUTHOR

A Tiny Farmstead in the Universe

109
Hutsul
The colorful inhabitants of the Carpathian Mountains and the subject of
Armenian filmmaker Sergo (Sergei) Parajanov's famous film *Shadows of
Forgotten Ancestors,* based on Ukrainian writer Mykhailo Kotsiubynsky's novel-
la by the same name.

110
coupons
Kupony were the initial basic monetary unit of the Ukrainian government
after it declared independence in 1991. They were later replaced by the
hryvnya.

110
A bear—that's half a *liudyná,* a person
Spoken in Ukrainian. The phrase *napiv-liudyná* with the accent on the *a*
instead of on the *y* would be dialectal.

113
on a broom, on a demon
Allusion to Khoma Brut, the hero of Gogol's fantastic tale of witches and
demons, "Viy."

113
seventy-seven
Seven and seven, that is, Seagram's 7 and 7-Up.

121
Vova
An unusual name for a dog. The name is a diminutive form of Vladimir,
the first name of Lenin.

122
chakra
Organ of feeling in Hindu philosophy.

123
magarych
Bottle of liquor used to seal a deal among the Hutsuls.

125
kinokephalos
From the Greek—a mythical creature with the head of a dog and the body
of a man.

125
Cocytus
The name of one of the five rivers of Hades from Greek mythology as well
as from Dante, along whose banks the unburied would wander for a century.
Its name means "river of wailing."

126
apofatikos and the *katafatikos*
Greek for, respectively, the negative and the positive.

129
play preference
Preference is the most popular card game in Russia and Ukraine. It's a variation of bridge and can be played by three or a maximum of four people.

129
Vysotsky
The famous Russian bard and Shakespearean actor Vladimir Vysotsky, who became a cult figure and symbol of opposition to the Soviet system in the 1960s and 1970s.

130
sverbivus
The plant *Rosa canina,* wild dog rose.

130
Athens
Afyny, the plant *Vaccinium myrtillus,* bilberry.

130
Aspen mushrooms
Orange-cap boletus mushroom growing near or under aspen trees.

130
dzindziura, zmievon, pidoima
Dzindziura refers to plants in the genus *Gentiana; zmievon* to *Scorzonera purpurea rosea;* and *pidoima* to the genus *Sanicula.*

130
Dikanka
The village that provided the title for Nikolai Gogol's collection of short stories *Evenings on a Farm Near Dikanka.* Klekh's prose pieces are also obviously about a *khutor,* a farmstead, like Gogol's.

138
the jot in the word "Ukraine"
The word УКРАЇНА in Ukrainian has diereses above the letter *ї*.

The Death of the Forester

141
the noseless one
The traditional depiction of death as a skull, that is, without a fleshy nose.

143
Czeslav Nemen
Popular Polish musician and singer.

143
POZOR
"Shame" in Russian.

144
Mukachevo
Town in the Transcarpathian Region near the border with Czechoslovakia and Romania.

165
Tonet chair
Furniture made out of bent wood by the Tonet company.

168
the stifling meeting room
A little shack at a construction site where workers change clothes and receive daily assignments.

172
a novella about this event
A reference to one of the stories in Isaac Babel's book *Red Cavalry*, in which he described the action of the First Cavalry Army led by the Revolutionary

General Semen Budeny in Ukraine and Poland during the Russian Civil War of 1918 to 1921.

172
Bulgakov, Olesha, Kharms

Mikhail Bulgakov, Yury Olesha, and Daniil Kharms were so-called fellow-traveler writers in 1921. Bulgakov is most famous for his novel *Master and Margarita*, Olesha for the novel *Envy*, and Kharms for his seemingly nonsensical poetry.

172
Zhvanetsky

Popular satirist who began his career in the late 1960s. He was extremely popular among the Soviet intelligentsia.

174
Cherubina de Gabriac

The name of a fictitious poet invented as a practical joke by Russian symbolist poet Maximilian Voloshin to mystify his colleagues at the symbolist journal *Apollo*. Voloshin's friend Elizaveta Vasilieva wrote poetry under this name. Vasilieva was a rather unattractive woman while Cherubina de Gabriac presented herself as a beautiful femme fatale.

175
Kiy, Khoriv, Shchek

The three brothers of legend who, according to *The Primary Chronicle*, founded the city of Kyiv, which was named after the eldest brother, Kiy. For a translation of the legend, see Serge A. Zenkovsky, ed., *Medieval Russia's Epics, Chronicles, and Tales*, rev. ed. (New York: Dutton, 1974), 48.

178
Sadovaya Vishnya

"Orchard Cherry Tree."

198
DYR, BOOL, SHYL

The first line of Russian Futurist Aleksei Kruchenykh's famous five-line nonsense poem. It can be found in Aleksandr Kushner, ed., *Poeziia russkogo futurizma* (St. Petersburg: Akademicheskii proekt, 1999), 206.

200

A carrot with a braid, a dungeon, a chamber . . .

Based on the Russian folk riddle "Morkov'" ("The Carrot"). It can be found in V. V. Mitrofanova, ed., *Zagadki* (Leningrad: Nauka Publishers, 1968), 86.

■ □ ■ □ ■

ABOUT THE AUTHOR

Igor Klekh was born in 1952 in western Ukraine and identifies himself as a Russian writer of fiction and essays. Since 1994, he has lived in Moscow, where he is a member of the Union of Russian Writers and the Russian PEN Club. His book *Intsident s klassikom* (*An Incident with a Classic*) was published in Russian in 1998. He has been nominated for the Russian Booker Prize and won the Yuri Kazakov Prize for best short story. *A Land the Size of Binoculars* is Klekh's first book to be translated into English.

■ □ ■ □ ■

WRITINGS FROM AN UNBOUND EUROPE

For a complete list of titles, see the Writings from an Unbound Europe Web site at
www.nupress.northwestern.edu/ue.

Border State
TÕNU ÕNNEPALU

How to Quiet a Vampire: A Sotie
BORISLAV PEKIĆ

A Voice: Selected Poems
ANZHELINA POLONSKAYA

Merry-Making in Old Russia and Other Stories
EVGENY POPOV

Estonian Short Stories
EDITED BY KAJAR PRUUL AND DARLENE REDDAWAY

Death and the Dervish
The Fortress
MEŠA SELIMOVIĆ

House of Day, House of Night
OLGA TOKARCZUK

Materada
FULVIO TOMIZZA

Fording the Stream of Consciousness
DUBRAVKA UGREŠIĆ

Shamara and Other Stories
SVETLANA VASILENKO

The Silk, the Shears and *Marina; or, About Biography*
IRENA VRKLJAN